Southern Roadie

Gregory P Robertson

This story is conceived from the mind of the author. Names, characters,
places and incidents are the product of the author's imagination.
Any resemblance to actual persons living or dead, business establishments,
events, or locales is entirely coincidental.

ISBN: 978-0-9906921-0-2
First edition 2014

For more information
about the author and the book, go to:
www.gregoryprobertson.com

Ralphster Magoo Publishing, LLC
Silver City, NM

This book is dedicated to those who served behind the breech and to those who lived beyond the spotlights.

Southern Roadie

M79 Grenade Launcher

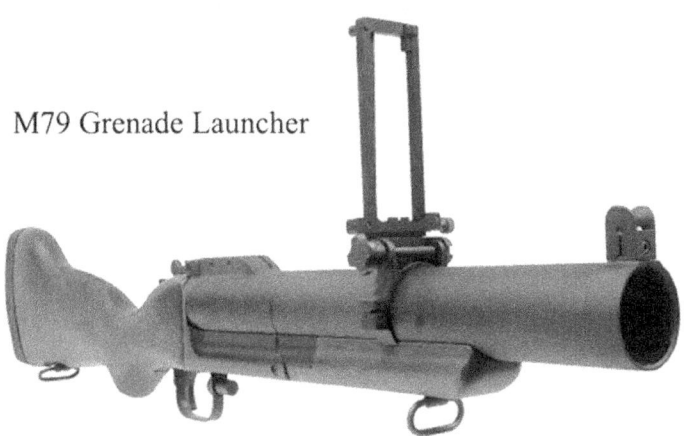

Chapter 1

Corporal Pham Tan Chu knelt at the edge of the tree line with a loosely rolled cigarette hanging lazily between his fingers. The American Army was coming. Intelligence from sympathetic villagers living near the sprawling base camp had confirmed it.

The unmistakable wop-wop of the American helicopter blades cut through the air. Corporal Pham rose as he unconsciously checked his AK47 to ensure that a round was in the chamber. The beating of the helicopter blades grew louder as Pham sank back from the edge of the tree line. Turning, he ran toward the ambush line as the first of the gunships fired rockets at the edge of the forest. He waved his yellow scarf toward the radioman hiding behind the line before he moved to his prepared fighting hole in the nearby gully.

Pham slipped into the hole and pulled the cover over the opening until only a small slit remained for him to see out. He settled in to wait for the opportunity for him to accomplish his primary order from the Battalion Commander, the capture of a live American soldier. If he were successful, he would have the honor of taking the prisoner back to Hanoi.

His heart lightened at the thought of seeing his three-year-old son for the first time.

Corporal Jeff Briggs leaped from the skid of the Huey as it touched the ground. The men around him scurried into a skirmish line ten meters from the beating blades. Fresh cordite in the air stung his nose. He knelt next to the machine gunner, pressed his M79 tight against his shoulder, and aimed at the tree line in the distance. The M79 Grenade Launcher, with its stubby large barreled single-shot shotgun look, was Jeff's weapon of choice. In the five months he had been using the weapon, he had gained a reputation among the troops for being able to hit anything he aimed at.

The thunder from the blades whirling above his head increased as the Huey lifted off the ground, moved quickly forward, and rose into the air. The dense air grew still as the line of choppers disappeared over the trees to the north. Monkeys slowly began to return to their incessant chatter as the danger of the blades disappeared. Sergeant First Class Slattery broke the stillness of the morning mist with a simple soft-spoken command.

"Forward to the tree line."

The skirmish line rose as one and scurried forward with their bodies hunched under the load of three days of rations and ammunition. Jeff moved forward in a trot with the grip of his M79 held tightly in his left hand while his right pushed the bouncing general-purpose bag of high explosive 40 mm shells against his holstered 45-caliber pistol. His helmet cocked to the left as he moved so he placed the end of the barrel of his M79 against the top of the helmet. He shifted his eyes left, front, and right as he moved scanning the shadows behind the tree line ahead.

The skirmish line disappeared into the tree line as the second wave of choppers approached from the south. Jeff moved into the shade of the large leafed trees and dropped to one knee, his M79 at the ready with his finger just outside of the trigger guard. He thumbed the safety off as he moved his finger inward until it touched the trigger. The engines of helicopters thundered as they landed to discharge their deadly human cargo. The sound of running feet accompanied by clanking equipment approached behind him as the chopper pilots drove their engines to a fever pitch as they lifted off for the return trip to the base camp.

A familiar voice whispered behind him. "Got your back, man."

Jeff turned his head toward the slight man kneeling behind him. The man's rifle pointed back into the landing zone, his eyes scanning for danger behind his friend. His finger was poised just outside the trigger guard of his M16.

"You took your sweet time getting here, Clarence."

Clarence smiled. His perfect white teeth gleamed against skin so black that it defined the color. "What can I say? I needed to stop to brush my teeth."

Jeff grinned at the often-repeated joke as he shifted his eyes forward toward the skirmish line.

Sergeant Slattery spoke again. "Forward fifty meters and set up a defensive line."

The mass of soldiers rose and crept forward as the beat of the third wave of choppers bit into the air. Jeff pointed his M79 forward and tilted up at a 30-degree angle as he stepped, his finger once again poised outside the trigger guard. The shuffling of Clarence's web gear and his labored breath behind him brought him a sense of security. Only the area to his front continued to bring the danger of injury or death. Jeff moved in a slight crouch while he held his weapon in his left hand as he used his right to shift the small branches from his path.

The platoon of soldiers forming the skirmish line reached a small depression forty meters in and spread out into a defensive line. The machine gunner and his assistant moved to the line while Jeff knelt slightly to the rear behind a fallen tree. Clarence took up a position five meters behind Jeff as he faced the ground they had just covered. Jeff opened his general-purpose bag, removed three gold tipped fragmentation rounds, and placed them next to his left knee. The fourth and last wave of choppers delivered the rest of the company to the ground. The choppers left the landing zone as the pilots hurried to head to their warm showers and hot food.

Not a soldier twitched to Jeff's front as the sounds of the jungle slowly returned. Tree monkeys once again chattered as the birds sang in the trees. Clarence's breaths came in short pants, like a cat after the failed chase of a lizard. Jeff's own breathing remained controlled with almost a relaxed nature to it. The muffled voices of the company command group drifted from the rear as reports went out on the radio and commands came in. Whispered grunts came from the mortar teams as they lugged the last of the ammo cases in from the landing field. The radio noise increased as a short command came forward.

"Scouts out."

Five men, who had been kneeling to Jeff's left, rose into crouches and moved past the protective line of M16s. The men slithered from tree to tree until their forms blended with the shadows. Their movement, though muffled, ceased the jungle sounds once more. The monkeys and birds seemed to hold their breath with the rest of the troops as the scouts disappeared into the shadows of the lower branches. The forest screamed a dangerous stillness. Jeff moved his finger into the trigger guard and onto the trigger as Clarence quietly duck-walked up on his right.

The scouts reappeared through the trees in a run as the jungle in front of Jeff exploded in gunfire and rocket trails. Screams of "Ambush" sounded along the line. Several of the scouts fell unmoving while others dropped behind trees to begin firing back toward muzzle flashes of AK47s. Jeff pressed the wooden stock into his shoulder and launched a round toward the muzzle flashes. He broke open the breech, loaded another round, and brought the muzzle back up. He pulled the trigger then watched the round as it flew toward several of the flashes. It exploded in the branches above them. The flashes ceased as he grabbed another round to load it into the chamber.

Sergeant Slattery ran up from the left and knelt beside Jeff. He fired his M16 toward other flashes before he grabbed Jeff by the collar and yelled into his ear. "Move to the top of the gully on the right to secure the flank."

Jeff dropped his pack, hoisted his general-purpose bag over his shoulder, and picked up the remaining round from the ground. He touched Clarence on the shoulder as he prepared to move toward the gully.

"Follow me."

Clarence got to his feet and touched Jeff's arm. "Be Careful."

"Always"

He did not look back at Clarence as Jeff moved from covering tree to covering tree. Clarence would be there like a wingman in a flight of jet fighters, rifle ready to take out any close in targets. Jeff reached the edge of the gully, lay down behind a fallen tree trunk, and dropped the general-purpose bag on the ground beside him. He poked his M79 over the trunk, sighted in on two men in NVA Sun Helmets as they ran down the other side, and squeezed the trigger. The M79 barked its distinct thunk then the round exploded in the chest of one man dropping both to the ground unmoving. Jeff loaded the round he held in his right hand as Clarence pushed up next to him to fire his M16 at targets in the trees across the gully. Jeff rose to one knee as he searched for the next danger. A rocket emerged from the trees and sped toward them. Jeff fired toward the start of the trailing smoke as he dropped behind the trunk.

The rocket exploded against the fallen tree. The old dead wood splintered and disappeared as Jeff's body blew backward. Clarence's body and Jeff's general-purpose bag spun through the air over the edge of the gully before the back of Jeff's head slammed into a tree. Darkness engulfed him.

The doorbell cut into the peaceful night of the second story bedroom. "Brrrring. Brrrring. Brrrrrrrrrrring."

Don threw back the covers and pulled on the t-shirt and shorts thrown out of the bed earlier as he stumbled toward the bedroom door. "Who the hell could that be at this hour?"

Sally slipped her nightgown over her head then reached for her robe. "Get down there and get whoever it is to stop before the girls wake up."

"Brrrring. Brrrring. Brrrrrrrrrrring."

Don switched the stairway lights on before he took the steps two at a time. Behind him, a small voice called into the night. "What is it, mommy?"

Sally's soothing voice flowed from the door of the girl's room. "It's okay. Y'all just stay in bed. Someone just needs to talk to daddy."

"Brrrrrrrrrrrrrrrring."

Don reached the front door and pushed his eye against the peephole. The spherically distorted head of a man with long black hair and a scraggly beard was standing in the yellow porch light. An old army pack hung loosely from his shoulders.

"Brrrrrrrrrrrrrrring."

Don pounded on the door. "Stop ringing the bell!"

The man stepped back half a step from the door as he looked at the peephole. A cut above his left cheek dripped blood into his beard and caked along his skin. His hair was tousled. The man did not move or speak. He just stared at the peephole.

Sally called from the top of the steps. "Who is it?"

Don pulled his eye back from the peephole and turned his head toward the stairs. "I don't know. It looks like a hippie that got mugged. Maybe you better call the police."

"Okay."

Don brought his eye back to the peephole and pressed it against the small glass port. The man outside stood silent, unmoving with his eyes focused squarely at the glint of glass in the door. Something in the man's eyes triggered a memory in Don. The vision of those eyes across a lunchroom table flowed back from the distant past into the present.

"Damn."

Don's hands fumbled with the deadbolt as he kept his eye pressed against the peephole. As the lock came free, he pulled the door open and stared at the bloody face before him.

The man smiled as Don came fully visible in the open doorway. "Hi, Don."

The man's eyeballs rolled into the back of his head as he sank. Don grabbed him to cushion the abrupt stop against the wooden porch. He cradled the man's head in his lap.

Don shouted up the stairs. "Sally. Don't call the police. Grab the first aid kit and bring it down here."

Sally slammed the telephone receiver into its cradle and scurried into the bathroom above. Her excited voice filtered through the hallway and down the stairs. "What is it?"

"It's Jeff Briggs. My old roommate from the Academy."

Blue jays sang through the open window as Jeff slowly opened his eyes. The curtains billowed inward gently as a ceiling fan slowly turned above him helping the breeze move the air around the room. Clean sweet smelling sheets nestled his body up to his chest. A teal wall and the painting of a kitten sitting next to a vase of flowers filled his vision as his focus clicked in on his surroundings. His arm ached as he slowly brought it to his face to explore the bandage on his left cheek. His hand next felt his hair, which curled over his bare shoulders. He struggled to raise his head from the mattress, but the pain only allowed him to lift it until he could see the open doorway.

Two small girls, no more than four years old, identical

in every way except for the color of their faded pajamas, stared open-mouthed and wide-eyed at him from around the edge of the door.

Jeff smiled at the two as he weakly spoke. "Hi, who are you?"

His arms could no longer hold him up and he collapsed on the mattress with a grunt. The girls ran away with their little footsteps fading as they scampered down stairs out of sight. Their two shrill voices raised in light screams before one went into kiddie speech.

"Mommy, the strange man is awake."

Two sets of heavier footsteps mounted the steps and the door pushed fully open. A woman with a stethoscope around her neck and a blood pressure cuff in her hand advanced toward him.

Behind her, Don's familiar face smiled. "So you finally decided to wake up."

Jeff looked at them both. "Don, what's going on?"

The woman pulled the covers from his chest and slipped the stethoscope into her ears. "Don't talk. Just lay there a minute while I check you out."

She placed the end of the stethoscope over his heart then moved it around his chest. "Breathe in. Now breathe out. Breathe in again. Now breathe out."

She dropped the end of the stethoscope and wrapped the blood pressure cuff around his arm. She pumped it up then listened to his artery as the pressure slowly came off. She removed the cuff and laid it to the side before she reached out to inspect the bandage on his face.

"How do you feel?"

"My left arm aches and my face itches. What's going on?"

Don sat on the edge of the bed. "Hopefully, you know more than us. You showed up at our doorstep three days ago all bloody and dehydrated. Sally took you to the emergency room at the hospital she works at and then brought you home."

Sally pushed the tape on Jeff's face lightly to reseat the edges. "I'm sorry, but they had to shave your beard off to stitch up the cut on your face."

Jeff looked up at her as he smiled. "Then I guess you're Sally."

Don shifted down the bed next to Sally. "That's right, you two have never met. We sent you a wedding invitation, but I guess the army wouldn't let you come home for it."

"Hi, Jeff. Don told me a lot about you and the time the two of you spent at the military academy."

Don smiled and put his arm around his wife. "And she still let you spend the night. Three actually."

"Don? What's going on? I don't remember any of that. The last thing I remember is that I was in Vietnam. A rocket exploded in front of me and threw me backward."

Sally took charge. "Jeff, before we go into that, I want to change your dressings and get some food into you." She turned to Don. "Honey, would you go heat up some chicken broth and toast a couple of pieces of bread. The two of you can talk after I leave for the hospital."

An hour later, as Jeff hobbled back from the bathroom with Sally at his arm, Don waited in a chair next to the bed as he leafed through the old military academy yearbook.

Sally helped Jeff into bed then pulled the covers up to his chest. "Now I don't want you out of bed except to go to the bathroom. Get as much rest as you can. Don can get you a book to read if you get restless."

She turned toward Don. "Fix him some noodle soup and crackers to eat. And don't talk about anything that will get him upset until he gets a little stronger. Talk about old girlfriends or something."

Don stood and kissed his wife. "Thanks, honey. I have classes from 12 until 3 so I'll let him get some rest. Why don't you ask your mother to keep the girls at her place until we get home, then I'll go pick them up."

Sally looked down at Jeff. "Take care. Everything looks okay. I think you just need to gain some strength." She wagged her finger at his face as she smiled. "And don't try to go down the stairs yet."

"Yes, mother," Jeff said. "I'll be a good boy."

Sally left the room. Soon the girl's excited voices came through the open window as the front door opened and closed. Their voices faded as the three walked down the street.

"How did you ever get that beautiful nurse to marry a sorry-ass guy like you?"

"I think she's just crazy. Only thing I can figure."

"Okay Don, now that she's gone. What the hell is going on? How did I get here from the Nam?"

"I don't know anything about that, Jeff. Like I said, you showed up on our doorstep three days ago. You were bruised and bloody as if someone had mugged you. The only things you had with you were an old army pack full of clothes, a wallet, and an id tag around your neck."

"What was in the pack?"

"A couple of changes of jeans, t-shirts, underwear, socks, a poncho liner, an army jacket, and a floppy hat. It looked like you'd been on the road for a while. The clothes were all dirty."

"What was in the wallet?"

"Your old expired driver's license, 15 dollars in bills, and a piece of paper with a name and address on it. You also had about a buck in change in your jeans pocket. The bills still in the wallet seemed strange since, like I said, it looked like you'd been mugged."

"Let me see the piece of paper."

Don got the faded leather wallet out of the top drawer of the dresser. He took out a tattered piece of paper from the side pocket and handed it to Jeff.

Jeff stared at the paper for a moment before speaking. "That's my old army buddy, Clarence. This must be his address down in New Orleans. I wonder if he knows what happened. The last time I remember seeing him was when the rocket hit. He—"

"What's wrong?"

"The rocket explosion blew him over into a gully that the NVA were trying to cross. That's the last time I saw him." Jeff's breathing quickened as he started to push himself up. "Come on. Help me out of bed. I've got to find out what happened to him."

Don moved to the side of the bed to hold Jeff down. "Don't you dare get up. You'll just fall over and Sally will have both our asses. You need rest to gain your strength. When you're feeling stronger, we'll call down there so you can talk to Clarence."

"He told me his family never got a phone."

"Then we'll figure out how you can go see him. For now, you're going to stay in bed. Okay?"

Jeff relaxed and Don removed his grip. "Okay. I don't want Sally to come down on you for my stubbornness. I'll rest until Sally says I can go."

"Jeff, tell me something. When did this explosion happen?"

"It was January 19th, the day before Clarence's birthday."

"What year?"

"1968, of course. Why?"

Don sat down on the bed and touched Jeff's shoulder. "Jeff, today is March 16, 1970."

Jeff relaxed in a wicker chair on the front porch as the twins played hopscotch on the sidewalk. Don opened the screen door, holding it while Sally carried out a tray filled with glasses of lemonade. Taking one each, they settled back into the calmness of the city evening. Cars moved by searching for parking places as the drivers waved to the people on the porches. Don and Sally held hands while they sipped their lemonade.

Jeff placed his glass on the small table. "I think it's time for me to start heading down to New Orleans."

Sally pulled her hand from Don's to touch Jeff on the sleeve. "Are you sure you feel strong enough to make the trip? From all the scars you have, you had several wounds over there. The one on your thigh looked really nasty. Something could still be wrong inside. I still think you should go to the VA hospital and get checked out further. They could get your service medical records."

"I feel fine. I'm running over a mile twice a day around the neighborhood. My wind is back and my strength is good. I feel almost as fit as the day I left Fort Bragg on my way to the Nam."

"I'll be sorry to see you go," Sally said. "You've been such a great help with the girls this last month. But, I understand that you need to find out what happened to the last two years of your life. You're welcome to come back to stay a while longer after you talk to Clarence."

"Thanks. And even more, thanks again for nursing me back to health."

Don set his glass down as he stared at his friend. "Have you had any more of those dreams?"

Sally raised her eyebrows. "What dreams?"

"Not so much dreams really. It's just sometimes at night I wake up thinking I hear gunfire through the window. Once it seemed so close that I slid off the bed and got under it."

"Maybe," Sally said, "you should go to one of those veteran support groups to talk about it with them before you go."

"Thanks for your concern Sally, but I'll be fine. Once I find Clarence and talk to him, I just know I'll get answers to my questions. Then I can figure what to do next."

"The two of y'all must have really been close."

"He was my best friend and was the only person I

really felt safe around over there. We looked after each other. I could talk to him about anything, even my fears. With him at my back, I knew nothing could hurt me."

Don reached into his back pocket and pulled out his wallet. He counted out five twenty dollar bills before pushing them across the table to Jeff. "Here's some money to get you there and to live on for a little."

Jeff stared down at the bills. He pushed them back. "You can't afford that. I can just hitchhike down there."

Sally pushed the bills back across the table. "Take it. You're just getting healed. You can't hitchhike that far."

Jeff pushed two of the bills back. "I can't take all that. The train fare to New Orleans can't be more than thirty dollars."

Don pushed the bills back at Jeff. "Take them. This way you'll have enough to come back after seeing Clarence. I don't want you showing up like you did before."

Jeff's eyes misted over as he gathered the bills and stuck them into his wallet. "Thanks." He turned his head toward the giggling girls as they continued their game.

Don sat still for a minute before breaking the silence of the three. He lifted his glass in a salute. "Well, here's to your journey. I hope it brings you everything you need." The three clinked glasses and then sipped the cool liquid. Don lowered his glass to the table. "So when do you think you're going to head out?"

"I'll go to the train station tomorrow and check the schedule. How do I get to the station from here?"

Sally pointed down the street. "It's about two miles that way. You can walk down to the park and cut right through it. Then, when you get to the road on the other side, turn left until you get to Broad Street. Turn right there and it's about a mile on your left. You can't miss it. It's a huge columned building with a domed roof."

"Okay," Jeff said. "I'll head over there after your mother picks up the girls tomorrow."

13

Sally sat up straight smiling. "We should send you off in style. Let's go out to dinner tomorrow night. Also, a Canadian band called Heaven Can Wait is playing down at the concert hall next to the college starting tonight. We could go to the show after dinner. My mother would love to keep the girls overnight to spoil them a little more."

"Where is the concert hall?"

Sally pointed down the street again. "You'll pass by it on your way to the station. It's on the right just before you get to Broad Street. It's called The String Factory."

Don raised his glass. "Let's do it. I'd love to take a break from studying. Calculus gets old real fast."

Jeff raised his glass as Sally raised hers. "It's a date," he said as they clinked their glasses once more.

Jeff waved goodbye to the twins as they walked away up the street with their grandmother. He turned the other way to head toward the trees that rose in the distance above the closely spaced two-story houses. The spring sun beat down on Jeff as he walked and his t-shirt was damp with sweat in less than a block. He shifted his Boonie hat on his head to cover the back of his neck with the brim. The shade of the park trees loomed ever closer. Jeff picked up his pace to get into their cooling shadows. A worn dirt path snaked into the edge of the park with a simple painted sign tacked to a tree. *To the other side.*

Jeff stepped onto the path and the air became instantly chilled. The sweat on his t-shirt turned cold so he fluffed it out from his skin. The trail twisted through the trees as the underbrush on both sides grew denser. Soon the street behind him disappeared. The traffic sounds became muted. The sunlight dimmed as he moved further into the trees.

Rifle fire cracked through the trees off to his left. Dirt fell from the front of his uniform as he shook his head trying to clear the ringing from his ears. The tree trunk, that had provided cover for him a moment before, lay splintered and burning before him. His M79 lay on the ground out of his reach half buried in debris. Jeff shook his head again blinking as he tried to take in the action around him. The explosions and screams that cut through the gunfire picked up in intensity as the ringing left his ears.

Behind him, Sergeant Slattery's voice boomed over the carnage. "Pour it into them. Sgt. Davis, take a squad from the reserves and plug the left flank."

Jeff crawled forward, picked up the M79, and looked at the left side of the stock. Etched in the wood was the date of June 21, 1968, the end of Jeff's tour. His dog tags fell forward from under his shirt swinging freely from the nickel-plated chain around his neck. He jammed them back under his shirt to get them out of the way. He broke open the breech of the M79, removed the spent round, and put a fresh round in its place. He moved forward, still in a crawl, until he could see past the remnants of the burning trunk into the gully beyond.

The bottom of the gully sat empty with no trace of Clarence. A path snaked in both directions with the edging grass bent to the left. He searched the edge of the gully on the other side. The NVA rocket position lay abandoned with the upper part of the rocket launcher hanging over the edge.

Jeff slid down into the gully to the path. Holding his M79 ready, he stepped carefully as he searched the ground to his front with a glance left and right every few seconds. His green general-purpose bag lay off the path to his right next to an empty fighting hole, its camouflaged cover tossed to the side. Clarence's M16 lay on the ground near the fighting hole half hidden in the leaves. Drag marks moved up the path away from the American lines. Blood spotted the grass on both sides of the path.

He moved, a slow step at a time, over to the fighting hole and dropped to one knee as he stuck the muzzle of his weapon into the hole before he peered into its empty shadows. Satisfied that it was empty, he looped the strap of his bag over his right shoulder and then lifted the M16 by the handle. He moved purposely up the path, his eyes ever moving, searching for danger.

Gunfire erupted to his left above the edge of the gully. He turned to face the threat as he pushed the stock of the M79 to his shoulder. The gunfire moved slowly past him, but out of sight over the top of the gully. Jeff slung the M16 over his right shoulder before he scampered up the slope until his eyes just cleared the top.

Three NVA soldiers in Pith helmets, AK47s pointed forward, moved in relays from tree to tree toward Sergeant Slattery as he worked to clear a jam from his M16. He dropped the jammed M16, drew his 45-caliber pistol, and fired it at the advancing enemy. Jeff rose from the edge of the gully to charge the NVA soldiers from their flank. The closest one stopped his advance and started to turn to engage him. Jeff fired the M79 straight at the man's chest. The round failed to arm but buried itself in his chest before it forced him violently against a tree.

The second closest NVA soldier turned to fire as Jeff dove behind another tree. He broke open the breech of his M79 to reload. Splinters flew from the trunk into his face as he loaded a short distance fragmentation round before snapping the breech closed. He rolled right, took quick aim at the soldier, and squeezed the trigger. The round entered the man's belly before it detonated cutting him in half. Jeff dropped the M79 and shouldered Clarence's M16 as he flipped the selector switch to automatic.

The third NVA soldier still concentrated his fire toward Sergeant Slattery. The Sergeant had dropped the empty pistol and had grabbed the barrel of his still jammed M16.

Jeff screamed at the top of his lungs as he rose from his cover to charge the remaining NVA soldier. The soldier started to turn to face him just as Jeff tightened his finger on the trigger sending a burst of automatic fire into the man. The man fell and did not move. Jeff twisted his head left and right as he searched for other targets before he moved to Sergeant Slattery.

"You okay?"

"Yea. Thanks, Blooper-man." He looked at the jammed M16 in his hands. "Damn 16s. Give me an M-14 any day."

Jeff pushed Clarence's M16 into his hands. "Here, take this. I've gotta find Clarence."

Without waiting for a response, Jeff moved back to where he had left his M79. He scooped it up, broke open the breech, extracted the spent shell, and loaded another fragmentation round. He pushed forward into the bushes at the edge of the gully. He stumbled through the bushes and onto the sidewalk, bumping into a man in a faded army jacket almost knocking him down. Jeff struggled violently with the man until he relaxed as he recognized the color of the cloth. The cars on the street slowed and other pedestrians stared as they moved sideways around the pair.

The man kept a grip on Jeff's forearms. He was tall and thin, almost gaunt, with wispy blond hair that hung to his shoulders. A trimmed goatee framed his mouth. His eyes, though they looked straight into Jeff's eyes, seemed to stare beyond him. Patches covered parts of the army jacket he wore with a few peace signs embroidered into the faded fabric providing contrasting colors to the green. A dog tag hung from a nickel chain and lay on top of his soiled t-shirt.

The man released Jeff's forearms as he took a step back. He reached for the hanging dog tag and stuck it back under his t-shirt. "Ya okay, man?"

Jeff ran his fingers through his hair before he wiped the sweat from his brow with the back of his hand. "Yea. I'm fine."

"You look scared."

"I think I was just living a nightmare."

"Bad dreams come on to bother ya, do they?"

"I guess that's what it was. It just all seemed so real."

"They do, that's fer sure. But don't worry, they don't mean nothing and it will all git better. It's over now."

"Thanks. Sorry about knocking into you."

"No problem. Do you know where you're going from here?"

Jeff pointed to the left. "I'm supposed to go down this way until I pass someplace called The String Factory and then turn right."

"That's the right way. You just go'on and enjoy your walk. Things will git better now."

The man turned and headed down the sidewalk away from Jeff. Jeff watched him walk away with the unmistakable gait of ten thousand klicks punctuating his step. The man disappeared as he reached the corner and the crowd waiting to cross closed around him. Jeff turned left and moved on with his own halting gait.

The buildings of the downtown college rose on both sides of the road as the trees of the park ended at the corner. Students in shorts with tie-dyed t-shirts on laughed together while they scurried along with books in their arms toward their afternoon classes. Flyers announcing antiwar rallies adorned telephone poles and peace signs flashed between the students. The occasional older male student moved purposely down the sidewalk, slightly slower than the younger ones. A slight headshake from some of them answered Jeff's ever-searching eyes.

After he passed by the high rises of the student dorms, the buildings reduced to single-story. Storefronts replaced the institutional buildings of the university offering food, drink, clothes, and smoking supplies through the gaily-colored ads plastered in their windows. The rumble of the heavy traffic on Broad Street sounded in front of him as he pushed his way through the lunchtime crowd.

The front wheels of a large truck stuck out of an alley and partially blocked the sidewalk. The crowd streamed around it moving into the street like a snake slithering in the grass. *Heaven Can Wait* adored the side of the truck in all the colors of the rainbow. In the alley behind the truck, grunting men and casters rolling across diamond plate steel provided a break to the rumble of the traffic ahead.

Jeff moved around the front of the truck with the crowd as he headed toward the street in front of him.

A man's voice yelled from the alley. "Oh, Shit!"

A cymbal crashed against concrete followed by the thud of a heavy case as it struck the ground. The sharp scream of a man in extreme pain silenced all of the other sounds. Jeff turned and ran into the alley.

Chapter 2

In the alley, two men grasped the folding handles of a large black case. They struggled as they tried to lift it from the ground. One of the men was tall and thin with brown skin and an Afro haircut twenty inches across. The other was big with broad shoulders, dark golden skin, and straight black hair that hung in a ponytail down to his waist. A third man, white with long brown hair, lay on the ground with his arm sticking under the edge of the case. The screams emanated from his mouth as his body jerked in convulsions. Jeff grabbed the folding handle on the case alongside the thin man. The big man spoke as his eyes met Jeff's.

"Okay, ready? One, two, three, lift." The case came a foot off the ground. "Roll out from under it, Sam."

Sam didn't answer as his screams continued unabated.

Jeff shifted his hand under the bottom of the case and took the load from the thin man.

"I've got it. Pull him out."

The thin man released his grip on the case and grabbed Sam's ankles. Sam's screams intensified as the thin man dragged him from under the case.

The big man looked over the case at Jeff. "Let's put it down. Your left edge first." The left edge met the ground. "Okay, now let it rock flat." The case settled and stopped.

The big man ran around the case while the thin man kept hold of Sam's feet. "I think his arm is broken."

The big man turned and ran toward the stairs. "I'll go call for an ambulance."

Jeff moved to the Sam's side, grabbed his good hand,

and held it tight. He grabbed the man's jaw with his other hand and turned his head until their eyes met. Forcing Sam's jaw closed until the screams were muffled, Jeff brought his face down so that his eyes were an inch from Sam's eyes.

"Look through the pain into my eyes," Jeff yelled at him. "Look through the pain into my eyes."

Sam's screams subsided to a whimper as he stared at Jeff.

Jeff softened his voice. "You're going to be okay. It is only a broken arm. You're going to be okay."

Sam stopped whimpering as he continued to stare at Jeff. Tears welled in the corners of Sam's eyes.

A siren bit into the traffic noise as the big man returned and knelt down next to Jeff. "Hold on Sam. The ambulance is on its way."

Jeff released Sam's jaw and lightly stroked his forehead.

The ambulance screamed to a stop in front of the truck. Its siren began to wind down from a fever pitch to a low moan. An attendant jumped from the passenger door, moved to Sam's side, and felt the twisted arm. He yelled instructions back toward the ambulance. The second attendant pulled a large case out of the back, opened it, and pulled out two short pieces of wood with a roll of gauze. They gently straightened Sam's arm before placing a piece of wood on each side then carefully wrapped the gauze around it. Sam began to whimper again as the attendants worked. Jeff continued to hold Sam's other hand while telling him that everything was going to be okay. Sam's whimpers changed to short quick breaths as the attendants tightened the gauze to the swollen arm. The attendants got Sam to his feet, walked him to the ambulance, and placed him in the seat in the rear.

"We'll take him to Richmond Memorial," the attendant said.

The ambulance left with its lights flashing while the siren built back to its fever pitch. It made the turn disappearing down Broad Street. The big man watched the ambulance vanish around the corner, then turned to Jeff and offered him his hand.

"Thanks, man. I don't think Russ could have lifted the end of the amp case by himself. By the way, people call me Mutluk. That was Sam that you helped. We're the Road crew for the band Heaven Can Wait."

Jeff shook the Mutluk's hand. "No problem. I'm Jeff."

"Let me give you a couple of tickets to tonight's show. It's the least I can do."

"Could you make it three? The couple I'm staying with and I were going to come to the show tonight. I owe them a lot."

"Sure." Mutluk reached into the cab of the truck and brought out three tickets. "Here you go. Say, would you like to make some quick money?"

"What do you mean?"

"We've still got to get this equipment up the back stairs into the hall. Russ is a great lighting man but he can't lift the heavy cases with me. If you help me get the big ones up into the hall and scattered on the stage, I'll give you twenty dollars U S."

"What do you mean U S?"

"Sorry. I'm Canadian. We say that to distinguish between U S and Canadian dollars. Anyway, it'll take us about an hour if you're game. It would really help us out."

"Okay. I have time. I just have to get to the train station to buy a ticket before it closes."

The two started walking toward the back of the truck.

"Where are you heading?"

"New Orleans."

"That's where we're heading. Well, eventually. It's the last stop on this tour." Mutluk pointed to the case that had broken Sam's arm. "Let's get this one first. You take that end and go up the stairs first."

Jeff pulled the folding handles out lifting his end as Mutluk lifted his. Jeff slowly backed up the stairs keeping the end of the case inches from the stairs. Mutluk lifted his end high, with his head disappearing behind the case as they slowly advanced up the stairs.

At the top, Mutluk lowered his end. "Back around to the stage steps. This one goes on stage at the rear."

They lifted the case onto the stage rolling it to the rear before starting back down the stairs toward the truck. Russ kept moving quickly by carrying smaller cases.

"So when are you getting to New Orleans? Maybe I'll bring my buddy Clarence and catch your show there too."

"We leave Monday for Columbia. Then it's Charleston, Savannah, Jacksonville, Pensacola, Mobile, and we finish the tour in New Orleans. The band plays a few nights in the majority of the cities with six in Charleston and five in Jacksonville. Most of the time there's a day or two between shows. We hit New Orleans on the 10th of next month."

They walked up the diamond plate ramp into the truck. Mutluk pointed to a case. "That one's next."

An hour later, Jeff sat on the edge of the steps as he rested his back against the railing. His sweat-soaked t-shirt clung to his shoulders while droplets of sweat gathered on the tips of his hair. A cold beer rested on the step beside him. Rock music, punctuated by the occasional equipment case lid slamming shut, filtered through the door from inside the concert hall. Jeff lifted the beer to his lips and let a slow sip pass into his throat. The truck sat parked in the lot across the street. The sidewalk, unobstructed now, teemed with students moving toward Broad Street to catch buses home. An older man, crossing the alley opening, looked up toward Jeff. A worn green army coat hung loosely from his shoulders. Jeff met the man's gaze with his own before the man turned his head and moved out of view.

Mutluk walked through the door with a twenty in his hand. "Here you go. Thanks a lot for your help." He leaned against the railing across from Jeff. "I just heard from Sam at the hospital. He's going to be okay, but he's going to be in a cast for eight weeks so he's heading back to Toronto. I was wondering if you don't need to be in New Orleans right away, maybe you'd be interested in working the rest of the tour with us. I'll pay you a hundred dollars US a week with a bonus hundred when we get to New Orleans. We pick up all motels and food. I drive the truck and Russ navigates. All you would have to do is work the load-in, set up, tear down, and load-out."

Jeff's mind was torn between hurrying to New Orleans to find out what happened after the rocket blast and the sacrifice that Don and Sally made when they gave him the hundred dollars. His friends won the battle.

"That sounds good. I'll do it."

"Well then, come on in so I can show you some stuff about set up."

Jeff followed Mutluk around as he grabbed cables from the floor to connect the different pieces of equipment.

Colored tape with numbers on the cables and painted colored numbers on the cabinets simplified the job. Jeff was soon grabbing cables as he moved around the stage on his own. He helped Mutluk stack the large cabinets of the sound system on top of each other before placing the smaller horn assemblies on top by himself. Mutluk dropped a bundle of cables by Jeff's feet. "That's for this side. I'll get the other side."

Russ busied himself wiring lights on a long truss suspended between two gantry lifts. When he finished the wiring, he showed Jeff how to crank up the lift. Together, they cranked them up in time to each other's rhythm. Jeff followed Russ while he laid the cables from the light trusses around the stage to the control box. Once again, colored tape, numbers, and paint dots guided Jeff in plugging in the connectors.

Mutluk called Russ over to an electrical fuse panel as he removed the front cover and placed it on the floor against the wall. A tangled mass of large wires crisscrossed next to the fuses within. Russ picked up the end of a large cable that had three wires sticking out. He carefully inserted each wire into a slot as Mutluk unscrewed and then tightened the wire clamps next to empty fuse holders. After he tightened the last clamp, he inserted fuses into the holders. Mutluk then secured a piece of cardboard over the exposed panel with Duct tape.

He held up the roll of tape toward Jeff and smiled. "Duct tape, the roadie's best friend. The musicians will leave you, the groupies will leave you, even the caterers will leave you, but Duct tape will stick with you all night and into the next day."

Jeff laughed. "What's next?"

"I've got to run through an equipment check while Russ tests and aims the lights. Why don't you get on stage and help me by speaking into each microphone in turn? I'll guide you from the mike at the sound board."

Mutluk's booming voice came through the monitor speakers from the darkness on the other side of the bright stage lights and directed Jeff from mike to mike. Jeff moved across the stage speaking into each mike in turn. "Test, 1, 2, 3. Test 1, 2, 3."

Russ turned the stage lights on in banks as he worked. He positioned the ladder beneath a bank of lights then climbed up with a crescent wrench held between his teeth like a pirate mechanic boarding another ship. The spot bulbs aimed at specific parts of the stage marked by X's of Duct tape while the flood bulbs bathed the entire stage in bright light color by color. Rock music continued to boom from a tape player on the edge of the stage.

Russ folded the ladder and carried it off the stage out the back door as Mutluk's voice came through the monitors.

"That's it. We're done."

A half hour later, Russ and Jeff were sitting at the top of the steps that overlooked the alley. Jeff grinned as he passed the joint to Russ.

Russ glared at him. "What you smilin' at, Boy?"

Jeff broke out laughing and coughed out the toke he had just taken. This was Russ's latest attempt to sound like a southern redneck. He had joked to Jeff that if he could sound like a local as the group toured the southern states, things might go easier.

Jeff recovered as he caught his breath. "I was just thinking that this is really good stuff."

Russ leaned against an empty equipment case and passed the joint back to Jeff. "Yea. It's real good."

Jeff took another lazy toke, passed the joint over to Russ, then leaned back against the railing as he looked toward the end of the alley. The older man in the army coat walked by on the sidewalk again and glanced in toward Jeff. He raised his head slightly with a nod. Jeff noticed a faraway look in the man's eyes, the same look that the gaunt man's eyes had. He turned his gaze down the sidewalk again and passed from the view of the alley.

Mutluk, walking from inside the concert hall, looked at the two and shook his head. "I need to let you know one of my rules, Jeff. I don't mind if you get high after the work is done. However, there's no smoking or drinking before we load-in or load-out. Also, no carrying pot when we're on the road. If the cops busted us in the truck, they would confiscate everything before they threw us in jail. If you want it, you need to get it locally a joint at a time. Russ has never had any problems finding it once we've finished setting up. We just can't take a chance with the local cops."

Jeff smiled up at Mutluk. "No problem. I probably won't do anything once we leave here. Richmond's fairly tolerant, but I can't say the same about anywhere further south. Clarence told me that New Orleans is pretty wide open and maybe Florida would be okay, but North and South Carolina and Georgia are still pretty redneck."

"Okay. As long as you understand." Mutluk took the joint from Russ, inhaled a long toke, and held it. He exhaled twenty seconds later. "Where'd this come from anyway?

Russ motioned toward the open concert hall doors. "Hall manager gave it to me."

Mutluk took another toke before passing the joint back to Jeff. "Pretty good stuff."

After another toke, Jeff passed the joint back to Mutluk before he let the sweet smoke flow from his lungs. "So, Russ. Are you from Canada too?"

Russ shook his head. "Nope. I'm from New York City. I normally work lighting Off-Broadway. But, I really want to act on stage."

"So why are you here and not acting?"

Russ shrugged his shoulders. "Not that many parts for Negros on stage. It's getting better, but still not enough to live on yet. I hooked up with Mutluk on this band's last tour when their normal lighting man couldn't get into the country because of a drug arrest. Mutluk called me up before they started this tour to see if I'd like to work this one also."

Mutluk passed the joint to Russ. "One night when you're really bored Jeff, you can get Russ to do the speech from Hamlet. It'll help you get to sleep."

Russ stood. He held his arm out in a dramatic pose. "To be, or not to be, that is the question. Whether 'tis nobler in the mind to suffer the slings and arrows of outrageous fortune, or to take arms against a sea of troubles, and by opposing end them? To die: to sleep." He bowed and sat down.

Jeff laughed and clapped. Mutluk shook his head as he turned toward the stage door. "Come on Russ. The band will be here soon for the sound check. Let's make sure everything is ready."

Jeff slowly stood holding onto the railing, slightly swaying. He steadied himself before he started down the stairs. "Well, I'm going to head back to my friend's house now. I'll see you later tonight."

Russ lifted the joint as he twitched his hand in goodbye. He pulled the stage door open. "Be careful."

Jeff started to answer without thinking. "Alwa—"

Russ had already turned and was walking through the stage door. Jeff hesitated as he looked back at Russ's retreating form. Those two words were the last words Clarence had said to him. They were their standard phrases as they went into combat together. Jeff continued to stare as Russ' form disappeared into the darkness of the hallway.

When the stage door shut behind Russ, Jeff continued down the stairs. He walked out of the alley turning left toward the school. The pot had left him so lighthearted that he whistled and hummed after shaking off Russ' words. The sidewalks, much emptier than during the afternoon, allowed his walk toward the park to go quickly. As he reached the edge of the park, the earlier trip through the center haunted him. His mode went from cheerful to stern as he turned right at the corner following the sidewalk for the long journey around the park. The hair on the back of his neck bristled as he peered out of the corner of his eye toward the bushes at the darkness within.

Jeff left the park perimeter sidewalk when he reached Don's street. With his mode cheerful once more, he smiled at the people as they passed him on the sidewalk. His steps were light when he bounded past the twins playing hopscotch before he mounted the steps to the house. Don sat on the porch swing, a glass of sweet tea in his left hand, an open calculus book in his right. His face concentrated on the page before him.

He looked up. "Get your ticket?"

Jeff sat down on the other end of the porch swing. He pulled out his wallet and retrieved the five twenties before he stuck them in the open pages of Don's book.

"Nope. Did better than that. I got a job and a ride to New Orleans. In addition, I got us free passes to the show tonight. And, I'm buying dinner."

Sally came through the door and sat down at the table. "You got a job? Doing what?"

"I'm going to be a roadie with the band Heaven Can Wait. The last stop on their tour is New Orleans. We'll get there next month on the tenth. "

Sally's face turned to a worried look. "Are you sure that you're feeling strong enough to do something like that?"

"I helped them this afternoon hauling the equipment up two flights of stairs and I felt fine."

Jeff went through the events that led up to the job offer. When he mentioned Pensacola as one of the stops, Don interrupted him. "Pensacola huh? Are you going to try to look up Pat?"

"Who's Pat?" Sally asked.

"That's the girl Jeff dated through high school. She was from Pensacola but went to the girl's school across town from us. We both thought they would get married one day."

Sally turned toward Jeff. "So what happened? Why did you break up?"

"We didn't really break up. Her parents wanted her to go to Vassar while I could only afford an in-State school. We wrote for a while, but after I dropped out of VPI to join the army, I lost touch with her. Hell, she's probably married by now."

"Well," Don said, "I think you should try to look her up. You two were good together."

"I don't know. I'd hate to go to her parent's house just to see her hanging on to some other guy. Anyway, enough of that. Are y'all ready for dinner? I really got the munchies."

Sally grabbed Jeff's head and turned his face so that her eyes looked straight into his. "Looks like you're feeling no pain. Is pot one of the fringe benefits?"

Jeff giggled. "It sounded like just a little bit of that goes on. Neither of the other two roadies holds while on the road. They just get some from people at the halls sometimes." He giggled again. "But they seem to get really good stuff."

Sally laughed back at him. "You're incorrigible, you know that. I'm not sure I want my husband hanging around you anymore. It took me too long to train him out of the habits you left him with from school."

"One other thing happened before I made it to the concert hall I need to tell y'all about. It was like a flashback or something."

Jeff went into a full explanation of the happenings in the park. Sally sat back and slowly sipped her sweet tea. When he finished, she looked at him with the concerned eyes of a trained nurse.

"Maybe you're just starting to remember what happened after the rocket explosion. I'd really feel better if you went to the VA hospital or maybe one of the veteran support groups downtown before you leave."

"Thanks for worrying Sally, but I really think if I just find Clarence, everything will be just fine."

Don laid his hand on Jeff's shoulder. "Okay, but you just keep our number handy. If you ever need help or just want to talk, call collect. We'll talk, or come get you, bail you out, or whatever."

Jeff's eyes misted. He rubbed his palms over them. "Thanks, Don. And Sally, thank you for all your help. Now come on, let's get those girls to their grandmother's so we can get some dinner. I feel like BarBQ with coleslaw."

After a messy dinner of pulled smoked pork, beans, creamy cole slaw, and beer, the threesome enjoyed front row seats at the concert. Sally and Don danced in the aisle to the driving beat of the band during the encores. Sally pulled Jeff up out of his seat and the three danced together through the closing notes. Singing the songs of the band, they walked home down the empty city sidewalks.

In the quiet of the guest room during the wee early hours of the morning, as the excitement of the evening wore off, Jeff lay half-awake in a semi-dream state. Gunfire sounded in the distance.

Late Sunday night, Jeff stood behind Mutluk and Russ in the control booth as the band finished the second encore. The audience, mainly college students, danced in the aisles pressing toward the front of the stage. Occasionally, a woman leaped up onto the stage only to be dragged to the side and dropped back to the floor by one of the large imposing security men. Mutluk stood slightly back from the soundboard, the levels set for the planned song with only the secondary master left to drop as soon as the band struck the last chord. Russ caressed his fingers against the slides and push buttons of the light board. The pulsating lights on the stage danced to his movements.

The music rose to a crescendo as the band went into the final series of the hard driving beats of their signature song. The lead guitarist leaped into the air and, as his feet hit the stage, the music stopped like a clamp had tightened hard against the strings of each guitar and drum. Mutluk's quick movement with his hand against the secondary master had done its job. Russ had released all the lighting buttons in time to Mutluk's slide. Only the reverberation of the two top cymbals sounded before they faded from the darkened stage. The crowd cheered while starting a rhythmic clap asking for another song. Russ then pushed seven buttons down on the light board while he kept his eyes focused on center stage.

The lead singer lifted his microphone to his lips as he mopped his brow with a green handkerchief. "Good night

Richmond! You've been great. Look for our latest album in the stores. See you next tour!" He threw the handkerchief out toward a young female student.

Russ lifted his fingers from the push buttons and the stage went dark. As the curtains closed in the dim light of the exit signs, the crowd clapped and hooted at the band. A cadenced clap began again from the crowd for the third time but quickly subsided as the hall manager flipped switches to turn on the house lights. The security men at the exits pushed the doors open moving the crowd down the stairs toward the street. Standing next to the stage's side entrance, the band's manager occasionally let a pretty woman through the door. Mutluk and Russ settled back into the folding chairs behind their control panels. They sipped soda from cans.

Jeff fidgeted with the new gloves that Mutluk had told him to buy. "How long do you wait before you start tearing the equipment down?"

Mutluk turned from watching the audience leave. "As soon as security gets the last of the stragglers out so they can shut the doors, the stage manager will open the curtain. That's the signal that the stage is ours."

"What do I do first?"

"Russ and I will disconnect the power cords and remove the power tap from the fuse box. You can go to stage left and find the four trunk sized cases with the word Cords stenciled on them. Bring them to center stage then open them up next to each other."

Jeff found the cases and placed them out as Mutluk had instructed. Mutluk finished rolling the large main power cable into a loop just as Jeff opened the lid on the last case. Mutluk threw the roll into the left most case, shut the lid, and twisted the catches closed. Then he disconnected each microphone cable first from the stage box then from the end of the microphone. Handling them with more care than the musicians had, he placed each microphone into a suitcase-sized case lined with foam.

He then showed Jeff how to loosely wrap and secure each cord around itself. "See the green tape in the center of each cord? That means they go into the cord case stenciled in green. The speaker cords have a red tape and the power extensions have white. Roll them all as I pile them and then throw them into the correct case."

Jeff rolled the mass of cords and cables as Mutluk and Russ dismantled drums, unstacked amplifiers, and reduced microphone stands to their lowest height. When Russ asked him, he cranked down the same lift he had cranked up on Thursday until the light truss was at a level such that Russ could remove the lights. As he removed each light, he handed it to Jeff, and Jeff placed it into different slotted cases depending on the color. Soon the stage was a collection of closed cases, pieces of light truss, and large unstacked speaker cabinets.

As the three took a break, Jeff surveyed the mass of equipment lying across the stage while he sipped on a can of soda. "How do you figure out what goes into the truck first?"

"It's easy," Russ said. "Each of the large cases has a number stenciled on it. We line those cases up along the aisle starting with number one near the door. Each smaller case has a number and a letter like 1A, 1B, and so on. We line those up on the floor in front of the stage. You and Mutluk will start taking the large cases down to the truck and I follow with small cases. The large cases go in and then I place the small ones on top of them to fill in the gaps. Mutluk sets a rhythm so that we don't get in each other's way. With the stairs here, I could pull ahead pretty quickly. But in other venues that let you roll everything, I would fall behind."

"That seems pretty easy."

Mutluk chuckled as he drained the last of his can of Coke. He threw it into a trashcan on the audience floor and headed toward the speaker cabinet on the left side of the stage. "I want to hear you use the word easy after we've taken about ten of these cases down to the truck. Come on, let's get the first one out of here."

Jeff pulled his new gloves on as he followed Mutluk toward the stack of speakers.

Mutluk rolled the sliding door on the back of the truck box down an hour later then slipped a large padlock through the closing handle. Jeff was standing behind him with a beer pressed up against his lips as he sucked the last drop from the can. Russ held a short joint to his lips and breathed in the sickly sweet smoke.

Pulling the truck keys from his pocket, Mutluk shuffled them around in his hand and then held out an alligator clip attached to the ring. "Here, clip that on this before you burn your fingers."

Russ secured the stub to the clip before handing it to Jeff.

Mutluk picked up his battered briefcase covered with used backstage passes. "We'll pick you up at your friend's house at ten. I want to get to Fayetteville by dark so we can find a motel for the night. Three of us sleeping in the cab of the truck is pretty tight. Then it will be an easy drive to Columbia the next day."

"Okay. I'll be ready."

Jeff strolled away down the empty city sidewalks. With the streets empty of traffic, the sound of his boots no longer remained hidden and the thud produced each time they hit the concrete echoed back from the storefronts. The buildings of the university were dark save for the occasional security floodlight. He crossed the intersections illuminated by alternating red and yellow signal lights, their control mechanisms clicking in time to the flashes. Few people passed him on the sidewalk, but a police car slowed as it cruised through an intersection in front of Jeff.

The brims of the officer's hats reflected the flashing lights as they scrutinized him.

When he approached the corner of the park, he turned right to follow the long perimeter sidewalk. The clicking of the traffic lights faded as he moved away from the intersection. Silence bit into the night but Jeff's ears picked up the sound of movement in the shadows to his left so he quickened his pace. He trotted lightly so that no sound came from his boots. A hand grenade exploded in the distance, followed by a sprinkling of fire from distant AK47s. M16s on full automatic answered the AK47s. Jeff broke into a full run as he crossed the street before diving behind a parked car.

The gunfire stopped.

He rose from his hiding place scanning the street as his eyes cleared the top of the car. Satisfied no danger existed on the street, he began walking again. Gunfire erupted from the bushes of the park and Jeff ran.

His running continued as he turned the corner onto Don's street. The gunfire stopped and the night was silent again. His hands shook as he reached for his keys while he mounted the steps to the house. He missed the first stab at the lock but made the second. Slamming the door behind him, he collapsed against it, his breath fast and hard. He stayed there shaking until exhaustion calmed him and then he stumbled up the stairs to bed.

Chapter 3

Jeff sat on the porch swing the next morning next to Sally as he sipped black coffee. His army pack leaned against the porch rail next to the steps. Sally, in her surgical scrubs with her hospital ID clipped to her collar, looked at the tiny watch that hung from the outside of her left breast pocket.

The morning rush hour had ended and the neighborhood settled into the sounds of young children as they played and the wind as it moved through the trees. City traffic sounds filtered down the street from several blocks away, providing a constant low rumble to the background. Don's voice filtered softly through the screen door as he worked to get the girls ready to go to their grandmother's for the day.

Sally set her teacup on the table. "Are you sure you won't reconsider and stay here until you can go see a doctor or at least talk to a VA counselor? Those flashbacks don't seem to be abating."

Jeff pushed his old Boonie hat to the back of his head. "Thanks for your concern, Sally. But, I really think finding Clarence is the best thing for me. I'm sure he can answer my questions about what happened. We talked a lot while we were over there and went through the same things in the field. I've also decided that I'm not going to talk to anyone else about it until I talk to Clarence. There would be too much to explain. If talking to Clarence doesn't work, I promise I'll go talk to the VA down in New Orleans."

"Okay. But remember, if you need our help, just call. I have vacation coming so I could drive to wherever you are, pick you up, and bring you back here. You're welcome to stay as long as you need."

"Thanks, Sally. That's really nice of you. I'll let y'all know what I find out after I find Clarence. By the way, thanks for the shaving kit."

"No problem. I think you look better without a beard."

The rumble of a heavy diesel engine accompanied by the sharp whoosh of air brakes came from down the street. Jeff picked up his pack as he stood up from the swing. Sally turned her head toward the screen door.

"Don, the truck's here. Come say goodbye." Sally stood and hugged Jeff. "You take care of yourself. Remember that you always have a place to stay here."

Jeff's eyes misted. "Thanks, lady." He pulled back while he wiped his eyes with his palms.

Don pushed open the screen door as the truck came to a stop in front of the house. The engine reverberating beneath the hood shook the wooden porch and vibrated the coffee left in Jeff's cup.

The twins ran out and grabbed Jeff's legs in their tiny arms. "Goodbye, Uncle Jeff."

Sally pulled the girls to her side as she stepped back from Jeff while Don approached. Don grabbed Jeff in a bear hug and patted his back. "You take care now. Send us some postcards from the road and call us if you can. Also, tell Clarence he's welcome to come back with you. I'd really like to meet him."

Jeff slowly broke from Don's embrace and pulled away until only their right hands remained in a grip. "I'll tell him. Maybe I can talk him into driving me back up here. He always said he'd like to see Washington."

Jeff stared at his old friend for a long moment until the truck air horn blasted behind him. "Thanks for everything. I'll be back." He turned and walked down the stairs.

The truck's passenger door lay open with the seat empty. Russ poked his head out from between the seats while he sat on the bed in the back. Climbing the outside step, Jeff handed his pack to Russ, settled into the passenger seat, and closed the door behind him. Mutluk shifted the truck into first gear and released his foot from the clutch. The truck lurched slightly as it began to roll forward. Mutluk quickly moved the stick shift into second.

He smiled at Jeff. "Welcome to the world of a Roadie."

The truck rumbled to the end of the street then Mutluk turned it south. After they motored through the city proper, they headed down Route 301 past the chemical plants lining the left side of road ending at the great docks of the James River. Fiery plumes of smoke rose high into the sky above their blackened brick smoke stacks.

The great warehouses of the southern tobacco companies lined the right side of the road, stretching beyond view. The sickly sweet smell of the drying tobacco whipped into the cab until Jeff rolled his window up to try to block the odor. Credence Clearwater Revival blared from the 8-Track player mounted below the dash.

The chemical plants and warehouses faded as the truck rolled into the farmlands south of the city until reaching the hamlet of Petersburg. Tidy shops and grocery stores bustling with patrons lined the road as they lumbered through the heart of the small downtown. As the truck left the city center, a sign directed tourist traffic toward the National Battlefield Park.

Jeff pointed to the sign. "There was a big battle called The Battle of The Crater fought here during the War Between the States. The Yankees tunneled under the Southern lines and blew up a bunch of gunpowder. The Yankees tried to breach the line, but got pushed back."

Russ glanced at the sign. "Do you know a lot about that war?"

"I was in high school during most of the Centennial Celebration. We learned about all the battles that took place in Virginia. Some of the people down here act like the war's still going or that the South didn't lose. There's also a bunch of people that still call it The War of Northern Aggression. It can be a mess sometimes."

They rolled out of Petersburg and into the flat farmlands beyond. Corn gave way to tobacco and cotton as they crossed the border into North Carolina. The maples and elms of Virginia disappeared and long needled pines replaced them. Small farming towns dotted the road as the tires ate up the miles and the sun rose higher into the sky. Mutluk turned into a truck stop south of Rocky Mount and rolled up to the pumps. A neon sign flashed on the attached diner welcoming hungry travelers.

An old man, standing in front of the truck stop office, looked down at a wooden barrel with a checkerboard on the top. Bib overalls hung from his flannel-covered shoulders and a hand rolled cigarette dangled loosely from his mouth. His partner in the game, dressed in worn coveralls also, slowly rocked in a rocker while he waited his turn. He puffed on a corncob pipe. Both men glanced up in a disturbed manner as the truck interrupted their game. The man with the cigarette looked at Jeff in the passenger seat and then at the side of the truck.

He pulled the cigarette from his mouth as he turned his head toward the service bay. "Leroy, get your lazy ass out here and catch the pump."

"Yes'em," came from inside.

A black man, dressed in soiled pants and a t-shirt so covered in grease that only the edge above his rope belt showed a hint of white, rose from under a car in the service bay and approached the truck. He wiped his hands on a greasy red rag while he slowly shuffled toward the truck with a slight limp in his right leg. As he rounded the front, Mutluk stepped down from the cab.

Mutluk smiled at the man. "Give me a hundred gallons of diesel."

"You got cash? Mr. Smith don't take none of them credit cards."

"Sure, no problem. I'll need a receipt."

Russ stepped from the cab and stretched his lanky body out. "Where's the restroom in there?"

Leroy looked at Russ as the pump counter dinged upward. "Ain't no bathroom you can use here." He looked over at Mutluk. "You neither. Closest place for colored is the BarBQ stand 'bout halfa mile down the road. They's got an outhouse around back. Good BarBQ too."

Jeff came around the front of the truck. "You want to get some burgers for lunch? Diner doesn't look crowded."

Leroy looked at Jeff before he flicked his head toward the diner. "They won't serve you in der neither. Y'all best git your diesel and move on down the road."

He replaced the pump handle in its cradle and switched off the pump. "That be twenty-two fifty-five."

Mutluk handed him two twenties.

"You's best wait here. I'll bring you the change and a receipt." He limped around the front of the truck.

Mutluk turned toward Jeff. "He said we couldn't use the bathroom here and we'd have to go use an outhouse down the road near some BarBQ place."

Jeff shook his head slightly. "That sounds about right for a podunk place like this."

Leroy came around the front of the truck with Mutluk's change. He piled the bills, coins, and hand-written receipt into Mutluk's hand. "Y'alls best head on out of the county. I heard Mr. Smith talkin' on the telephone 'bout your truck."

Mutluk shoved the pile into his pocket. "Think we can still stop at the BarBQ place?"

Leroy shrugged his shoulders. "Just makes sure that y'all park off the road. Watch your speed, Sheriff's 'round here somewhere. County line's about five miles on down. You take care now." He limped slowly around the front of the truck.

Jeff half-smiled at Mutluk and Russ. "Come on. Let's head out. Carolina BarBQ is good."

Mutluk pulled the truck slowly back onto the road running through the gears in a slow methodical manner. An old gray Ford pickup backed out of the diner parking lot, falling in behind them. Jeff noticed the truck in the side view mirror but didn't say anything.

Mutluk slowed as he pulled the truck onto the shoulder at the roadside stand identified only with a handwritten sign advertising BarBQ. The pickup from the diner passed by the stand and pulled off the road about a hundred feet further down. Jeff looked down the road toward the pickup truck and motioned toward it.

"Y'all go hit the outhouse. I'll get us some BarBQ sandwiches and Cokes to go. I don't think we should hang around here. We're being followed. We can eat at a pull off in the next county."

Mutluk and Russ walked around the rear of the stand toward the outhouse while Jeff went to talk to the old woman behind the roughly nailed counter. In minutes, the three were back in the cab. The smell of pulled pork splashed with vinegar sauce filled the air. The bag sat unopened on the floor as Mutluk kept his eyes on the road ahead with an occasional glance toward the speedometer. The pickup truck pulled into place behind them after they passed it.

Mutluk shifted his eyes momentarily toward the side view mirror. "Who do you think is in the pickup?"

Jeff kept his own gaze focused on the reflection of the pickup in his side. "If I had to guess, I'd say probably they're Klan."

Russ stuck his head between the seats, pushed Jeff aside, and looked into the mirror. "Klan? There's Klan down here? I thought that was just a bunch of guys that marched in the cities."

"There's Klan everywhere down here. Some areas are more active than others are. Just settle down. As long as we keep going they won't bother us in daylight."

The two-vehicle convoy gathered speed slowly as Mutluk ran through the gears. He stopped shifting in third high to hold the truck at forty-five miles an hour. They passed a speed limit sign on the right with a fifty printed on it. Jeff sat back in his seat while keeping his gaze loosely on the pickup behind them.

Two miles from the county line, a police car came up fast behind them. The driver of the pickup dropped back to open up space as the speed limit changed to sixty. Mutluk shifted into fifth high. The police car settled into place behind him as Mutluk accelerated to fifty-five. The light on the top of the police car remained unlit. The hairs on Jeff's neck bristled as he kept vigil through the side view mirror. "Cop car just pulled in behind us. He hasn't turned his light on yet."

Mutluk glanced in his side view mirror. "Got him."

The county line sign appeared as the truck drove around a curve. The light on the top of the police car behind them remained unlit. Mutluk shifted his eyes constantly between the speedometer, the side view mirror, and the road ahead. His knuckles blanched on the steering wheel.

Jeff kept his eyes focused into the mirror as the Wilson County limits sign flashed by. He relaxed and turned his eyes forward. "The cop car and the pickup are turning around."

The open farmlands of central Carolina gave way to clothes stores, gas stations, and used car lots as Mutluk drove into Fayetteville as the last of the evening sun faded from the sky. The black of the night was lost in the glow of the flashing neon signs. An unlit sign on the side of the road announced Fort Bragg three miles ahead. The stores changed to bars and strip joints as the turn to the base came upon them. The truck made slow progress through the crowded street.

Jeff motioned to Mutluk. "How about you park in that lot over there and let's go get some dinner at the Dew Drop Inn. It's coming up on the right next to the alley. The airborne troops go to it sort of as a tradition after they get their wings. Good food and great beer. I went there a bunch of times before I shipped out and have always wanted to go back."

Russ looked at him from between the seats. "You sure it'll be okay? I'm still shaken up about that thing outside of Rocky Mount."

"It'll be fine. I used to see vets in there all the time talking to the new troops. There might even be some of the guys I served with in there. Come on. I'll buy."

Mutluk turned the truck into the dirt lot. He set the air brakes with a loud whoosh letting the engine cool for a minute before he shut it down. The heavy idle of muscle cars cruising the street replaced the rumble of the diesel. Occasionally, a driver revved his engine and squealed the tires in an attempt to impress one of the few women walking on the street.

The three roadies headed through the crowd past flashing neon signs that advertised burgers, beer, and strippers as Jeff led the group toward the door of the Dew Drop Inn. Soldiers in dress greens, a few with large-haired women held tight to their sides, crowded the sidewalk forcing Mutluk, Russ, and Jeff to walk in single file.

Jeff pulled the door open just as four soldiers stumbled out. Causing a break in the crowd, they reached the sidewalk and leaped toward the street. Shouts of Geronimo came from the four as they stopped short of the busy roadway before they staggered down the sidewalk.

Jeff led his small group into the smoke-filled dimly lit bar. The seats at the tables were full of soldiers with the tabletops stacked with overturned shot glasses and empty beer bottles. Soldiers crowded around the few women scattered amongst the tables. Pool games flourished with quarters for future games lining the rails. Country music blared from a jukebox in the corner.

Jeff smiled taking it all in as he slid onto a stool at the bar near the side exit. While Mutluk and Russ followed him, their gazes warily eyed the crowd around them. Jeff sat on the stool surveying the familiar scene of a dozen soldiers vying for each woman. His mind went to the day of his first pass off base after receiving his jump wings. His buying drinks in an attempt to flirt with those same women had gotten him nothing except an empty wallet accompanied by a hangover that tortured him during the next day's training. The bartender passed in Jeff's peripheral vision.

Jeff spun on his stool toward the bar. "Can we get three beers and some burgers here?"

The bartender stopped as he pulled a case of beer from the cooler below the bar. He looked at Jeff then shifted his eyes to Mutluk and Russ. "No."

He walked down the bar and set the case of beer on the floor. He emptied the case into another cooler throwing the empty box down the rear hall before he came back in front of Jeff to reach back into the cooler.

Jeff stared at the bartender. "Do we need to sit at a table to get burgers now? I used to eat at the bar when I was stationed here."

The bartender pulled another case of beer from the cooler. He stared at Jeff with his jaw set in a grimace. "I said no, hippie. Now take your other hippies with you and leave before I throw you out." He turned and started to head down the bar.

Jeff grabbed the man's shirt collar. The case of beer fell from the bartender's hands and it crashed to the floor.

The breaking glass overpowered the wailing music of the jukebox. Jeff shouted above the music. "My money was good enough for you when I was stationed here. What's changed?"

The bartender reached below the bar and came up with a club in his hand. Grabbing the back of the bartender's head with his left hand, Jeff bounced the bartender's face off the bar while he grabbed the club with his right. The bartender fell to the floor behind the bar and did not move.

The jukebox fell silent. The room became still.

Mutluk grabbed Jeff by the collar. "We've got to leave."

Jeff turned toward Mutluk before he looked out into the bar. Soldiers had left their seats and moved toward them. Several yielded pool cues like clubs. Jeff faced the advancing soldiers with the bartender's club raised in front of him. The exit sign glowed to his right. He slowly backed toward the door, pushing Mutluk and Russ behind him with his free hand.

They flew out the door in a run. Moving into the alley, they turned toward the street with soldiers close behind them. Other soldiers, who had left the bar through the front door, closed off that exit to them. A standoff ensued with the soldiers surrounding them as the three roadies circled with their backs to each other. Jeff scanned the faces of the soldiers as they slowly circled. He held the club loose across his chest. Threats came across the narrow void from the soldiers.

Jeff studied each face and the mannerisms they presented as he circled. A sneer here, a grimace there, a pool cue held in a particular manner caught in his ever-searching eyes. He quietly called out the dangers that he saw to Mutluk and Russ. "Mutluk, the guy third from the right with the pool cue, he'll be the first to attack from that end. Russ, watch the guy standing closest to the wall, he's trying to work his way around to our flank."

A small gap appeared between the open door from the bar and the line of soldiers. The soldiers in the door were standing back as the ones in the alley advanced slowly. "Mutluk, get the keys to the truck into your hand. Get ready to charge the line near the door. Head to the truck after you get past the line. I'll protect your rear as y'all run down the alley."

Russ answered Jeff. "I'm not leaving you here."

Jeff kept his eyes focused toward the danger spots. "Do it. Get to the truck and lock yourself in. These guys may hurt me, but they will kill y'all. Mutluk, you ready?"

"Yes."

"I'm going to charge the front line to draw their attention. I'll take out the biggest danger first before I try to break through to the street. Most of these guys won't fight. They'll just back up to watch. Hopefully, an MP patrol will come by quick and save me. I'll count to three. Give me a second before you move." Jeff continued to scan the crowd as several soldiers advanced toward them a half step at a time.

A soldier, wearing a garrison cap, looked in on the action between the shoulders of two soldiers. The nose below the brim of the cap bent slightly off center to the right at an angle that caught Jeff's attention and he snapped his gaze to the eyes above the nose. Those eyes looked indifferently down the alley at the scene, but Jeff knew those eyes. The eyes had stared at him in formations during training and in the heat of battle. Eyes that could be both menacing and comforting at the same time. The head turned as the figure started moving from the alley. Only the garrison cap remained visible above the heads of the soldiers while it moved down the street.

Jeff raised himself to his full height as he yelled toward the figure just before it disappeared behind the wall. "Sergeant Slattery!"

The figure stopped and the front of the garrison cap turned toward Jeff. The voices in the crowd of soldiers quieted somewhat at the mention of the name, though the more aggressive soldiers continued their rants. The figure moved behind the sea of shoulders until the body beneath the cap stepped into the open as it pushed through the front line of the soldiers.

Sergeant First Class Ray Slattery, in impeccable dress greens sporting four rows of ribbons over his left breast pocket, moved forward with his standard cautious gait. The soldiers surrounding the trio further quieted as he stepped beyond the closest aggressors. Even the most drunken and aggressive soldier stepped back. He moved until his face was a foot from Jeff's stern gaze, each set of eyes staring at the other's.

The corners of Sergeant Slattery's mouth curled up ever so slightly and a small amount of the tobacco-stained teeth inside showed between the lips. Jeff relaxed his stance at the sight of what he guessed was a smile, though he had never seen one on the face before. Ever so slowly, the corners of the mouth went further up until the teeth were fully exposed.

Sergeant Slattery finally broke the silence. "Hello, Blooper-man. Damn good to see you."

The Sergeant backed up slightly from Jeff as he moved to the side of the trio. "Stand down," he roared. The soldiers in the alley went silent. "Take a knee."

The soldiers obeyed the command without hesitation. All went down on a knee as a group though several fell onto their sides. Their comrades-in-arms quickly helped them back to their knees. Sergeant Slattery walked slowly past Mutluk and Russ as he scanned them from head to toe. He looked out toward the kneeling soldiers as a pair of MPs walked into the alley. Sergeant Slattery waved them away. They turned back toward the street as they resumed their patrol.

Sergeant Slattery moved back next to Jeff before he turned toward the crowd of soldiers near the street. "Troops, I want to introduce you to Corporal Jeff Briggs, though based on his present appearance and company, I would have to say ex-Corporal Briggs. He was the best damn M79 gunner I have ever known. He could put a round into a beer glass at a hundred meters and not disturb the foam."

The Sergeant turned his head toward Jeff. "He was also one of the best combat soldiers I ever saw fight. You are all lucky he didn't get his hands on you. Reveille formation tomorrow would have been sparse with the number of you he would have put on sick call. And if any of you had hurt him, you would then be enemies of mine." He turned his head back toward the assembled soldiers. "Now, as you were and leave us."

The troops rose quickly from their knees, scurried out of the alley, and back toward the bar. In less than ten seconds, only Sergeant Slattery and the three roadies remained standing in the alley.

Jeff stuck his hand out toward the Sergeant. "Thanks, Sarge. Things were getting a bit dicey there for a minute."

Sergeant Slattery took Jeff's hand shaking it warmly. "Call me Ray. You're obviously a civilian now. In addition, it would take a hell of a lot more than this to even the score. What the hell are you doing here, Jeff? And who are these two guys?"

"The big guy is Mutluk and the skinny one is Russ. I'm working as a roadie with them for a band. We're on our way to Columbia and stopped for the night. We tried to have a beer in the Dew Drop. Things went a little wrong."

Ray stuck his hand out to first Mutluk and then Russ. "Call me Ray. Any friend of Blooper-man is a friend of mine. Come on, I'll buy you that beer."

"We really ought to go find a motel for the night," Mutluk said.

Ray shook his head. "You won't find a motel around here." He turned toward Jeff. "Why don't the three of you stay at my house for the night? We can have that beer and you can tell me what you've been doing. Sarah can put something together for dinner. It might be leftovers, but I promise the beer will be cold."

Jeff looked at Mutluk and Russ. Mutluk shrugged his shoulders. Russ looked around the alley and then out at the soldiers moving along the street. "As long as we get away from here, I'll be happy."

"Good," Ray said. "Let me go call Sarah to tell her we're coming. Where are you parked?"

Jeff pointed down the street. "We're in a truck parked in the vacant lot next to the Shell Station."

"Okay, I'll meet you there in five minutes. How big is the truck?"

"It's a 35-footer," Mutluk answered.

"Just follow me up the drive to the house. There's room for you turn around at the end of the drive." Ray turned to Jeff, grabbing him in a bear hug. "Damn, it's good to see you." He released Jeff before heading into the bar to make his call.

After a dinner of cold fried chicken, potato salad, and corn on the cob, Jeff and Ray sat on chairs at the porch table, each with a beer in their hands. Mutluk leaned against the front steps watching the fireflies as they slowly danced through the air. Russ's off-key singing emanated from the downstairs shower. Droplets of water formed on the ends of Jeff's damp hair and slid onto the collar of his clean t-shirt.

"Thanks again for the food and shower, Sarge, uh, Ray. I hope we didn't put you out too much."

"Like I said before, it'll take a lot more than this to even the score."

A minute later, Russ opened the screen door as he shaped his hair with a large pick. "Boy, that shower felt good. I also never thought a flush toilet would be so nice."

Ray looked at Jeff with a quizzical expression.

Jeff smiled. "Russ got introduced to Jim Crow today. We stopped south of Rocky Mount for gas."

Russ sat down in a chair at the table and pulled a beer from the bucket of ice. "Who's Jim Crow? Was he that colored guy at the truck stop?"

Jeff let out a muted laugh as he started to lift his bottle to his lips. He looked at Ray. "You'll have to excuse him. He's from New York City." Jeff turned his head toward Russ. "Jim Crow refers to a bunch of old laws that kept colored folks away from whites in the South. The federal courts have ruled them illegal, but the locals still run things that way in many places, mainly out in the country. You shouldn't have any problems near the concert halls in the cities though."

Ray took a sip from his beer. "Damn archaic laws. After two tours of fighting and dying in the bush with troops of all colors, I don't have time for that shit."

Jeff set the empty bottle on the table. "We also were followed for a while by what I guess was a pickup full of Klan and a Sheriff's car. They left us after we crossed into Wilson County."

Rising from his seat on the steps, Mutluk walked over to Ray. "Well, I'm turning in. We need to get an early start so we can get to Columbia to set up. It should be an easy load-in though. Road manager said the loading dock is at the same level as the stage. Good night, Ray. Thanks for everything."

"No problem, Mutluk. You had better take the bed. I don't think the folding cots will hold you."

Russ finished his beer, placing the empty upside down in the bucket. "I'm going to turn in too. See you tomorrow. Or I guess it's see y'all tomorrow."

Jeff giggled. "Russ is a want-to-be actor and is trying to learn how to speak redneck while he's down here."

"I'm not a want-to-be actor. I'm an out-of-work actor."

Ray laughed. "Ain't nothin' wrong wit dat."

After the two went in through the screen door, their footsteps echoed down the hardwood floors before they faded into the bedroom. Just as the sound of the guestroom door closing came through the screen, light gunfire echoed in the night air.

Jeff jerked his head toward the sound. "Do you hear that?"

Ray cocked his head upward. "That's just night fire exercises at the Fort. It'll go on until about midnight."

"I remember those exercises. I thought they were so real until we were actually in a night firefight."

Ray turned toward Jeff and set his beer on the table. "Listen, Jeff, have you ever thought about coming back in? I could get you posted here in the training cadre. They'd probably bring you back in as a three-stripe Sergeant. Your experience might help keep some of these young troops alive."

"Thanks for the confidence, Ray. But, right now, I just need to find Clarence to talk a few things out. Then maybe I can figure out where I belong."

"Okay, I can understand that. You two were as thick as thieves over there. But, think about it. If you decide you want to do it, give me a call. I'll come to wherever you are and bring you back."

"Sure, Ray. I'll let you know."

The men sipped their beers as the gunfire sounded in the distance.

Later that night, Jeff awoke on one of the folding cots. Listening for a minute to the distant gunfire as it filtered through the open window, he thought about Clarence and Vietnam. He then fluffed his pillow, turned on his side, and soon fell into a fitful sleep once again. Only Russ' light snoring broke the silence of the night.

The next morning broke with the classic North Carolina mist suspended over the pond visible through the trees. White-tailed deer munched grass along the driveway while rabbits hopped away at the slightest noise.

The truck idled with its deep rumble as Jeff said his goodbyes. "Thanks again, Ray. I'll let you know what happens."

"You take care of yourself, Jeff. Just remember there's always a bed and a beer waiting here for you."

The two men shook hands before Jeff climbed into the cab. Before he could close the door, Ray climbed up on the step and looked in at Russ. "Y'all take care, ya hear?"

Jeff broke out laughing as Ray dropped from the step closing the door behind him. Mutluk shifted the truck into gear to start down the driveway. Russ watched as Ray's figure diminished in the side view mirror. "Nice guy."

"He is that."

Chapter 4

Mutluk slid the rear sliding door of the truck down and slipped the padlock into the catch. Jeff and Russ were sitting on the edge of the dock upwind from the exhaust of the idling diesel. The streets were quiet after the last show at the Columbia Memorial Concert Hall. Only the lights of an occasional campus police car patrolling the university area showed past the glow of the dock lights. The first hint of dawn etched the sky behind the twin residential student towers that rose to the east.

Mutluk flipped his ponytail over his shoulder as he motioned toward the front of the truck. Jeff and Russ slid down from the dock slowly making their way up to the passenger door. As they approached the cab, Russ pulled quickly ahead, opened the door, and climbed in.

"I get the bed."

Jeff let Russ disappear between the seats. "Take it. I'd rather look at the scenery. This drive is the way that I used to go to Rocksville with my grandparents when they would pick me up from the train."

He turned toward Mutluk as the big man settled into the driver's seat and pushed in the air brake knob. "You sure you're okay with me missing the load-in and set up in Charleston? I could always make my way back to Rocksville tomorrow on the bus or hitchhike."

"It's fine. The Charleston hall is a union place. As soon as the cases hit the dock, the union stagehands have to take them to the stage to stack them where I tell them. I want you there though for tear-down and load-out. You and I can be in the truck putting everything into place while

Russ stays on the stage telling them what to bring out next."

"Sounds like a pretty easy thing."

Mutluk looked left and right before pulling into the street. "It's about the easiest load-in we have. It gets a little ridiculous though. We have to lay out the extension cords from the amps to the power box, but the union electrician has to plug them in."

Mutluk shifted into third low as he pointed the truck down the quiet road. He guided the truck through the college area while the sun lightened the sky to the east. A few hard-partying students still sat on their front steps to have one last beer before going to sleep. The truck moved onto the main road past the blinking stoplights, harsh street lamps, and the occasional young child delivering the morning paper.

A city patrol car pulled in behind the truck. Mutluk's face tightened as he began to shift his eyes from the mirror, to the road, to the speedometer, and then back to the mirror. He visibly relaxed when the police car turned around as the truck passed by the city limits sign. Russ snored softly in the bed in the back. The lightening countryside came into view as they left the outskirts of the city, careful to obey every speed limit.

The little crossroad towns came and went as the truck rolled on US route 21 through the dawn of the day. Jeff rolled the window down as he looked for familiar landmarks. The old gas station at Oak Grove came into view through the morning mist with its dirty and dim hanging lamp slowly swinging in the light breeze. Jeff and his grandfather stopped there for gas coming from the train. While the black attendant filled the tank, his grandfather talked to the farmers in the shade of the front porch over a game of checkers. Jeff would run down to the pond to skip rocks while looking in the reeds for snakes and frogs. Before they resumed their trip, his grandfather would buy him an RC Cola and a Moon Pie for the rest of the ride to Rocksville. Jeff always had to promise not to tell his grandmother about the Moon Pie, for she was against those store bought sweets. She was always against anything new fangled.

He still missed his grandparents, but he was glad that his great-grandmother, Mama Hazel, was still alive. Many nights he had slept at her little house, just up the dirt road from his grandparents. In the mornings, he would gather eggs from the hens in the yard. After making him a breakfast of eggs, smoked country ham, grits, and fresh biscuits with homemade jam, she would read a passage to him from her old worn bible. He really didn't understand all that she read, but she seemed so happy when she shared it with him.

The truck drove on into the early morning hours as the dawn came fully awake. Road signs announced that they were approaching Orangeburg, the closest large town to Rocksville. Jeff's grandparents would take him with them on their monthly trip to buy things that were not available in the small general store in Rocksville. Jeff looked forward to the trips. He would ride in the back of the pickup with Bessie, the black woman that cooked meals and cleaned house for his grandparents. She had always called him Honey Child. When the weather was good, they would each stare out their own sides of the truck at the passing landscape as the pines, mulberry trees, and Spanish moss created a continuous ripple of shade and sun. When it rained, they would huddle together under the tarp.

Mutluk's voice broke Jeff's solitary thoughts of the past. "What route do I take to get to that town you want us to drop you at?"

"Stay on 21 through Orangeburg. You'll get on US 78 at Branchville. Then it's only about 15 miles further up to Rocksville."

"Okay."

Jeff went back to his thoughts of yesterdays while the landscape became fully visible. The sun peeked its glow through the morning mist bathing everything in a red softness. It was fully above the mist as they entered the City of Orangeburg. Traffic on the road increased making Mutluk constantly shift his eyes from mirror to road to mirror.

Mutluk, without stopping his shifting eyes, spoke to Jeff. "Keep that map handy and look for the route signs. I don't want to miss the turn and accidentally end up trying to turn around in some police parking lot. I'm still a little spooked from the other day."

Jeff left the map in the door side pocket. "Don't worry. I know the way from here."

They passed by the old Tri-county Hospital where Jeff's grandfather had taken him when he was nine after breaking his arm climbing the big old oak tree in the Carter's backyard. The cast stayed on for three months and had made him the center of attention when elementary school started up back in Richmond that fall.

"Take a left at the next stop sign."

Mutluk made the turn. Main Street, with its shuttered stores framing one busy diner, opened in front of them.

Russ pushed his head through the seats as he whistled softly. "Look at all those pickups. I bet they're all Klan good old boys. Keep driving, Mutluk."

Mutluk kept the truck slightly below the speed limit as they moved past the line of parked pickups. Several of the men standing on the sidewalk talking turned to watch as the truck went by. Jeff held his hair behind his head so they would have trouble seeing it. Relief flowed through him when he saw through the rear view mirror that they had gone back to talking with no further attention to them.

As they crossed the railroad tracks leaving town, Jeff pointed to the upcoming intersection. "Take the next right."

The sun shone brightly above the trees as the truck

rolled eastward away from the town. The buildings and houses of the town had given way to small irregular farm fields. Black sharecroppers outside their worn out shacks in faded bib overalls prepared to work those fields. Before Jeff had left for the army, he would have paid top dollar for a pair of overalls that worn to get the natural look that seemed so cool at the time. He guessed that the bibs that the black men wore were the only ones they owned. Some of the men led old mules out into the fields to plows or rickety wagons. His grandfather had told him years before that the coloreds would never get tractors because they weren't smart enough to run them. Jeff knew better now.

As the truck entered the crossroads town of Branchville, Jeff directed Mutluk to turn left onto US 78. They left the small collection of stores that passed for a town as the railroad tracks joined the path of the road on Mutluk's side of the truck. Jeff knew those tracks well for they ran straight through Rocksville. He used to place pennies on the tracks when he was young and watched as the trains flattened them into shiny oblong pieces of copper. The flattened copper would fetch a nickel each back in the Richmond suburbs from his classmates. His grandfather took them from him one year when he found out. He told Jeff that he could go to jail for destroying government property.

His smile left him as he realized that was the last year he had been down here. A drunk driver on the road back from Orangeburg had killed his grandparents three days later. They were returning home after putting him on the train back to Richmond at the end of the summer. When Jeff got off the train, his mother had told him about the accident. Tears formed in his eyes as he thought of those two people that he loved so dearly. One thing he had prayed was that his grandfather still was not upset with him when he died. He wiped his eyes as he turned to face out the truck window. The sign announcing that they were

5 miles from Rocksville came into view.

Jeff nudged Russ as he pointed at the collection of worn sheds and pens on the land next to the sign. "Those were my grandfather's chicken coops and pig pens. I couldn't tell you how many eggs I collected from those coops and how many corn cobs I fed to the pigs."

Russ looked at the coops and pens. "How come you didn't end up one of those redneck boys?"

"Just lucky I guess. Why don't you hand me my pack? I'll be getting out in just a few minutes."

Russ reached back, brought out Jeff's well-worn army pack, and handed it to him. Mutluk pulled the truck to the shoulder as the truck came to the flashing red light that signified the center of the little town.

Jeff turned to Mutluk before he stepped down from the cab. "Just stay on this road. It takes you straight into Charleston. I'll see you Monday."

Russ slid between the seats into the passenger seat. "How are you going to get down there?"

"I've got cousins here that work in the shipyards down there. I'm sure that one of them will give me a lift."

Russ closed the door, giving a wave as Mutluk pulled the truck through the intersection accelerating slowly away.

After he adjusted the Boonie hat on his head, Jeff hefted the pack onto his shoulders. He turned left onto the sidewalk of Main Street toward Mama Hazel's house. Only a few shopkeepers were out as Jeff strolled down the street. He went past the general store where a man prepared the sidewalk displays for the morning shoppers.

Jeff recognized the man as an older version of the person that used to sell him firecrackers. Jeff gave a wave and a "Morning" as he walked by. The man stared back with the hard look of disgust on his face. Moving slowly along, Jeff looked into the windows of the closed shops. The displays in the windows appeared to be the same as the last time he had walked this way. Dated clothing, canned goods, and faded advertisements filled the shop windows. A tractor chugged by on the street, a young boy at the wheel. Jeff waved, but the boy only stared back.

When the stores ended, Jeff turned left down the railroad tracks that cut through the center of town. The tops of the tracks were a mix of shine and rust and grass grew between the ties. He walked along balanced on the left rail, his arms held out like airplane wings. At the next road crossing, he turned left and started down Reedville road. Mama Hazel's house was just a mile down the road. His grandparent's old house was next door to hers. Jeff wondered what relative had inherited it as he started the familiar walk on the old country road.

Jeff picked his way through the grass on the shoulder of the road as pickup trucks headed the other way toward the farm fields, chicken ranches, or the small downtown. Faces stared at him from the rolled down windows and two of the drivers spit in his direction, but Jeff didn't notice. Only the thought of Mama Hazel with her wonderful kitchen full of the smell of morning biscuits filled his mind.

The town's dentist occupied the building on the corner of Reedville Road and Railroad Avenue. Dual doors marked the separate waiting rooms, one was marked Whites while the other read Coloreds. The stately worn houses of the town's old money sat back from the road on the left. Sitting porches wrapped around three sides of the ground floor of each house and the sleeping porches above the east side lay hidden by screening maple trees. Old slave quarters sat rotted, overgrown with ivy at the rear of several of the houses. The occasional carriage houses, long turned into garages, sat with their doors open. The noses of shiny Buicks poked out from buildings too short for their current charges.

Jeff marched past these familiar comfortable sights toward the Y in the road ahead. The Reedville Road jogged to the left while the Old Reedville Road went to the right. Mama Hazel's house lay down the old road another half mile, but years of little use had allowed nature to shrink the road on both sides until only a lane and a half remained for traffic. Whenever two pickups met on the road, a rare occurrence in itself, one would go onto the grass on the shoulder to allow the other to pass. On a normal day, the drivers would stop to visit for a few moments before going on their way. The road had been this way since before Jeff had first walked into town alone when he was only five.

The woods on the right, known as Milspaul Woods, grew deeper and thicker as Jeff got closer to the split in the road. Stately yellow pines rose high into the air above his head. Their needles smelled strong of sap as the last of the morning dew disappeared from the grass on the shoulder. Ivy worked up the tree trunks and around bushes to form an almost impenetrable barrier along the road. Long strands of Spanish Moss hung from the branches above like the webs of spiders waiting for a huge prey. The woods appeared thicker than he remembered.

Jeff looked into the woods wondering if the old tree house he had built with the Carter boys still stood in that forest of his youth. Vines might cover the old fort by now. Maybe some other children had commandeered it after the Carters moved to Washington after Jeff had stopped visiting.

A path exited the overgrown shoulder into the woods just before the Y, a path that Jeff had taken many times before. It led to the houses he sought beyond the bend. Without a second's hesitation, Jeff stepped from the shoulder onto the defined trace. He pushed past an ivy-covered bush that had grown out across the path. The forest closed in behind him.

A vine, fallen across the path for so long that roots from it had taken hold, trapped his ankle. He pitched forward as he lost his footing and rolled into the gully. His helmet flew off his head, bouncing along the slope to the path at the bottom. He instinctively gripped the stock of his M79 with his left hand and brought it close to his chest. His roll stopped as he hit the bottom of the gully. Jeff quickly knelt, brought his weapon to his shoulder, pushed the safety until it clicked, and turned his head as he took in his surroundings. The muzzle of the M79 followed his eyes. He blinked as the sounds of gunfire and explosions from the raging battle above the gully hit his ears. The pines of the Milspaul Woods had morphed into the large leafed banana bushes with the signature clinging vines of the sub-tropics. Deep-throated M-60 machine gun fire came in bursts above the gully as Jeff grabbed his helmet.

Jeff rose and moved cautiously up the gully. A rocket whooshed from the right edge of the gully in front of him exploding somewhere above the edge to the left. Screams emanated from the direction of the explosion. The smoke trail left by the rocket betrayed the position of the launcher team. Jeff threw himself against the right slope. Crawling along the side, he listened to the battle raging above him. As he reached the area below where the rocket had launched, Jeff heard two voices in the singsong rhythm of the Vietnamese. He slithered up the face of the gully with his M79 pointed in front of him, silently wishing he had loaded a black-tipped shotgun round.

He buried his face in the wet leaves as a rocket launched above him with a loud whoosh of flame. Bits of burnt cordite drifted down around him from the trail of smoke burning his exposed skin. Equipment rattle came from the top of the gully. The rocket team was preparing to abandon their position to move to a new one. Jeff waited for another second before he dug the toes of his boots into the soft dirt and pushed himself up to the edge of the gully. He raised his M79 to his shoulder as his head cleared the edge.

An NVA soldier, with a rocket launcher on his shoulder

raised so that it pointed into the air, was turning away from the gully. A holstered pistol hung from his belt. A second soldier was on one knee gathering RPG rockets from the ground into his arms. An AK47 hung upside down from his right shoulder. He dropped the three RPG rounds and grabbed for the AK47 as he saw Jeff rise up. His left hand had just touched the barrel when Jeff fired. The blue tipped grenade left the barrel and drilled into the man's chest. It lodged there without exploding, the spin distance too close for it to arm. The heated round sizzled as blood began to flow from the sides of it down the man's chest. The soldier stared at the round before he fell over backward. Grabbing the warm barrel of his M79, Jeff continued his advance.

The other soldier had dropped the rocket launcher and had turned toward Jeff as he struggled to draw his pistol. The muzzle of the pistol had just cleared the holster when Jeff swung the butt of his M79 across the man's face. The man spun around down to his knees, dropping the pistol to the ground. Jeff went down to one knee, grabbed the stock of the M79, and bashed the man's face with the butt again. The soldier fell backward and brought his hands to his face. Jeff drew his 45-caliber pistol and shot the man in the head before turning back toward the other soldier.

The soldier on his back had stopped writhing, but blood continued to seep around the sides of the unexploded round. The projectile had cooled so the blood no longer sizzled but it flowed down both sides of his tunic. Jeff looked down at the soldier's blank face before holstering his pistol. He slung the M79 over his shoulder, grabbed the man's AK47, and launched himself back over the edge of the gully.

Jeff rolled to the bottom of the gully, checked for movement nearby, and then searched the path that ran down its length. A blood trail with boot drag marks showed that the NVA had taken Clarence up the path. He reloaded his M79 with another blue tipped round before setting the safety and then slinging it again over his left shoulder. He checked that the AK47 was loaded then flipped the selector switch to semiautomatic before he started cautiously moving up the gully toward his friend.

As he moved, NVA machine guns unleashed short deadly bursts above him to his left. He pushed around a clump of vines that had encased a rotted stump. The NVA machine guns were behind him now above the lip of the gully so he slowly crawled up the side. When he reached the lip, he raised his head just until his eyes cleared the leaves and twigs. An NVA machine gun position was ten meters from him to his left set up in a small depression. Another was behind a bunker of stacked logs about fifty meters further away. Both were spitting bullets in short deadly bursts toward his platoon.

Jeff laid the AK47 on the ground and brought the M79 to his shoulder. He gripped the trigger guard with his left hand as he placed his right hand under the wooden forward stock before flipping the safety to fire. Raising the muzzle of the M79 while he judged the distance, he looked out at the machine gun further away. He squeezed the trigger until it clicked and the familiar thump of the discharging weapon hit his shoulder. Without waiting for that round to hit, he shifted his attention to the nearer gun as he broke open the breech while reaching into his ammo vest for a short arming fragmentation round. The assistant machine gunner had turned his head toward him and was tapping the gunner on the shoulder. The gunner turned his head and then lifted the muzzle of the gun as he turned it toward Jeff.

Jeff glanced back toward the further machine gun as his round hit home and the gunner flew over the stacked logs. The assistant gunner lay with his legs at an unnatural angle. Jeff rammed the new round home and snapped the breech closed. He pointed it toward the machine gunner and raised the muzzle just above level.

The round flew from the muzzle and hit the machine gun as the gunner brought it down to bear. The explosion broke the gun into two pieces. The gunner and the assistant flew backward out of the depression. Wisps of smoke filtered from their clothes where the pieces of hot shrapnel embedded in them.

Gunfire sounded behind him and bullets chewed the leaves above his head. Jeff sank below the edge of the gully as he dropped the M79 to the ground. He picked up the AK47 as he rolled over onto his back. An NVA soldier was standing on the opposite bank of the gully with his AK47 tilted slightly as he dropped his now empty magazine to the ground and reached into his left pouch to get another. Jeff raised the borrowed AK47 to his shoulder and fired three quick rounds. Splotches of black followed by spurting red blood appeared on the soldier's chest and belly as he crumpled to the ground. Another NVA soldier reached the edge of the gully. He turned his head turned toward his now still comrade. He had just started to turn toward Jeff when two bullets from Jeff's rifle hit him in the chest. Jeff pulled the trigger again and the hammer clicked on an empty chamber. Jeff threw the rifle down into the gully, reached behind himself, and grabbed his M79. He reloaded it as he scanned the opposite bank for more soldiers. There was no more movement across the gully.

M16 gunfire moved closer to him as members of his platoon advanced forward toward the destroyed machine gun nests. NVA riflemen filtered backward through the heavy vegetation firing short unaimed bursts toward the Americans. Jeff slowly lifted his M79 vertically into the air with his left hand as he raised his other hand to show his position to the advancing troops. A rifleman turned his M16 toward Jeff, then with a nod of recognition, turned it back toward the retreating NVA. Sergeant Slattery crumpled a map in his hands while he moved behind the skirmish line, a radioman tucked up close behind him. The

Sergeant held the radio handset to his ear and yelled quick commands into the mouthpiece. Jeff climbed from the gully and stood as the line passed him. He approached the sergeant as he handed the radio handset to the radioman.

"Saw you get those two MGs, Blooper-man. Good job."

"You better get some security over on the other side of the gully. I destroyed an RPG detail and got a couple of riflemen. They seem to be trying to move around our flank."

The sergeant turned his head toward the radioman. "Radio for a squad of the reserve platoon to get sent up here to protect the right flank." He turned back to Jeff. "Company thinks we ran into a battalion of regulars. Two more companies are being choppered in behind us and another two are going to land about two klicks further out to act as a blocking force."

He looked down at his map before he turned toward a Staff Sergeant moving behind the line of advancing troops. "Take the line about fifty meters further and you should get to the edge of the tree line. Set up defensive positions there. They'll probably hit us with mortars and a ground assault as soon as they regroup." He turned back toward Jeff. "The Lieutenant and Sergeant Lee are dead. I need you to take over Second Squad."

"Clarence is missing. I need to look for him. There's a blood trail and drag marks going up the gully."

The Sergeant looked toward the gully and then back at Jeff. "Okay. You want any help?"

"Give me an M16 and a few magazines. Let the line know I'm out there so no greenie gets nervous when I'm coming back in and fires on me. I'll follow the drag marks until I either find him or I meet too much resistance."

Jeff took the M16 as the Sergeant held it out and then slipped the sling over his shoulder. Sergeant Slattery opened his right ammo pouch, withdrew three magazines, and gave them to Jeff.

"You take care. If they hit us hard before the reinforcements get here, we may have to pull back so the artillery and the gunships can do their work. I won't be able to stop them for you."

Turning toward the gully, Jeff slipped the magazines into his general-purpose bag. "I understand. I'll be back as soon as I find Clarence."

The Sergeant grabbed Jeff's shoulder as he unclipped a purple smoke grenade from the front of his own combat webbing. "Here, pop this when you're coming back in so we'll know it's you."

Jeff took the grenade, shoving it into his bag. "Thanks."

Jeff turned again and ran toward the edge of the gully. A stump caught Jeff's boot as he pushed through the brush at the edge causing him to pitch forward. Tires squealed skidding toward him as his chest hit pavement. His Boonie hat flew off his head and he rolled left as the front of a car slid toward him. It stopped just as the bumper passed above his face. The front right tire touched his leg. A car door slammed and rapid footsteps approached from the driver's side. Jeff wiggled his body back from under the bumper while looking up at the approaching figure. Tan pants then a tan shirt came into view as his gaze continued upward. A deputy sheriff badge on the tan shirt reflected the sunlight. The deputy pulled a pistol from his holster as Jeff stared wide-eyed at him as he struggled to get up under the weight of his pack.

"Stay where you are, Hippie. What are you running from?"

Jeff stared at the hole in the end of the barrel. Small at first, it grew larger with each second that he focused on it. He finally answered weakly while he fought through heavy breaths as he worked to take in his surroundings.

"I'm just trying... to find Clarence."

"Who's that? Another one of your hippie friends? Get up. Face the car. Keep your hands where I can see them.

You make one false move and I'll send you to hippie hell."

Jeff slowly turned on his belly and rose onto his knees. He cautiously got to his feet as he moved his hands toward the hood of the patrol car. The deputy placed the pistol to the back of Jeff's head.

"Drop your pack on the ground real slow like."

The pack slid off Jeff's shoulders and thudded as it hit the road.

"Place your hands on the hood of the car."

Jeff's hands flinched as they touched the hot metal.

"Watch it. I get paid extra for saving the cost of a hippie trial."

A pickup truck pulled up on the road next to the patrol car. "You need any help, Bruce?"

"No, this little girl is about to shit in her pants. I'm going to take her in to let the sheriff figure out what to do with her."

"Okay. Just let me know if you want me and the boys to do anything."

"I'll have the Sheriff let you know."

The deputy moved the gun to Jeff's back. He ran his hands up and down Jeff's sides and legs. Pulling one of Jeff's arms behind his back, he forced Jeff's face onto the hood.

The cold steel of handcuffs contrasted with the burning heat of the hood as they went first around one wrist then other. The Deputy ratcheted the cuffs on Jeff's wrists until the metal pressed against bone. He then roughly pulled Jeff from the hood and pushed him toward the back of the car. He opened the rear door, shoved Jeff into the back seat, and forced his legs in before he slammed the door. Jeff slowly struggled to sit up in the rear seat. The deputy walked to the front of the car, picked up the pack and the hat then shoved the hat into the pack. He hesitated a moment as he looked toward the woods before he walked to the driver's door and threw the pack into the passenger's seat. He grabbed the radio mike as he slid into the car.

"Mabel, this is Bruce. I'm coming in with a hippie that I think is hopped up on locoweed. I found him running out of Milspaul Woods. Sounds like there's another one out here somewhere. See if you can get Bubba to come down here to patrol around to look for him."

Bruce slammed the car into gear spinning the tires as he pulled away with the lights on and the siren howling. The drive to the town lockup was quick. When they got to the small building, Bruce pulled Jeff from the back seat and pushed him toward the front door. A small bell attached to the doorframe dinged as Bruce used Jeff's chest to push the unlatched door open. A large woman with big hair looked up from a magazine as they came into the room. Two microphones on stands sat on the desk in front of her with static hissing from the attached radios.

"Hey, Mabel. I'm going to put this hippie in the lockup then go see if I can find the other one. When's the sheriff due back?"

"He should be back in an hour or so. He radioed in about a half hour ago that he was heading to Bob Wicker's place to tell him that his son was brought in drunk on the 'shine again last night. Bobby's still sleeping it off in the cell. Then the Sheriff was going to his mother's house to visit her for a spell."

Bruce guided Jeff into the hallway and held him against the cell bars as he unlocked the door. He positioned Jeff in the doorway.

"Stand there and don't move, Hippie."

Bruce unlocked the handcuffs before he pushed Jeff into the cell, slamming the door shut. The bars of the jail resonated with an off-key musical note as the door clanked shut.

Bruce snickered as he walked out of the hallway. "You better hope Bobby there doesn't wake up 'fore the sheriff gets back. He don't like hippies."

He slammed the dividing door closed and the hallway went dark. Jeff glanced down at the loudly snoring man in the bottom bunk. Vomit had splashed on the floor next to a discarded pillow. Jeff stepped around the pile before he lifted himself onto the top bunk. The smell of corn whiskey permeated the urine-saturated air so Jeff rose up on one elbow to try to gather some fresh air through the small barred window. Only the heat of the cell flowing out the window provided any air movement and that was in the wrong direction.

Jeff's t-shirt, sopping with sweat, clung to his body, adding to the dankness of the cell. Jeff finally slid down from the bunk, peeled the t-shirt over his head, and hung it through the bars of the cell. He laid his face against the cold steel of the bars wondering what would come next. Hopefully, they would soon allow him to contact his Great-grandmother. The radio in the office squawked an occasional conversation that was covered up by the snoring Bobby.

The bell on the front door dinged and Bruce's voice filtered through the closed hall door. "Any word from the Sheriff yet?"

"He should be here any minute. He radioed in on his frequency a little bit ago that he had stopped some Yankee for speeding. He was escorting them to the clerk's office for them to pay the fine before he let them leave."

The bell dinged again a minute later. "Morning Bruce. Morning Mabel."

"Morning Sheriff," the two responded.

"Sorry I'm late. Momma wanted to read a long passage before I left. You know how she is once she gets started in her bible."

"How's she doing today?" Mabel asked.

"Actually real good. She had Bessie dress her in her best housedress. She said she felt like she might have company today. What's all that stuff on the table?"

"I picked up a hippie running out of Milspaul Woods. Said he was looking for somebody named Clarence. I thought he might be high on some loco weed, so I brought him in to check him out. I've got Bubba out checking the area to see if he can find the other one."

"Anything in his stuff we can charge him with?"

"Nothing there but some dirty clothes, a worn hat, an old army jacket, a shaving kit, and a wallet. Only thing in the wallet is a couple of twenties, an expired Virginia driver's license, and a piece of paper with an address in New Orleans."

"Let me take a look." The room went silent for a moment. "I'll be damned. Bruce, get the cell keys."

The Sheriff opened the door to the cellblock and marched quickly in with Jeff's driver's license in his hand. Jeff stared at the sheriff's face as he moved closer to the cell door. The face reminded Jeff of his grandfather, yet was different from what his mind told him he should be seeing. The Sheriff stopped at the door to the cell, looking in at Jeff before he spoke.

"What's you name boy?"

"Jeff. Jeff Briggs."

"Where were you heading when my deputy picked you up?"

"I was on my way to my great-grandmother's house."

"What's her name?"

"I only know her as Mama Hazel."

The sheriff turned toward the deputy. "Open the cell, Bruce."

The sheriff stepped back as Bruce turned the key and swung the cell door open. Bruce then stepped back from the open door with his hand on the butt of his pistol.

The sheriff moved Bruce aside. He stood in the open doorway of the cell. "Take your hand off your pistol, Bruce. He's kin. This is my brother's grandson."

Chapter 5

Jeff hung the thin towel on the hook next to the door of the jail shower room then pulled on his last clean t-shirt. The water had been tepid, but cleansing the salty sweat gained from his hour in the cell and the dirt from the woods had been refreshing. He shoved his dirty t-shirt into the pack before he opened the door to step into the jail hallway. The urine encrusted smell of the cellblock air contrasted to the fresh scent of the soap his great uncle had given him. The Sheriff had even made Bruce get some shampoo for Jeff from the store.

Jeff brushed out his wet hair as he walked down the hall past the cell that his former bunkmate still resided in. Bobby was sitting red-eyed on the edge of the bunk bed. He twisted his head to look at Jeff as Jeff started by the cell. He leered at Jeff with a drop of drool hanging from the corner of his mouth.

"Damn hippie fag. Sheriff had no right to put the likes of you in here with me. You best hope I don't find you out on the road after I get out. Me and the boys'll take care of your pretty ass."

Jeff stopped to glare down at the man. His eyes focused with an intensity that always showed through when a threat moved into his life. Bobby shrank back on the bed as he turned his eyes from Jeff's stare. Jeff shook his head slightly before he continued toward the open door to the office.

The smell of bacon filled the air as Jeff walked into the room. Two plates, covered in foil, were sitting on the table along with two glasses of tea with ice. The sheriff motioned toward the table while he rose from his desk chair as Jeff entered the room.

"I had the diner send over some bacon, eggs, grits, and sweet tea for us. If you'd rather have a soda pop, I've got some in the fridge in the back room."

Jeff sat down behind one of the plates and removed the foil. The smell of cooling grease flew into the air. "Sweet tea is fine. Thanks, Uncle Bill."

Bill slid into the seat across from Jeff. He lifted a strip of bacon from the plate and stuck it into his mouth. "So what caused you run blindly out of Milspaul Woods? Bruce said he almost ran over you. Were some of the boys chasing you?"

Jeff stopped chewing as he looked at his Uncle. He slowly started chewing again until he swallowed. He sipped some sweet tea before he answered. "I just got turned around in the woods. It's been awhile since I tried to find my way in there."

"I guess it has been a long time since you were down here last. How long you plan on staying?"

Jeff scraped some grits onto his spoon. "I've got to be in Charleston on Monday. I'm working my way to New Orleans as a roadie with a touring band. They're heading to Charleston now. They dropped me off so I could visit with Mama Hazel."

"How are you gonna get there?"

"I figured that somebody I'm related to here works at the shipyards and maybe I could catch a ride."

"I'll call your second cousin Tom. He works there. I'm sure he would give you a ride."

"Thanks. If he can't do it, I'll just hitchhike."

Bill glanced at Jeff's hair. "Probably wouldn't be good for you to be alone on the highway around here. I'll let the boys around here know who you are, but I'd stay close to the house or with me or Mabel. Some of them might not get the word."

Jeff knew what Uncle Bill meant and who the boys were. "Don't worry. I don't plan to do anything except visit Mama."

"So how did you hook up with this band? Is that what you do now?"

Jeff related the story of the injured roadie. "It's really just a way for me to get to New Orleans to visit my old army buddy, Clarence. I just want to talk a little about something that happened over there."

"So that's the Clarence that you mentioned to Bruce when he picked you up."

"Yes. He and I went through a lot over there. We used to talk a lot. It's just something I need to do."

Uncle Bill sipped his tea and remained silent for a minute after Jeff finished speaking. "Did your mother ever talk to you about your Uncle Gary?"

"Nothing except that he was killed in Korea."

"He returned from Europe after the war ended in 1945 and started keeping his own company. He was the town's only combat veteran that came back. Before the war, he was the class clown. After it, he rarely smiled. He finally went back into the army in 1948. Said he wanted to be near his old comrades. I think he just needed to talk to someone who had been through what he had."

"I didn't know that."

Bill pushed back from the table. "I'll tell you what. I'll loan you our spare car so you can drive straight to New Orleans. That way you can find your friend without waiting for that band to make it there. You can drive the car back when you're done. Then, maybe you'll think about staying on here amongst your kin. You used to like living down here in the summers."

"Thanks for the offer, but I committed that I would work all the way to New Orleans. I wouldn't want to break my word to them."

Bill smiled. He reached across the table and put his

hand on Jeff's arm. "Your grandfather would be proud to hear that you take your word seriously. But, if you change your mind, you're welcome to stay with us as long as you want. We moved into your grandparent's house after they died. You could stay in your old room."

A stab of pain hit Jeff's heart. He slightly deflated as he lowered his head. After a moment, he recovered his composure. "I figured somebody inherited it or bought it. I never really thought about somebody else living there."

"Someone needed to live near your Mama Hazel to help her, so we took on the job."

"How's she doing? I haven't seen or talked to her since the funeral."

"She's okay but getting more frail. You know she just turned ninety. I had to disconnect the stove a couple of years ago. She would forget that she had something on a burner. Almost burnt the place down a few times. She tried several times to get a friend's son or grandson to turn the stove back on until I put the word out not to. We only let her have an electric kettle to make tea now. Mabel fixes breakfast and dinner plates for her. We kept Bessie on cooking and cleaning for us. She spends part of each day over there helping Mama get dressed and cleaning her house."

Jeff smiled as he put down his sweet tea. The memories of Bessie cooking in his grandparent's kitchen flooded into his mind. He could almost smell the frying chicken, the sweet potato casserole in the oven, the apple pies cooling on the windowsill. "How's she doing? I really used to like her cooking."

"She's getting along fine I guess. Her husband died in a tractor rollover a few years ago. Most of her kids moved away either to Charleston or above Virginia. She lives now with her daughter and her family."

"Do you think it would be okay for me to stay over at Mama Hazel's house while I'm here? I'd really like to spend most of my time with her."

"I don't see a problem with it, but you'll have to ask her. She keeps reminding me that it's still her house."

"She always was a little independent."

Bill chuckled. "That's one way to say it. I'm her son so I can call her stubborn. Listen, I'll run you over there. You can use the washer at our house to clean your clothes then hang them on the line at Mama's to dry. If you need anything else, just let me or Mabel know."

"Thanks."

After finishing their plates of food, the two headed out to the patrol car. As they drove through the now awakened town, Jeff looked out the passenger window at the still familiar sights of his childhood. Farm people bustled around on Main Street in their ritualistic morning trip to town after delivering fresh eggs to the store. Black men in bib overalls waited in a vacant lot behind old wagons filled with fresh garden vegetables and jars of homemade jam. White women moved around the wagons picking out the best produce and jams from the stacks while black women, their eyes downcast, walked behind them carrying cloth bags filled with the purchases that their employers had made. The black women would meet up with the wagons on the edge of town in the afternoon to pick over whatever remained.

A group of young white men, cigarette packs rolled into the sleeves of their white t-shirts, drank sodas and smoked in the shade of the Shell station. They turned their eyes toward the patrol car as it moved past so Bill gave a small wave to the crowd. The car glided past Milspaul Woods while Jeff searched for signs of his earlier terror. The pine trees waved in the late morning breeze as the sun filtered through the branches. No sign of the battle remained.

Bill stopped the car in front of Mama Hazel's house and put it in Park. Jeff stared back into his past. The Gardenia bushes set below the porch had burst forth with their white flowers and framed the bottom of the gray columns. Yellow Jasmine grew on each side of the steps. The porch glider, a little more faded with rust peeking through on the edges, still held its place on the left side. Flowering tomato plants in old miniature half-barrels faced the sun on the right with a sweating watering can on the deck next to them. The sunlight glistened off the bright green leaves.

Chickens clucked from the back yard as a familiar voice called to them.

"Here chick, chick, chick. Come on little chickens. You's gotta eat to keep us in eggs. Here chick, chick, chick."

Jeff turned toward Uncle Bill and smiled. "Doesn't sound like much has changed here. I wonder if Bessie will let me gather the eggs now."

"The only reason she wouldn't let you before was because you kept dropping them. You really were the most fumbled fingered kid I ever saw."

Jeff laughed, opened the door, and slid out of the seat. He leaned in through the window as he shut the door. "Hopefully, I've gotten better. Thanks for everything, Uncle Bill."

"No problem Jeff. You go on and visit with your Mama. Mabel and I will be over about five with dinner for all of us. If you need anything, just head on over to the house. Backdoor is still unlocked."

Jeff backed away from the window as Bill put the car in drive. As the sound of the engine faded down the country road, a door slammed in the back of the house. A voice, weaker than years before but still recognizable, filtered above the low clucks of the chickens.

"How many eggs today, Bessie?"

"Them's chickens really did you well, Mizz Hazel. There's over a dozen in the basket and I still needs to check behind the coop."

"You keep half of them for yourself and take the rest over to Mabel when you head back. Maybe she'll let you bake us a cake. I still think someone special's coming to visit."

"Yes'em."

Jeff set his pack on the front steps before he wandered around the left side of the house. The majestic magnolia tree in the side yard seemed larger than before as it provided shade from the morning sun to the side of the house. A tire swing, its rope frayed with age and too low for Jeff's legs now, hung from the branches. An electric fan, dutifully oscillating back and forth, spun slowly in the open kitchen window while birds landed on the sill below for crumbs of bread scattered by a gentle hand. Jeff continued past the edge of the house to the fence, stopping as the chicken coop came into view.

A black woman, as large as he remembered, bent to gather eggs from the hen's secret places behind the coop while they clucked and worked to impede her movements. A white headscarf, so clean that it shined like a beacon, topped the head with a gray frizz now framing the smooth skin of her round face. She straightened up after retrieving the newly discovered eggs and then bent backward slightly to ward off the years. She shooed the chickens away from the feed pail, picked it up, and turned back toward the house.

As she turned around, she caught sight of Jeff standing by the fence. She pulled the egg basket and the feed pail close into her as she quickened her pace toward the protection of the house. She moved to a spot between the porch steps and the fence. Stopping, she set the eggs and feed down. She folded her arms while staring hard at Jeff.

"What you doin' around here? You ain't got no business in dis yard. Go on now, 'fore I call out."

A voice called out from the porch. "Who's out there, Bessie?"

Jeff slowly smiled. Bessie reached to the wall and picked up a broom. She held it like a club, prepared to defend her charge.

"I said git."

"I thought I was your honey child, Bessie," Jeff said.

Bessie's eyes grew wide as she dropped the broom. She raised her hands above her and looked to the sky. "Praise the Lord. You've brought back my honey child. It's little Mister Jeffery, Mizz Hazel. He's come back to us."

Bessie ran to the gate as Jeff moved along the fence. She flung it open and grabbed Jeff's head, pulling it into the folds of her bosom. Tears fell from her cheeks as she slowly rocked Jeff's body against hers.

"Thank you, sweet Jesus. Thank you. You's brought him back to us. Thank you, Lord."

Bessie released Jeff from her hug but kept her hands on his shoulders. "Let me look at you. Why you's skinny as a coon in winter. I's got to fix you something to eat." She pulled him close again and hugged him tight.

Mama Hazel walked up beside them. "Let him go, Bessie. Let me see my Jeffery."

Bessie released Jeff and he turned toward the tiny woman leaning on a cane before him. She was shorter than memory served him and looked frailer. Her hair was the same brilliant white from before and remained pulled into her trademark bun. Jeff opened his arms as he moved toward the woman.

"Hi, Mama. I've missed you."

He enveloped her in his arms until her head rested softly on his chest.

She whispered. "I've missed you too."

He slowly stroked her hair as he rocked her lightly. They stood there for what seemed like an hour to Jeff, but only minutes passed. Jeff released her from his embrace and stood back while he held her hand in his.

"You're looking great Mama."

"Don't go lying to an old woman, Jeffery. Help me up to the porch. I need to sit and you need to explain to me what you're doing here without letting me know you were coming."

Jeff took her arm and together they slowly mounted the stairs to the porch. Mama settled into her well-worn rocker and Jeff moved to his old place on the hanging swing. Bessie followed them onto the porch, waiting with the pail of eggs. The chickens pecked at the forgotten pail of feed.

Mama looked at Jeff for a moment before turning toward Bessie. "You go on to Mabel's and take her those eggs. You be needin' to fix extra for dinner so's my Jeffery will have enough to eat. Go'on now."

"Yes'em"

Bessie turned toward Jeff. "You's gonna be here long enough for me to see you again?"

"Yes, Bessie. I'll be here until Monday morning."

"Okay, Honey Child. I'll be back tomorrow. Maybe you can help me get the eggs likes you used to."

"That'd be great Bessie. I'll see you tomorrow."

Bessie picked up the egg basket then made her way down the steps. She shut the leaning wooden gate before following the path across the small field toward Bill and Mabel's back door. Jeff watched Bessie as she traced the steps that he had made so many times those many years before. She disappeared into the back door before Jeff turned his head back toward Mama. She sat slowly rocking with her eyes fixed on him.

"So why didn't you let your Mama know you were coming? You 'bout gave Bessie a heart attack."

"I'm sorry Mama. I just figured out a couple of days ago that I could come visit."

Jeff explained the band and his heading to New Orleans to find his friend.

"I don't want to put a damper on your parade, but how do you know your friend is in New Orleans or even alive?"

"He's alive, I can feel it. As far as him being in New Orleans, I've been carrying this in my wallet."

Jeff opened his wallet and pulled out the worn paper with Clarence's address. He held it in front of Mama's eyes for her to read.

"How long you had that ratty piece of paper?"

"I don't know. Probably since 'Nam. But it's the only direction I have right now."

"Sounds to me like the Lord is guiding your footsteps in this. You just listen to him and everything will be fine. Get my bible from inside. I want you to read a passage."

The screen door squeaked as Jeff went into the old kitchen. The same worn lived-in appearance emanated from the room as it had ten years before when he had left it that last summer. However, the changes due to Mama's age were apparent. The smell of baking bread was absent and a vase of fresh cut flowers from Mabel's garden rested on the stove. A few more chips that were not Jeff's fault pitted the otherwise shining porcelain sink. The jars that once held flour, sugar, and baking powder sat cleaned and empty. The fan on the windowsill oscillated slowly as it blew the slightly frayed flowered curtains in its breeze.

Jeff walked to the stand that held the old large family bible and gently folded the ribbon place keeper into the page that Mama had stopped on that morning. He closed the bible and started to lift it, but hesitated. He carefully opened it to the page that started the family tree. Placing his finger first on his name, he traced backward through time up the page. He hesitated under Uncle Gary's faded name as Jeff thought about what might have caused the man to go back into the army. Perhaps Uncle Gary searched for an understanding of his experience as Jeff did now. Sergeant Slattery's offer crossed his thoughts as his finger left Uncle Gary's name and continued upward.

His finger traced further back to the time of the War Between the States. Ancient names sat on single lines with no charges after them, the carefully penned-in years of 1863, 1864, and 1865 beneath them. These names, that had simply been a curiosity before and the basis of a school report once now became men such as himself that had faced the horrors of battle. However, these men who had lost their lives to these horrors were now laying in graves in out of the way fields across Virginia and Pennsylvania. Jeff closed the bible and lifted it into his arms.

Mama spoke as he sat down on the hanging swing. "Open to Isaiah 42."

Jeff folded the pages back and then gently set the bible on Mama's lap. She moved her fingers down the page to the bottom, flipped the page, and traced with her finger along the edge. She stopped a few verses down.

"Here it is. Read it for me Jeffery."

Jeff took the large bible from Mama. "I will lead the blind by ways they have not known, along unfamiliar paths I will guide them; I will turn the darkness into light before them and make the rough places smooth. These are the things I will do; I will not forsake them."

Jeff closed the bible as he turned his face to Mama. She stared back into his eyes. "You just follow what the Lord is telling you, Jeffery. When he's done with you, you let me know what he showed you."

"I will Mama."

"Have you given any thought about what you're going to do after you find your friend?

"No. I really haven't thought about anything except I need to find him and talk to him."

"Well, when you've got all your answers, you talk to the Lord to see what he wants you to do. If he doesn't guide you anywhere else, you think about coming back here. You belong back here with your kin. I never did like your father taking your mother away to that city, even if it was Richmond"

"I'll think about it Mama, but I don't know. I'm not sure where I belong. Once I find Clarence, maybe I'll know where I need to go."

"You do that Jeffery, you do that. Now help me inside to my room. All this excitement has worn me out so I want to take a little nap. You can go visit with Mabel and Bessie. I'm sure they would like to chat. Bessie probably has some fresh biscuits with ham slices you could have."

"Now that sounds wonderful. I'll do that."

Sunday dinner at Bill and Mabel's house was akin to a homecoming for Jeff. Great Uncles and Great Aunts, Uncles and Aunts, first and second cousins with a few once or twice removed, assorted husbands, wives, girlfriends, and boyfriends filled the tables set up under the large magnolia trees in the back yard. Jeff couldn't remember many of the names other than those he had known when he used to visit in the summers, but it seemed that half the town was related to him. Mama Hazel sat on the relocated glider as she received well wishes from the throng. A little black girl slowly waved a large fan of peacock feathers to ward off the flies from her. Jeff sat next to Mama Hazel. Together they shared a plate of food.

Bessie and several other black cooks worked throughout Saturday on the feast. Bessie's brother Tom had spent the night in the backyard roasting a whole pig while he also tended the smoke house where hams and chickens dripped juices onto each other. Besides the roasted pig and the smoked meats, bowls of fried chicken, candied ham with pineapples, dirty rice, macaroni pie, peas, lima beans, corn on the cob, and collard greens filled two long tables placed together. A separate table held sweet breads and fresh rolls with butter and honey. Dessert overflowed on a fourth table with donated sugar cookies, peach cobbler, pineapple upside down cake, cherry pie, angel food cake, rhubarb pie, and pound cake. The black women standing behind each of the tables filled every plate presented to them to overflowing as they smiled and said "Yes·em" to any comment or question asked.

A separate table held pitchers of sweet tea, sweet tea with lemon, sweet tea with pineapple juice, and water brought up from the spring on the back of some uncle's farm. Bottled sodas for the children swam in a washtub full of ice off to the side. The black man that kept the pitchers filled and poured from them would reach into a box under the table upon request of the men to pour a shot of a clear liquid from one of several Ball-Mason jars hidden there.

That night, Jeff sat on the front porch glider drinking sweet tea while the crickets rubbed their legs in their mating song. The front screen door creaked as Mama pushed forward into it. Jeff pulled the door open and Mama shuffled over to his side. She bent down, kissed the top of his head, and then laid her hand on his cheek.

"I'm sure goin' to be sorrowful tomorrow when you're gone. I do wish you'd stay. You used to enjoy being here in the summers. You could make a good life here. I saw how some of those young girls looked at you."

Jeff blushed. "It's tempting Mama. There are many good memories here. I'm just not sure where I belong yet. I need to find Clarence to settle my mind about what happened and where I've been. Then maybe I'll come back."

"Well, I'll pray that the Lord looks after you and brings you back to me. You always got a place here. I asked Bill today to go see the lawyer tomorrow to change my will to leave you this place when the Lord calls me home."

"Now don't go talkin' like that, Mama. You're going to be here forever. I'll write you when I figure out what I'm going to do."

"All the same, it's going to be yours. Now, you got everything ready for tomorrow?"

"Yes, Mama. Bessie cleaned my clothes and made some sandwiches to take. Cousin Tom is picking me up at five to take me down to Charleston. I already have the clock wound and set. I've still got to take a bath tonight."

"Well, you stand up here and give your Mama a hug.

I've got to go lay these tired bones down."

Jeff hugged her tight as he kissed her forehead. "I'll stick my head in before I leave to say goodbye."

Mama averted her eyes as she shuffled through the doorway while Jeff held the screen door open. She slowly moved down the long hallway before disappearing into the room she had slept in for over sixty years. The door squeaked closed. The night lay still as even the crickets had quieted from Mama's bumping of her cane. Jeff picked up his empty glass from the side table and carried it down the hallway to the kitchen. He grabbed a spoon to take a last mouthful of peach cobbler from under its protective cover. Then, he took another before closing the cover and placed the spoon in the sink. He flipped off the light as he made his way to the small bathroom.

When he turned the switch, the white tile gleamed a sparkling white under the single bulb. Bessie had laid out a clean towel for him and left a bottle of shampoo. Kneeling, Jeff adjusted the taps on the old claw foot tub until the water flowed pleasantly hot. As he stood to remove his shoes, he blinked as the ground gave way beneath him and he fell down the slope of the gully. Gunfire sounded from above the edge while Sergeant Slattery's voice boomed commands over the din. After he stopped at the bottom, he rose to one knee bringing his M79 to his shoulder as he pushed the safety off. He blinked rapidly and shook his head as he looked in all directions.

Nothing moved in the gully as Jeff scanned his surroundings trying to make sense of the shift in reality. The spotty blood trail and drag marks stretched away as his mind adjusted to the situation. He rose into a crouch moving silently forward up the path. He cocked his head while he listened to the combat happening above him. Dueling mortar tubes thumped behind him and to the front. American and NVA voices shouted warnings and commands above the edge of the gully as Jeff moved. The screams of the wounded came from all directions in the universal language of pain. An NVA machine gun opened up to the left in front of him. The gunner lay on the gully slope as he fired through the brush. His security team, their uniforms clean and helmets unblemished, poked the muzzles of their AK47s through the foliage watching as the green tracers disappeared toward the American lines.

Reaching into his vest, he brought out a fragmentation round, laying it on the ground next to him. He then aimed the M79 toward the machine gunner, the muzzle lifted slightly above horizontal. He squeezed the trigger and the deadly projectile left the muzzle toward the unsuspecting crew. Without watching the flight of the grenade, Jeff broke the weapon open, extracted the spent shell, and pushed the new round in. As he slapped the breech closed, one of the machinegun security team twisted his head toward him and shouted a warning. He began to swing the muzzle of his AK47 around, but it caught in the bushes. As he pulled the muzzle backward, his eyes grew wide as Jeff shouldered the M79. Turning his head, the assistant gunner looked toward Jeff. The other members of the NVA security team remained transfixed by the stream of tracer bullets flying from the muzzle of the machine gun.

The first round exploded next to the machine gunner just as Jeff squeezed the trigger again. The first blast threw the gunner to his side as the helmet of the assistant gunner flew backward off his head. Even at this distance, Jeff could see blood fill the man's face before he collapsed out of sight. The second round exploded alongside the three members of the security team. Two of them writhered on the ground as they tried to pick hot shrapnel from inside the back of their uniforms. The third did not move. Jeff charged toward the position as he reached into his ammo vest and pulled out black-tipped buckshot round. He ran screaming as he broke open the breech, threw the spent round out, and loaded the buckshot round. He closed the distance rapidly as one of the security team recognized the danger, stopped picking at the hot shrapnel, and began to bring his rifle to his shoulder. The man pulled the trigger and bullets whipped past Jeff's left side before the muzzle climbed harmlessly into the air. Jeff pulled the trigger as he pointed the muzzle of the M79 at the soldier from five meters away. The buckshot slammed into the man, pushing him backward into his still convulsing comrade.

Jeff continued running, leaping over the prone soldier as he switched the M79 from his left hand to his right. He pulled his KBar knife from its sheath on the side of his left boot and wrapped his fist around the handle with the blade pointed down. He plunged the tip of the blade into the wounded soldier's chest falling on the hilt to drive the blade home. The soldier's spasmodic movements slowed before they stopped.

Jeff raised his head as he quickly scanned the area through the bushes. He withdrew the blade and wiped it clean on the dead soldier's shirt. Small arms tracer fire crossed above him, red heading to the right with green heading to the left. A rocket, launched from cover on the right, left a smoke trail that blossomed behind as it flew to its explosive end. NVA soldiers left covered positions firing as they quickly withdrew away from the American rifles. The unmistakable roar of an incoming American artillery round bit into the air.

The first round landed two hundred meters to Jeff's front as he turned back into the gully. He ran down the slope searching the ground for a spot of cover. Having about twenty seconds before the full barrage began; he turned back to his original path moving cautiously but quickly. His foot slipped slightly on a patch of mud as he sidestepped a small tree growing in the center of the gully. Water from the last evening's storms had filled a depression on the left side.

The first rounds of the barrage hit the ground above

the gully. Jeff dove into the cold water and grabbed roots with his right hand. He held his breath as the concussions from the exploding rounds smashed his eardrums. A ringing sound filled his brain. A round hit twenty meters away, blasted a tree trunk across his back, and flipped him over in the water.

The barrage ceased as bright light filled the inside of his tightly closed eyes. The weight of his ammo vest was gone and his M79 no longer rested in his hand. The sides of the depression had closed around him. He reached his hands up and felt slick smooth edges just above the water. He lifted himself up slightly until his eyes broke the waterline.

The bright single bulb in the ceiling reflected on the shiny white tile. The chrome handles and the tub spout gave multiple surreal reflections of him as his eyes focused closer in. The soap in the dish dripped sudsy bubbles while a layer of oily suds floated on the surface of the cold water. Jeff looked around at the rest of the room. His clothes lay loosely stacked on the toilet seat with the clean towel left by Bessie still folded on the side stand. The alarm clock in his room dinged softly through the wall.

Jeff stood grabbing the towel from the stand as he stepped onto the mat. He dried himself before wrapping the towel around his waist. He stepped off the mat and looked into the medicine cabinet mirror. His face looked haggard. Blood slowly seeped from the inside of his left ear.

Chapter 6

Jeff leaned against the wall on the left side of the stage in Charleston with a half-empty beer bottle listing lazily in his left hand. The concertgoers exited through the back door while they talked excitedly about their favorite songs. The Monday evening show had sold out, as did the show for the next night. Nothing had gone wrong with any of the equipment so Jeff had only sat in the rear of the control booth or off the side of the stage as the band went through its act. He had learned the band's act was a set procedure so that encores were actually planned into the timing.

Mutluk came through the side stage door with a six-pack of beer in his hand. "You ready for another?"

Jeff held his beer up into the light and stared through the bottle. "No, I'm good."

"Want to go to a party down by the beach? The guy that owns the hall, Clay, has invited the band down there. He has rooms we can crash in for the night rather than that fleabag we had to check into. It sounds fun to me."

"I'm game. Sleeping to rolling waves at the beach sounds better than listening to horns honking in the city. Russ going?"

"Yea. He already left with the band. A couple of women are going to give us a ride. They're waiting up at the soundboard. I just have to grab Russ's and my travel bags out of the truck. You want me to grab your pack?"

Jeff drained his beer, throwing the bottle in the trashcan next to the stage. "I'll get it."

They walked into the darkened alley where the truck had sat cold for four nights. After retrieving their belongings, they locked the truck before heading back into the hall. It was almost empty as they reentered through the stage door. Heading up the aisle to the raised control platform at the back of the hall, Jeff saw the two women standing on the platform. Their features showed in the dim lights of the soundboard.

A mass of blond curls cascaded over the shoulders of the taller one. Dark mascara above her blue eyes contrasted to the blond curls. She wore a tie-dyed t-shirt and cutoff jeans that were so short that they would have been illegal in Richmond. A cigarette hung lazily from the corner of her mouth as she pointed to some control on the soundboard that had caught her eye.

The other woman, short and slightly built, had hand-stitched flowers decorating the blue jeans she wore. Her faded green t-shirt had a hand painted peace sign across the front. Jet-black hair, parted in the middle of her scalp, hung over her shoulders then straight down her back to her waist. A leather headband, also etched with peace signs, held the hair off her face. Dark, almost black, pupils lent a mysterious appearance to her being when she looked up as Jeff and Mutluk approached, but became inviting when she smiled.

Mutluk dropped his and Russ's bags on the seats behind the soundboard and held the six-pack up toward the women. They each took one. "Girls, this is Jeff."

He pointed to the tall woman and then the shorter one. "This is Margo and that is Mary. Why don't you wait by the stage door while I shut the rest of the equipment down?"

Mutluk began flipping switches on the pre-amp rack to the right of the soundboard.

Margo twisted off the top of her beer as she spoke. Her cigarette danced between her lips. "Pleased to meet ya."

Mary nodded slightly as she stared into Jeff's eyes. "You have the most beautiful blue eyes."

"Uh... Thanks," Jeff said as he picked up his pack and

slung it over his shoulder. He grabbed Mutluk and Russ's bags from the floor before leading the women to the stage door.

The three stood by the door as Mutluk moved around the stage flipping switches on the equipment. After he finished moving across the entire stage, he signaled to the union electrician to shut off the main breakers. The clunk of the breakers echoed through the empty hall as the electrician switched them off causing the hall lights to go dark. Only the exit lights lit the way as Mutluk jumped from the stage to retrieve his briefcase from the control booth.

Margo opened the stage door every few puffs as she flicked her ashes outside before letting the door close while she took another drag. The smoke wisped around their heads and up into the light of the exit sign.

Mary kept her gaze on Jeff in the dim light. "So what do you do with the band?"

"I just carry and hook up whatever Mutluk tells me to. I've only been working with them for a couple of weeks. Mutluk and Russ are showing me how to operate things during the show, but they still run it."

"So what do you do when you're not working with them?"

Jeff avoided his loss of memory. "Nothing really. I was in the army a while ago, but now I'm just traveling with the band down to New Orleans to look up an old Army buddy."

Margo's face hardened toward Jeff as Mutluk picked up the bags from the floor before pushing open the stage door.

"Let's go," he said without a backward glance.

Jeff held the door as the two women moved through it. Mary lingered near him. She pulled car keys out of her pocket and pushed them toward the Margo. "Here Margo, you drive."

Margo's voice carried to Jeff's ears as she walked away

in a huff, her cigarette dancing between her lips again. "Great, now I have to act as a chauffeur to a baby killer."

Jeff stopped as the words hit his soul. While still in Vietnam, he had gotten letters from friends who had left Vietnam telling him that students were calling them baby killers. He knew he had only killed soldiers as part of his duty, never a civilian, most certainly never a child.

Mary glanced back at him as he came to a standstill. She offered her hand out to him. "Don't worry about her. She's opinionated about the war and can be little crass at times. Come on, Clay's place is big so we can avoid her there."

She walked back to Jeff and took his hand into hers. "Don't worry. I'll protect you from her."

The ride to the beach was both relaxed and tense. They climbed the rollercoaster-like Grace Memorial Bridge as Mary pointed out landmarks in the city lights behind them through the rear window. While they coasted down the final slope of the bridge, the small town of Mount Pleasant appeared before them with few lights showing at the late hour. Margo turned the car off Route 17 onto the side road that headed toward Sullivan's Island. After one more small bridge, a sign announced that they were crossing onto the Isle of Palms.

Mutluk talked during the ride about growing up in Canada along with stories of other tours. Margo missed few chances to comment on how Canada treated their Indian population better than the US and how the Canadian government doesn't go around sending its army out to kill innocent people. Jeff sat muted in the backseat at these comments with the only condolence being Mary's hand gently stroking his.

The road shifted to the right to follow the beach. The houses became further and further apart until only one remained in the distance. Bright lights emanated from all the windows. The cars on the road ahead turned toward it.

The tires of the car slipped on the loose sand as Margo entered what passed for the driveway and brought the car to a hurried stop on the sparse lawn. She slammed the door as she left, never looking back at Jeff. Mutluk grabbed his and Russ's bags before he hurried to catch up with her.

Jeff stayed still in the back seat watching Margo stomp away as cigarette smoke trailed from her head. His gaze remained fixed on her back while she moved quickly toward the brightly lit house. Mary stayed with him, holding his hand as she rubbed her fingers lightly across his knuckles.

After a few minutes, she gripped his hand tight. "Come on. Don't worry about her. Let's go inside to the party."

"What's she so pissed about? She doesn't know me or what I did in the army."

"She's just mad about everything the government does. She helps organize all the anti-war rallies and protests every week at the draft board."

Jeff turned until he looked at Mary's dark eyes. "And how about you? Are you pissed at me too?"

She squeezed his hand lightly before she spoke. "I don't know you or anything about you. One of my brothers was in Vietnam a couple of years ago. I know from talking to him that few people over there enjoyed killing. He said he just did a dirty job and was glad that he got out okay. He's up in Atlanta at Georgia Tech on the GI bill now."

"What unit was he with?"

"He was in the Fifth Marines. He said he was stationed somewhere in the northern part of the country. The names of those places are always too hard for me to pronounce. How about you?"

"I served with the 417th Parachute Regiment in the central part of the country."

She pulled on his hand harder. "Come on. Let's go have some fun! I'm thirsty and would really like a beer. I'll help you avoid Margo and protect you. We could go for a walk on the beach."

Jeff let Mary pull him from the car and then lead him into the house. Music blared throughout while people crowded the entry hallway. They pushed through the people as Mary led Jeff to a stairway. After reaching the top of the stairs, Mary led Jeff down a hallway to a closed door. Pulling out a set of keys, she unlocked the door.

She kicked her shoes off as she walked inside. "This is my room. You can leave your pack in here. It will be safe."

"You live here?"

"No, I live in Columbia to attend college. Clay lets me have this room for when I come down to his parties or for a weekend on the beach. Oh, I forgot to mention, Clay's one of my brothers."

Jeff placed his pack on the bed. "How many brothers do you have?"

"Seven. No sisters. I was the last one born so I grew up pretty protected."

"Do they still protect you?"

She removed the headband from her head and threw it on the dresser. Grabbing a beach blanket from the top of a trunk, she headed back toward the door. "No. They learned early on that I could take care of myself. Come on, let's go get some beers and maybe some smoke and go sit on the beach."

She took his hand again as she led him down the stairs. Jeff picked up four cans of beers from a tub while Mary grabbed a joint from Clay. She then led him out the back door down the stairs to the beach. Together, they walked up the beach until they were away from the lights of the house and the music became subdued enough to hold a quiet conversation.

"Is this your first time in South Carolina?"

"No, I used to spend my summers in Rocksville with my grandparents until I was twelve. I still have relatives there. In fact, I just spent the weekend visiting my Great·

grandmother."

"I know where that is. We used to pass through it going back and forth to Columbia until they opened up 178 straight to Orangeburg."

"I remember when that opened up. One day there was lots of traffic on Main Street then the next day it was almost empty. My grandfather said the new road would kill the town. From the looks of it last weekend, it did."

"Do they still live there?"

Jeff turned his head out toward the waves as his eyes misted, glad the darkness hid them. His voice broke slightly. "No. They died when I was twelve. That's when I stopped visiting and started spending my summers in Richmond."

Mary took Jeff's hand into hers. "I'm sorry. I didn't mean to bring up a bad memory for you."

Jeff turned his head toward her. "Thanks, but it's okay. It's just that last weekend was the first time I had been back since their funeral ten years ago. Things are still a little fresh. How about you? Where'd you grow up?"

She pointed back toward the house. "Born and raised right here in this house. Clay bought it from the parents when they moved up to Columbia after my father got a job with the Governor's office. I live up there near them, but I come down here most weekends. It's a lot more fun here with Clay. Did you ever come down here to the beach when you were younger?"

"Not here. But my grandmother would drive me down to Hilton Head Island outside of Savannah to visit my cousins a couple of times every summer."

"Did you like it there?"

"It was okay. Most of my cousins down there were teenagers so they didn't want to hang around a little kid. I spent most of my time playing with the one cousin that was three years younger than I was. At first, it felt like I was babysitting her, but we became friends toward the end."

Mary spread the blanket on the hard sand of the low tide and took two of the beers from Jeff. "I'll go put these in the water to stay cool. Why don't you sit down and relax."

Jeff opened the other beers as he sat on the blanket. The sound of the party in the house drifted across the open sand as gentle evening waves broke on a sandbar beyond the light. Mary returned, sat down on the blanket across from Jeff, and lit the joint. She took a long draw on it before offering the burning weed his way. She smiled her closed lips toward Jeff as he took a toke.

They passed the joint back and forth without talking until it was half-gone. After Mary lightly crushed the burning end until the red glow disappeared, she placed the remnant on the corner of the blanket. She turned toward Jeff and moved closer. The light of the moon, just starting in its waning journey toward new, produced a shimmer in her hair. She reached up with her hands, brushed the hair away from his face, and then locked her fingers behind his head.

"I have a confession to make. I saw you at the show in Columbia. That's when I noticed your eyes. I knew from talking to Clay that the band was playing down here next so I decided to come down here for a few days of Spring Break. Did I mention that you have the most amazing eyes? They're soft, but intense."

Jeff smiled as he relaxed in her grip. He moved his mouth closer to hers as he placed his arms around her neck and softly spoke. "I can't say anyone has ever told me that before."

Mary pulled him closer until their lips were only an inch apart. She opened her lips slightly with a soft seductive smile. "It's true. A girl could get lost in those eyes."

She drew his lips to hers. She kissed him softly at first, then with an intensity matched only by the hard drumbeat of the rock music emanating from the beach house. Her tongue found his as they sank down onto the blanket, hungry in each other's arms. Mary pulled her lips away from Jeff's then rolled on top of him. Her hair fell past her shoulders onto his chest and face as a hint of coconut shampoo drifted into his nose. She straddled him and held his hands tightly in hers.

Jeff stared up at her excited eyes. "How far are we going to take this?"

Mary smiled as she dropped his hands, lifted her t-shirt over her shoulders, and threw it to the side of the beach blanket. "I tell you what. Let's go for a swim."

"I don't have a swimsuit."

Mary smiled as she bent down and whispered in his ear. "We don't need swimsuits."

Jeff turned his head toward the beach house as the noise of the revelry notched up. "How about them?"

"Don't worry about them. Let's just worry about us."

Mary stood, offered Jeff her hand, and helped him up until they both stood bathed in the moonlight. She lifted his t-shirt over his head and threw it on the blanket. Then, she shifted her mouth to his as his hands reached for buttons of her jeans. Her chest rose and fell as he worked each button in turn, from the top to the bottom. She backed away slightly as she shifted her hips while he pulled down on the denim until the pants fell to the ground. As she stepped out of them, she pulled him tight until she found his lips again. Her hands moved from his neck to his belt.

The last of their outer clothing dropped to the blanket and they embraced tightly. The heat of their bodies mingled as Jeff moved his hands up and down her spine.

She grabbed his hands from behind her. "Race you."

She ran toward the gentle surf. Jeff ran behind her in a race he didn't plan to win but planned to tie. His legs hit the cool water as a wave pushed foam around his calves. Mary moved determinedly into the surf until the water reached her panties and the tips of her hair brushed the water's surface. Jeff pushed quickly forward and just as he reached for her shoulders, she dove into a wave, disappearing into the rolling surf.

Jeff struggled through the surf for two more steps before diving toward to the bottom where he thought she hid under the water. He found only sand beneath his hands before a passing wave lifted him from the bottom. Kicking his legs to push himself down, he searched the bottom for her with his hands. The water beneath the waves stilled as mud oozed through his fingers. A bright light flashed behind him and a moment later, a concussion wave pushed him deeper into the mud while a burst of pain came from his right forearm. The back of his helmet bit into his neck.

Jeff held his breath and kept his eyes closed beneath the tepid water. The concussions from the shelling seemed to be moving away from him. He gripped the mud with the fingers of his right hand while his left gripped the stock of the M79. After a few more seconds, he slowly began to bring his knees down as he pushed upward with his arms. He stopped as his nostrils gained air. He inhaled deeply while he moved his eyes across the broken forest. A hint of coconut lay lightly on top of the cordite-laced atmosphere. Trees smoked with pieces of red-hot shrapnel embedded in their trunks. An NVA Pith helmet, bloody with gray parts of its former owner inside, lay upside down at the edge of Jeff's watery pit.

A snake, searching for a safer place to be in, swam past him as he rose to his knees and shifted around to face the path up the gully. Burning craters pockmarked the soil as though a giant pickaxe had dug into the earth leaving smoking embers in its wake. The shells had obliterated the drag marks and blood trail, replacing them with only carnage and ruin. The screaming roar of another incoming 105 MM round hit Jeff's ears. He dove beneath the water, grabbed the thin roots at the bottom with his fingers, and pulled himself down until his face met the mud. The shell exploded in the trees above him and the concussion drove the air from his lungs.

Jeff gagged as muddy water filled his throat. He dropped his M79 as he instinctively pushed himself up out of the water. His knees sank into the bottom of the water-filled depression as they took the full weight of his body. Shells exploded around him as the faraway artillerymen walked the barrage back at him. Sizzling shrapnel flew past his ears pinging off his helmet. He coughed one last time, gulped air to fill his lungs, and dove back into the muddy brown water. Jeff held to the bottom with his right hand clutching to a root while he searched blindly with his left for his weapon. He touched hard metal with his thumb and wrapped his fingers around the large muzzle. The concussion of the shells sent pain into his ears. Then, all went quiet.

Jeff waited until his lungs wanted to explode before he slowly raised his head to let his nostrils take in a breath. He blinked the tepid water from his eyes as he searched the area around the makeshift pond. Broken trees lay twisted and fragmented as smoke oozed from jagged holes blackened by the burning shards of death. The air was silent save for an occasional pop and sizzle as hot shrapnel found new drops of water to destroy. He stood up from his watery retreat with slimy mud clinging to his knees until his movement caused it to drop leaving splotches of brown that soaked through to his skin.

Brown water trickled from his right sleeve into the blood that seeped from the shrapnel gash on his arm. The two mixed into a rust drip that fell from his arm to the surface of the water. The droplets formed momentary circles of contrasting color that disappeared in an instant. Jeff raised his arm to his eyes to examine the wound. The small piece of shrapnel had cut a path three inches long and a quarter inch deep. The capillaries caught in the path of the burning metal had been instantly cauterized. Only where Jeff's movements had broken that seal was there a slow seeping of bright blood.

Jeff sank into a prone fighting position on the edge of the depression. He opened the breech of his M79, withdrew the round, and looked down the barrel at a mass of mud. As he turned his head checking around him, he shook out the mud before washing the barrel clean with the slimy water before returning the round to the chamber. He lifted the stock to his shoulder and scanned the area again for noise and movement.

The cry of wounded soldiers calling for help broke the post bombardment silence. No movement or noise seemed near so, as exhaustion overcame him, Jeff shifted to his right until he was behind a fallen tree trunk and then onto his back to rest for a moment. As he twisted, his helmet fell over his eyes. He clicked the safety of the M79 rearward while he lifted his right hand up to shift the helmet back. His hand touched flesh as Mary collapsed onto his chest as the muscles of her torso quivered.

Her breath came ragged and short. "God... That was...amazing. I've... never felt... such energy... come... from a man."

She laid her head sideways on his chest as she continued to breathe in short labored breaths. Afterglow vibrations pulsed through her body and moved through to Jeff's stomach. He placed his left hand on her bare back and lightly stroked her glistening skin as his ears took in the steady beat of the music pulsating from the house in the distance. His senses searched for danger, but only Mary's body existed near him.

After a few minutes, Mary's breathing became soft and even. She moved off Jeff until she was by his right side with her right leg over his thigh. His right arm lay buried beneath her body as if she wanted to hold him there for later with her right arm draped over his chest. Her breathing steadied further and soon a soft snore emanated from her throat. Jeff remained vigilant until exhaustion drove him to close his eyes seeking sleep.

The moon had moved into the western sky as Jeff woke when Mary shifted her left hand to his head and touched her lips to his neck. He twitched and pushed away as he sat up quickly, his breath ragged and short. He twisted his head violently left and right while he scanned the beach all around.

Mary moved backward quickly in an upside down crawl. Her eyes were wide as Jeff shifted hastily into a defensive posture as he squeezed his hands into fists.

She covered herself with her arms as she stopped crawling. She screamed at him. "What's wrong?"

Waves lapped at the hard sand of the peaceful beach as small crabs moved in the moonlight along the retreating edge of the water. The music from the house had ended and only a few lights shown in the windows. Quiet voices echoed across the sand from two people sitting on lounge chairs under the patio light. Jeff settled his knees onto the sand and pushed the air out of his lungs in one last tension release before his breath slowed into a steady rhythm. Mary's eyes remained wide and her body tense as though she prepared for escape from this wildman.

He sat backward, bringing his feet forward. He looked down to the water's edge at the crabs scurrying in their search for food and lied. "Sorry, I think a crab bit my toe."

Mary brought her hand to her heart as she stood. "You scared me."

She picked up her t-shirt and pulled it down over her head. She smiled at Jeff as she picked up her jeans from the sand. "Why don't you put on your clothes so we can go to my room? I can think of better things to do than let the crabs bite us."

Jeff held the rolled up beach blanket under his left arm as they strolled hand in hand to the house. Few cars remained parked across the front lawn and the driveway was clear. A light in the upstairs of the house went dark as they mounted the stairs. Mutluk and Russ were sitting on the porch swing sipping from half-empty beer bottles.

Russ turned toward the couple as they reached the porch. His face gained an inquisitive look to it as they came into the yellow cast of the bug light. "Hey, Jeff. What happened to your arm?"

Jeff looked down at his arms. A three-inch gash on his right forearm slowly seeped blood.

Wednesday was an off day that the roadies spent at the concert hall repairing cords, cables, lighting fixtures, and microphones before repacking them into the proper cases. The floor of the stage lay covered in the electronic equipment, as was the area in front of the stage. The massive speaker cabinets lined the walls at the rear of the stage. Rock music, blaring from a radio on the ledge of the sound booth, entertained the roadies as they worked.

Russ was sitting on the edge of the stage with a screwdriver in one hand and a pile of lighting cables on each side of him He took a cable from the right pile, tightened the screws on each plug, and then threw it into the pile on his left. Jeff sat on the audience floor with a smaller screwdriver as he worked on two piles of microphone cables. He grabbed a cable from the pile on his left, tightened the two screws that clamped the end connector to the cable before tightening the screw that held the end to the connector body. He repeated the process the other end of the cable then threw the cable into the pile of his right.

Mutluk moved along the rows of speakers and electronic equipment with a work belt that held a pouch of different sized screwdrivers. He inspected the different cabinets inside and out and then closed the inspection panels before he methodically tightened each screw in turn.

Jeff looked up toward Mutluk as he threw a just

completed cable into the pile and reached for another. He absent-mindedly scratched at the bandage on his arm. "How often do you do this?"

Mutluk straightened up from the cabinet he was working on, leaning against it. "I like to do this every couple of weeks. It's best to do it when we get a chance like this to have the hall for a full day so we can lay everything out to take our time. Otherwise, we have to do a little at a time the night after a show before we load-out. Then it's fast and dirty. Doing it like this is better so we can get everything tight.

He pulled the back of the main amp rack off. "If we didn't do this occasionally, we'd have more problems with the setup or during the shows. The band gets real upset if their microphones stop working or a light goes out during a song. They're a little sensitive like that."

Russ chuckled. "Especially the bass player for this group. He's a whiner."

Mutluk smiled as he leaned against the amp rack. "I think you're just still mad at him because he left with that girl you were flirting with that night in Washington."

"That's true. But he's still a whiner."

Russ threw another cable into the completed pile. He looked at Jeff as he leaned back on the stage with his hands behind him. "We'll run a resistance check on all the cables before we pack them. If any of them are showing anything wrong, I will show you how we resolder the internal connections to fix them. If one breaks during a show so you have to replace it, you could fix the broken one backstage." He grabbed another cable from his right and set the screwdriver to the screws.

Light came from behind them as the stage door opened and three bodies in silhouette moved onto the stage. Jeff turned his head, smiling when Mary's face became visible when the stage door closed behind them. Margo passed by Jeff without a glance as she headed across the stage toward

Mutluk. The third shadow morphed into Clay as he moved across the stage toward the back office.

Clay waved to Mutluk. "Don't mean to bother you. I just gotta pick up a couple of contracts to read on the trip to take Margo and Mary back to school. We'll be out of your hair in a minute."

Mary sat down next to Jeff, her smile ending in twinkling eyes. "How's your arm today?"

Jeff looked down at his right forearm and the neat bandage that covered the wound. "It itches a lot less than yesterday. Whatever that ointment was you put on it when you changed the bandage this morning worked."

"That's good. You best leave that bandage on for a couple of days and then take it off so the wound will finish healing in the air. I still don't understand how you hurt it."

"I'm guessing I just cut it on a piece of metal or shell while we were playing in the surf."

"I don't know. It almost looked burnt. I fixed enough of my brother's cuts and scrapes growing up to see a lot of different ways for boys to hurt themselves. This looked different from a slice."

Jeff smiled at her before he kissed her on the cheek. "I don't know what to tell you, my attention wasn't really on my arm at the time."

Mary blushed. She then pushed a piece of paper into Jeff's pants pocket. "Well, I just wanted to say goodbye and give you my address and phone number up in Columbia. You're welcome to come up to visit after you finish your visit with your friend in New Orleans. I live in an apartment with two other girls so you could just stay in my room with me. Think about staying for a while. You could go visit your great-grandmother during the week and we could come down here on the weekends. Clay always has a party Saturday nights."

Jeff glanced toward Margo. "How about her?"

Mary laughed. "Don't worry. She doesn't live with me

nor does she come down here much. Her parents live here, but she can only take so much of them and vice versa. They're conservative and they also support the war."

"It sounds like a nice offer. I have been thinking about coming back to spend more time with Mama. I'll give you a call after I get to New Orleans."

"That sounds wonderful. I'll even borrow my brother's car to drive down on a weekend to pick you up if you'd like."

The office door closed with a solid thud. "Let's go ladies. I want to get back here at a decent hour." He turned toward Mutluk. "If you finish up before I get back, make sure the doors lock solid. The key to the beach house is under the flower pot to the left of the steps."

Mutluk turned from Margo. "No problem, Clay. We'll see you later."

Margo hugged Mutluk, turned, and headed toward the stage door. Her face grimaced as she passed Jeff.

Mary placed her arms around Jeff's neck pulling him close. "Hurry back to me."

She kissed his lips and then stared into his eyes. "You really do have the most beautiful blue eyes."

Pecking him on the lips again, she stood and headed toward the stage door behind Margo. Jeff watched her as her silhouette moved into the bright light of the outside before it disappeared behind the closing door. He turned his attention to the next cable in the pile.

Chapter 7

Mutluk down shifted the truck to keep it below the speed limit as they entered the downtown of Savannah. "Look at the directions, Russ. Don't start gawking at women. You'll get us lost like you did in Charleston."

"He got y'all lost?"

"Wasn't my fault, I tell you. The directions were wrong."

"The directions were right. You just missed the turns because you were looking at the women."

"Well, we got to see the harbor with all those cannons."

Russ turned from looking out at the road toward Jeff. "Hey, Jeff. I meant to ask you. What were all those cannons doing in a neighborhood of big houses?"

"Oh. You were at the Battery. That's where the first shots of The War Between The States were fired. They were all aimed at Fort Sumter out in the harbor."

Russ scratched his head. "I notice you always call it The War Between the States. In New York, the teachers always called it The Civil War. What's the difference?"

Mutluk lifted the clipboard from the seat, holding it up in front of Russ' eyes. "Russ, keep your eyes on the directions and the streets."

Jeff glanced at the clipboard. "Drayton Street. I'll help you look for it."

Jeff moved his gaze back to outside the truck toward the street signs as Mutluk drove the truck through the city traffic. "That's just the way I always learned it. I guess the state's rights thing is what the teachers pushed at us in school. Like I told you before, there're a lot of people down here that never really accepted the defeat. It's kind of like how they never say the word north. Most people down here call North Carolina just Carolina. They also never say they're going north. They just say they're heading up Virginia way. It's like nothing's beyond Virginia."

Russ scratched his head as he kept looking at the street signs. "That's weird. I mean— " Russ pointed across Mutluk's face. "Mutluk, there's Drayton. Turn left. The concert hall should be four blocks up on the left after that."

Russ turned back toward Jeff. "Anyway, it's weird that you never say north. Anything else weird? I mean I see the discrimination against Negros all around, but anything else?"

"Sure. They hate Yankees too. When I was visiting in the summers in Rocksville when I was a kid, my Uncle Bill was a deputy. He used to let me ride with him when he would run speed traps out on highway 15 at the edge of town. He would wait until a car with plates from New York, Pennsylvania, or New Jersey came by. Then, he pulled them over for speeding no matter how fast they were going. He always said they owed us for all the damage they did when Sherman marched through the South. And my Great-grandmother never says a curse word except when she talks about Damned Yankees."

Mutluk pulled the truck to a stop in front of the concert hall where the marque announced Heaven Can Wait for four nights. "This is it. Let's go see how the load-in looks. The road manager said it would be easy, but he's lied before."

The load-in went as easy as promised. In less than three hours, the equipment was set in place with most of the connections done. After he finished cranking up his side of the light tower and as he held the ladder that Russ stood on to aim the spots, Jeff let his mind drift back to Mary and the fun they had shared for those few days in Charleston. Going back to her after finding Clarence would be an easy thing to do, but something still didn't feel right with it. It was as if South Carolina wasn't where he belonged. However, Jeff knew that since he had promised he would call, he would have to honor that no matter what happened. Anyway, going there for a while would give him time to visit with Mama again. That would be a good thing.

Mutluk shouted from the backstage door. "Hey Jeff, there's some girl at the door asking for you. She says she's your cousin."

Russ looked down from the top of the ladder and smiled at Jeff. "You got more groupies on this tour than the band. Go ahead. See what this one wants. I can finish aiming these by myself."

Jeff jumped down from the stage, pulled his worn-in gloves from his hands, and headed toward the door. He pressed and smoothed the adhesive tape that held the bandage to his forearm where sweat had loosened it.

Russ called after him. "See if she's got a friend."

On the loading dock outside the backstage door, a tall woman in a nurse's uniform waited for him. Wavy red hair fell below her shoulders. Sun-darkened freckles covered a little peaked nose. Thin lips broke into a smile as he moved into the light of the loading dock. "Your hair isn't as long as daddy said Uncle Bill described it. But it would still give daddy a heart attack if I brought a boy home looking like that."

Jeff kept a solid look on his face with his shoulders tense. "Well Joyce, I never could do anything right with you or him."

"No, you couldn't. Anyway, I never cared about what either of them said. By the way, I'm Helen, not Joyce."

Jeff smiled as he relaxed his stance. Memories of helping his little cousin build sandcastles while they played in the surf flooded his mind. He stepped forward with his arms open and she met him with hers. They hugged, not uneasily like cousins at a wedding, but as past friends, both ostracized by the older cousins years ago.

Jeff broke the embrace but held onto her hands as he looked her over. "Damn! You've grown up. I think you were nine the last time I saw you."

"You've grown too. And I won't even hate you for calling me Joyce."

"You two still at opposite ends of the world?"

"About the same as you and she would be if she saw you now with long hair working with a rock and roll band. Anyway, she didn't say anything about wanting to see you after Uncle Bill called Sunday night. But mommy did want to know if you would have time to stop by, maybe for dinner."

"Well, I'll have to check. The band plays here through Monday night and then we head to Jacksonville on Tuesday. I'll have to ask Mutluk if I can take off for an evening."

Helen cocked her head. "What's a Mutluk?"

Jeff grinned as he released her hands to pull open the stage door. "He's the head Roadie. Come on in. I'll introduce you. Can you stay for the show? I can get you a pass."

"Thanks for the offer, but I'm on my way to work. I'm on the night shift at the hospital. I'm off the next two nights though."

Jeff led Helen around the road cases to the stage stairs. Mutluk and Russ were standing on the front of the stage.

Russ tapped Mutluk on the shoulder as he pointed toward the two. "See, I told you. He's got his own groupies."

Jeff smiled at the comment. "I wish. This is my cousin Helen. Helen, this is Russ and Mutluk. Russ operates the lights and Mutluk does the sound and runs the crew."

Helen offered her hand. "Please to meet you. Any friends of Jeff's are friends of mine."

Jeff turned to Mutluk. "What's our schedule between now and Jacksonville? Helen's parents would like me to come to dinner if there's time."

"Nothing really going on. Since we took time yesterday to do the maintenance, everything should be working okay. You can take a night off no problem. Only issue we have is that the road manager told me that none of the hotels around here let coloreds in. Closest one is about a mile away. Also, the laws here say that whites can't stay in colored hotels."

Russ shrugged his shoulders "I told you, you go ahead and stay at the hotel. I'll sleep in the back of the cab."

"Nope. We're in this together. I'm not splitting up the crew just because of a stupid law. I'll roll my bag on the floor here with you. There's a bathroom with a shower backstage."

Helen broke into their conversation. "Listen, if you'd like to come and stay at my place until Tuesday, you'll welcome. I live in my parent's old house on the beach." She turned her toward Jeff. "It's that place on Tybee Island where we lived at when you used to visit. The parents bought a place on Wilmington Island to be nearer to the city and their store a couple of years ago. I rent the beach house from them."

"I remember it. Nice place. Right on the beach surrounded by sand."

"There've been a few more houses built since then but it's still pretty isolated."

Jeff looked over at Russ and Mutluk before returning his gaze toward her. "You sure your parents won't mind?"

She laughed. "They won't know until it's too late. Anyway, who I bring there is my business, not theirs."

"Is there room for me to park the truck there?" Mutluk said.

"Yea. You can just pull off the road right in front of the house. The sand is packed hard there."

Mutluk smiled. "It sounds good to me if it's okay with Russ."

Russ nodded his head in agreement. "I'm game. We just stayed at a beach house outside of Charleston. It was a lot of fun playing in the surf throwing a... a..." He turned toward Jeff. "What was that thing called again?"

"A Frisbee"

"Thanks. It was fun learning to throw that Frisbee around. The concert hall owner even gave me one to keep."

Helen turned toward Jeff. "Good. I'll write you directions. Y'all can head over there tonight to stay. I'll meet you there tomorrow morning. Key's on top of the doorframe. I'll call my parents to see what night they want to have dinner."

She turned toward Mutluk and Russ. "I have a pickup that I can use while y'all are here so you have my car to run back and forth. That way you won't have to move your truck every evening from the island."

Mutluk grinned. "That would be great."

The afternoon sun beat down on the foursome as the low waves rolled in breaking against the beach with a soft splashing sound. Dressed in her green bikini, Helen laid with her eyes closed in the full sunshine on the beach blanket while Jeff, in shorts with a t-shirt, stayed on the other side of the blanket under a beach umbrella. The sun had reddened Jeff's skin the first day so he had resorted to the shade of the large colorful umbrella to keep from looking like a cooked lobster. White lotion covered his nose. He sipped on sweet tea to kill the taste of the salty air.

Even though it was a Saturday afternoon, only a few other full-time residents in the distance laid out on blankets under beach umbrellas on the otherwise empty beach. The end of the fishing pier a half mile up the beach toward Virginia appeared crowded with weekend anglers. A few boats trolled offshore with their owners looking for the prizes of Black Sea Bass and Bluefish.

Mutluk and Russ stood at the water's edge on the hard-packed sand throwing a blue Frisbee. The Frisbee would leave Russ's hand in a wobble, dive toward the ground, then hit the sand before rolling on its lip toward the surf. Mutluk had to run to the Frisbee to retrieve it each time. Mutluk had mastered the art of spinning the disk flinging it to Russ' hand every throw. Laughter punctuated the ocean's gentle roar as the two chased the disk between them in the bright sunlight. Their darker skins seemed to be unaffected by the harsh rays of the sun.

Helen opened her eyes as she raised herself up on her elbows. "Kinda reminds me of us playing years ago."

"It does that. I just don't remember my skin getting so red so fast."

"You worked on your grandpa's farm with your shirt off all the time so you got tan before you would come down here. Anyway, I remember having to put suntan lotion on your legs."

"Oh-yea. Forgot that part. I would smell like a coconut for a week afterward."

"Anyway, have you thought any more about what you're going to do after New Orleans?"

"No, haven't really thought much past it. I guess it depends on what Clarence has to say after I find him."

"Well, just know that you can come back here to stay as long as you want. I missed your visits when you stopped coming after your grandparents died."

"I missed seeing you too."

"Anyway, I could talk to the guy that runs the marina. I went to high school with his son. We could probably get him to hire you to pump gas and move boats around. He'd be cool about your hair."

"Thanks, I'll keep it in mind." He set his tea down on the cooler, stood, and pulled his t-shirt off. "Come on. Let's go for one last dip before we have to get ready to face your parents and sister."

He grabbed her offered hand and the two raced down

the beach toward the surf where Mutluk and Russ struggled with making the Frisbee work. Mutluk picked up the Frisbee thrown at him by Russ as Jeff approached the water's edge.

"Go long," he shouted.

He cocked the Frisbee hard to his side before he let it fly. It sailed up before angling down toward the ocean.

Jeff ran down the edge of the surf with his head turned toward the flying disk as it arced to the right toward the water. Jeff leaped into the air, pulling the Frisbee into his arms. His feet hit the wet packed sand just as a breaking wave moved onto the beach. The wave, pushing his feet out from under him, covered his body in water. The rip current of the retreating wave pulled him out into deeper water.

The Frisbee slipped from his left hand while he tried to get a grasp onto something. He finally worked his fingers down into the packed sand to stop his uncontrolled slide.

Jeff brought his head above the turbulent surf as he rose to his knees. The sky above him shown clear blue and the salty water of the ocean dripped across his lips. A stinging sensation radiated from his right forearm.

The gash had opened up and blood slowly oozed down his arm. It mingled with the salt water on his skin before the watery red mixture dripped away, disappearing into the turbulent water. Jeff covered the gash with his left hand as he uneasily struggled to his feet.

Helen ran up to him. "Are you okay?"

"I cut my arm on something in Charleston and it just opened back up."

"Let me see." She lifted his hand away before gently brushing the sand from around the wound. "You must have slid across the sand on it. Strange, the edges are red and solid, almost like they had been burned. Let's get you up to the house to clean this up. It's almost time to get ready to head over to my parents anyway."

In the pickup on the way to Wilmington Island for dinner, Jeff lifted the edge of the tape of the fresh white bandage, peering beneath it at the gash.

Helen took her right hand off the large steering wheel, grabbed his left hand, and pulled it into his lap. "Stop picking at it. It's going to itch, but if you pick at it, you'll just inflame it more. I'll get you a couple of aspirin to deaden the itch a little when we get to my parent's house."

Jeff moved his left hand under his leg. "Okay, I'll sit on my hand. You keep both hands on the wheel. I still can't get used to you driving. I guess you're still nine in my mind."

Helen returned her hand to the steering wheel. "I've probably been driving longer than you. We can get our driver's license at fourteen in South Carolina. I got mine on my birthday."

"Is Joyce going to be there tonight?"

Helen shook her head. "Momma said no. She gave some excuse, but like I said, Joyce really didn't seem interested in seeing you. It's just as well anyway; you're going to get enough comments from my father about your hair."

"I'll just smile and take it for the good of the evening."

"If you guide the conversation over to your time in the army, he'll probably treat you better."

"Not much I want to talk about from then."

"Well, get him to talk about his time in the Navy. He keeps going on all the time about his service on a cruiser in World War II. Anyway, once you get him going, we'll never get him to stop. At least it will shut him up about hippies and your long hair."

"Sounds like a plan."

Helen turned the pickup into the packed seashell and sand driveway of a two-story house perched on the edge of the inlet that ran from Wassaw Sound to the fishing docks of Savannah. A floating dock stuck out from the land into the inlet with a ski boat tied up to the end of it. Seagrass infested the gravel path that led from the garage to the water's edge until it disappeared beneath the rippling surface on the channel.

Helen pointed to the water. "There're lots of crabs in the channel. Momma said Daddy caught a bunch for dinner tonight."

"That sounds great. I haven't had fresh crab since I was down here before the grandparents died. I did go to Fisherman's Wharf in San Francisco before I shipped out and had some cups of crab. They just weren't as good as the fresh crab here though."

Helen stopped the pickup as the front door of the house opened and her parents stepped out onto the porch. As Jeff stepped out of the pickup, Aunt Rose turned toward his uncle. "You behave yourself. He's family."

Jeff and Helen were sitting on old rusted lawn chairs next to the dock and both sipped from cans of beer. A bucket, with an opener tied to a string, held two more cans buried in the ice. A deep water fishing boat made its way slowly up the channel past the dock in the evening twilight. Its wake gently bobbed the dock before softly rippling into the beach. Red and green flickers from the reflection of the running lights raced sideways across the water like miniature flashlights held in the mouths of fish. The stern light broke the coming darkness as it reflected the white churning from the twin screws. The white froth left a visible trail that stretched beyond the bend.

Helen and her aunt had guided the dinner conversation to non-explosive topics such as Jeff's visit to Rocksville, the coming summer tourist season, and Uncle George's time in the Navy. Jeff's ears had perked up when his uncle talked about the cruiser getting shelled and hit several times by the Japanese warships. Uncle George's quick changing of the subject at Helen's mention of men being wounded or killed sparked a question in Jeff's mind that he decided to save for a more private time later.

Jeff finished his beer and reached for the bucket. "You ready for another, Helen?"

"No, I've always been a slow drinker."

Jeff opened the can with the opener. Footsteps crunched on the seashell drive behind them.

Uncle George's voice broke the calmness of the scene. "Helen, your mother wants to talk to you a minute before you leave."

Helen rose from her chair and headed toward the house. As she passed by her father, she gave him a kiss on the cheek. "I better go see her now. We need to head out soon anyway."

Her figure melted into the twilight as her footsteps crunched up the drive.

Uncle George reached into the bucket and grabbed the last can of beer. He opened it before walking to the end of the dock. It bobbed up and down under his footsteps. Jeff rose from his seat to follow him. They stood side by side on the edge of the dock as the sound of the fishing boat faded up the channel while its retreating stern light turned the water behind into twinkling shimmers like the stars overhead. The trail of foam slowly faded as the boat moved further toward its berth. Only the slapping of fish jumping out of the water after bugs broke the night stillness.

"It seems a lot more peaceful now than it did when I used to visit. Guess that's because you're on the inlet rather than the ocean."

"When you came here before, you and Helen created most of the ruckus, running around playing 'till we sent y'all to bed. But, this is a lot quieter than the old beach house with the surf coming in all the time."

Jeff took a swig from his beer, hesitating before he spoke again. "You mind answering a couple of questions about your time on the ship during the war?"

"Depends upon the questions."

"I'm guessing since you changed the subject when Helen asked about casualties you must have seen friends wounded and killed."

"That's true."

"Did you ever dream about it later? I mean, like relive the moments."

Uncle George lifted his beer to his lips as he quietly stared into the darkness. A fish leaped into the air near the dock and splashed salt water on their legs when fell into the inlet with a bug in its mouth.

He finally whispered out an answer. "Dreams? No. I wouldn't ever call them dreams. I used to have nightmares where the faces of my shipmates would pass by me trailing blood."

He turned to face Jeff. "Why do you ask, son? Do you have nightmares like that?"

"Maybe. That's why I want to find Clarence to have a chance to talk."

Uncle George placed his arm around Jeff's shoulder. "I thought that you going down to find your friend in New Orleans was just an excuse to party. Now I see that it's something you need." He took another sip from his beer. "One of the good things we had on the ship is that we spent six more months on patrol with no action before the war ended and we came home. Those of us left alive had a lot of time to talk about the losses and come to grips with them. That's one of the things I think they're doing wrong in this war. They pull you out of the jungle and a week later you're back home. You're alone, away from the friends you fought with. That's too fast. Too damn fast. You never have a chance to talk and get it behind you. I was in pretty good shape by the time I left the ship because I had time to talk it out. Even then, I would still wake up at night sometimes in a sweat for a couple of years."

Uncle George turned until he faced Jeff. "If you'd like, I'll drive you to New Orleans to help you find your friend.

I'll even wait for you and bring you back here. You could stay here 'till you decide what you want to do next."

"Thanks for the offer, Uncle George. But, I committed to working with the band until New Orleans. I'm going to fulfill that promise. Not really sure what I am going to do after that. Helen offered to let me stay with her also, but my life is too uncertain to make any promises. I just don't know where I belong."

"Okay. Can I give you some money to help you on your way?"

"Thanks, but no. The band pays me and takes care of my room and meals on the road. I'll be okay."

"Well if you need anything, just call. I'll help you with whatever you ask."

"Thanks."

Uncle George finished his beer and turned up the dock. "I better go see what's going on in the house. Your aunt is making up a bunch of crab salad for y'all to take back. I'll send Helen back down if they're done. You can just relax here 'til they're ready."

Jeff turned to face the water as Uncle George's footsteps stepped off the dock. The graveled crunched beneath his feet before fading into the night. In the now dark night, a splash from a fish sounded as it jumped at a bug. The chug of another boat on the inlet heading toward Savannah entered the night. The chugging of the diesel echoed across from the far shore. The echo sounded like well-timed gunfire. Jeff turned and ran up the dock toward the house. He caught up with Uncle George halfway there.

Jeff and Helen waved their goodbyes out the windows until darkness enveloped the car as they left the driveway turning south on the two-lane road. Bugs raced by the headlights with the occasional unlucky one being splatted on the windshield while the lucky ones blew around the car past the open windows. Jeff stuck his hand out the window, flying it up and down in the racing breeze. Helen drove one handed as she rested her free arm on the door. The broken yellow line down the center of the dark road measured the miles back to Tybee Island.

Helen pulled the pickup into the empty carport and shut down the engine. Only the bug light beside the entry door lit the night as the sea breeze blew the curtains through the open kitchen window. Waves broke on the sand beyond the light and gave a gentle roar to the night.

Helen turned in the yellow light toward Jeff. She twirled her hair in her fingers. "Doesn't look like they're back from the show yet. Want to go sleep on the beach and listen to the waves like we used to?"

"Yea. That would be nice."

"You go on down. I'll put away the crab salad then grab a couple of beach blankets. Want a beer or two?

"Sure."

Helen headed into the house as Jeff strolled down the path between the dunes then onto the soft sand of the upper beach. The rising half-moon reflected on the unsettled waters of the ocean giving a line of light that stretched from the beach to the horizon. Jeff kept walking until his feet hit the flat compacted sand left by the retreating tide. His feet settled into the dampness and left unseen prints that would disappear before the rising of the sun. He walked until he felt the ending roll of the surf touch his toes. The Milky Way stretched out across the clear sky, the stars forming a bright strip that lit the dark sky with a glow like a night light in a hallway. A flash of lightning from a squall over the horizon lit the edge of the end of the stars. Jeff closed his eyes while he drank in the sounds of the waves breaking against the unseen edge of the sand shelf beyond the shore.

Jeff shifted his helmet back from his eyes. He blinked as the trees of the jungle came into focus above him. The sound of movement touched his ears from behind him on the other side of the tree trunk. He slowly turned over, carefully raising his head until his eyes could see the area ahead. In the filtered sunlight that snaked through the canopy above, the muzzle of an AK47 stuck out from between the branches of a tree trunk blown down across the gully. The face of an NVA soldier peered from behind the rear sight of the weapon. Sweat dropped from Jeff's eyebrow down to his lash. He blinked it away.

Helen's voice came from behind him as her hand touched his neck. "Jeff, Are you okay?"

"Get down," Jeff screamed.

Jeff pulled her close to his side as he dropped to the sand. Helen struggled from his grip, rolled away, and gained her feet. Her breathing was quick, almost panicked.

"What's the hell's wrong, Jeff?"

Jeff looked up at her as the sound of the surf once again filled his ears. Helen looked at him with eyes that were wide with fear. She stood there tensed. Ready to run. He pushed himself up from the sand until he sat cross-legged. The gentleness of the surrounding beach worked its way into him slowing his breathing.

"Sorry, I guess I fell asleep and was having a nightmare."

Helen relaxed her stance and sat down on the sand next to Jeff. Laying her chin on his shoulder, she placed her arms around his neck. Her eyes met his and they stared at each other for a long moment before she moved her mouth toward his lips. She kissed him, gently at first. Then passion took over.

Chapter 8

Jeff relaxed into the kiss at first. But, after a few seconds, he pulled back to stop it. He pushed Helen away as she tried to move toward him again.

"What's wrong? You used to kiss me before."

"That was just two kids fooling around then. We're not kids anymore and we're still cousins."

Helen laughed softly as she tried again to move closer. "We're second cousins, not first. There's nothing wrong with this. Your grandparents were second cousins. So were Mama Hazel and Great-Gramps."

Jeff kept his arms tensed to keep Helen away. "I'm sorry Helen. It just doesn't feel right to me. I like you okay and all that. You were my best friend both down here and when you would come to Rocksville, but I've never thought of you any other way but family."

Helen relaxed. She slid away slightly while smiling at his questioning face. "Jeff, I've loved you for a long time. Since we were kids. I was scared I'd lost you when you when to war. I promised myself that I'd tell you how I felt if I ever got to see you again. Anyway, I'm sorry if that scares you, but it needed to be said."

Jeff relaxed backward and placed his hands in the sand behind him. "Visiting with you was one of the things I really missed after my grandparents died. I always felt that I not only lost them, but I lost you too. But, what could I do about it? I was just a kid being led around by adults. I couldn't just come down here by myself."

"I felt the same way. I even tried to get my parents to let me visit you up in Richmond, but daddy said no."

"But why me? Sure, we were good friends, but I went on to have other friends. I even had a girlfriend throughout high school."

"Did you love her?"

Jeff turned his eyes toward the breaking waves. "Yea. I guess I did. At times I think I still do."

"What happened to the two of you?"

He turned his eyes back toward Helen. "We headed to different colleges. Her parents wanted her to go to Vassar. All I could afford was in-state tuition at a school in Virginia. I lost touch with her after I dropped out and enlisted. She's probably married by now. How about you? You must have dated guys around here."

She bent her head downward looking at the sand laying between them. "Sure, I dated. I even thought a few of them loved me. In the end, those guys only wanted one of two things, my discount at my parent's sporting goods store or to get into my pants a few times. Either way, after they got what they wanted, they found a reason to break up."

Jeff placed his hand on the back of Helen's neck. "I'm sorry."

She looked directly into his eyes. The glint of a tear lined her lower lid. "You were the only guy I've ever known that was always honest with me. Even now, you're not telling me what I want to hear, but you're saying what's true in your heart. That's one of the reasons I love you."

"We did have something special when we were kids."

Helen rose up on her knees and moved closer. "That's just it Jeff. We're not kids anymore. You're here now but you're going to leave me again in a couple of days. I don't want that to happen. I want you to stay near me. I want us to have a chance to form something. If it doesn't work, at least we would have tried."

"I don't know Helen. It still seems weird. I never got that first and second cousin or first cousin once removed thing—"

"That's what my parents are to you."

"What?"

"They're your first cousins once removed."

"I thought they were my uncle and aunt."

"No. Daddy just didn't want you calling him Cousin George."

"Well, maybe I could get past the second cousin thing, but—"

Helen held her hand up for him to stop. She lost her smile. "Somehow I knew that there was a but coming."

She started to raise herself up from the sand. Jeff reached out, pulling her close so that he held her head to his chest. She struggled for a moment, but then stopped, relaxing in his embrace.

He gently stroked her hair. "You never would let me finish what I wanted to say before you took it wrong. You're going to have to work on that. Now as I was going to say before you interrupted me. But—I need to find Clarence and get a bunch of questions answered before I do anything else."

Helen sat up, placed her hands around his neck, and looked straight into his eyes. "Just promise me that you will come back before you make any decisions. I just want to try... us." She waited a moment and then grabbed the sides of his head. "Promise!"

Jeff laughed as he grabbed her hands from his head, holding them gently. "I promise. Now, let's just go lie on the blanket and get some sleep."

She kissed him lightly before hugging him. The two slowly moved back into the soft sand where Helen had spread out the beach blanket. They brushed the sand from each other's backs as they had done as children. Together they lay down on their backs next to each other with their hands intertwined.

As they relaxed, headed toward sleep, Helen pulled Jeff's hand over her heart and held it tightly there. With the surf rolling in the background, Jeff stared up at the stars of the Milky Way. As Helen's heartbeat moved through his palm, his eyelids grew heavy. When he closed them, rifle fire erupted off in the distance.

Jeff blinked and held his breath as the NVA soldier behind the rifle sticking through the foliage turned his head in his direction. The soldier cocked his head slightly as if to listen before he resumed the slow scan of the area. The muzzle moved away from Jeff toward the center of the gully. After a long moment, the face and the muzzle withdrew back behind the trunk. Jeff breathed again.

He pulled the safety slide on his M79 back until the F indicator was covered. As he shifted to the right for better cover, he glanced down at his right arm. A rust colored thick mixture of blood, mud, and water streaked across the arm from the gash. Jeff stared at the blood oozing from the bottom of it.

His external senses reeled back into play as American voices in the distance shouted commands to move forward. AK47s fired full automatic as the screams of newly wounded soldiers quickly replaced the shouts. Jeff rose from his knees, moving forward, stumbling through the mud as it sucked at his boots until he regained solid footing on the floor of the gully. He focused his ears toward the firefight for a moment, then turned back onto the path.

Jeff moved in a low crouch as he picked his way through several broken trees. Clarence's M16, still slung over his shoulder, made the movement a struggle as branches caught the muzzle pushing him backward. The land beyond the first line of broken trees lay relatively undisturbed for a short distance with only an occasional fallen branch impeded his progress. Drag marks scoured the ground at the center of the gully while blood spots on the leaves marked his way like breadcrumbs dropped by fairytale children.

The battle behind him raged as mortars from both

sides joined the fight. Ahead of him, through a second line of downed trees, equipment rattled as men moved toward the blockage. Jeff moved to the side of the gully and pushed into a large clump of leafy bushes. He lay facedown in the center placing the M79 on the ground to his left. He shifted Clarence's M16 off his shoulder, pulled the charging handle back slightly to check that a round was in the chamber, and then tapped the forward assist with the palm of his right hand. He peered through the foliage toward the equipment rattle.

Green-clad figures appeared through the broken branches of the fallen trees quickly picking their way past them. Ten NVA came through before the flow through the mangled trunks ceased. The quiet singsong voice of the leader directed the group into ambush positions on the edge of the gully just down from Jeff's hiding place. Jeff slowly shifted the muzzle of the M16 toward the threat but kept his eyes focused toward the line of broken trees up the gully. No more equipment rattling came from beyond the twisted trunks with their shattered branches. Jeff shifted his eyes back toward the line of NVA as they settled into firing positions while checking their weapons. He looked up the gully back toward the path. A blood spot reflected from a leaf. The bushes on his side of the gully provided cover to the line of broken trees and Jeff mentally picked a course past the tree line to resume his search. He looked back at the line of NVA as the leader spoke softly as he moved the open palms of his hands in a downward motion. The troops settled further on the bushes breaking branches at the edge of the gully. The leader pushed a branch to the side and peered through the opening.

Jeff reached forward with his left hand and broke several small branches until a six-inch hole opened up straight toward the line of NVA. He raised the M16 to his shoulder shifting the front blade until it settled just above the head of the NVA leader. Jeff's breathes came steadily as he never let the sights of the M16 move from that fixed position. As the leader raised his hand slowly like the start of a chopping motion, he rose slightly as he opened his mouth to yell. His head centered in Jeff's sights. Jeff quickly squeezed the trigger twice.

The leader fell forward on the slope with the front of his head gone. A soldier to his left glanced at the fallen leader and then at the edge of the gully behind them. He turned his gaze toward the bushes at the bottom just as Jeff shifted his sights before squeezing the trigger twice again. The man fell in a clump down the slope.

Two members of the ambush party rose while they turned their weapons toward the opposite side of the gully as they searched for this danger to their rear. Jeff sighted into the one further away ready to squeeze the trigger when an American machine-gun fired. Red spray erupted from the chests of the two NVA soldiers as the bullets found their marks. The helmet of another member of the ambush team flew backward as another machine gun round blew off the back of his head. Jeff shifted the muzzle to the right until the sights were centered on an NVA kneeling behind a tree before he fired twice again. The man dropped to the ground on his right side and remained still.

The remaining four NVA soldiers spun their heads around as they searched for the danger behind them. Two slid down the slope and began running toward the fallen trees just beyond Jeff. Jeff clicked the selector switch to automatic and centered the sights on the lead soldier as he moved past the opening in the leaves. Jeff pulled the trigger, holding it back as the bullets spit from the muzzle.

Bullets cut across the side of the chest of the soldier causing him to fall just as the second soldier ran into the fusillade. He spun around, dropping in a twisted clump. The M16 clicked on an empty chamber. Jeff dug into his general-purpose bag looking for a full magazine.

The last two NVA soldiers began a fast crawl down the

slope toward the twisted group of fallen trees with the relative safety they represented. Jeff estimated at the range to the two men as he grabbed his M79 from the ground next to him. He rose from the center of the bushes as he brought the weapon up into an under the shoulder firing stance with the muzzle raised ever so slightly above the targets. One of the soldiers swung his AK47 toward Jeff, firing just as Jeff pulled his own trigger. The bullet from the AK47 stung as it tore through the left sleeve of Jeff's fatigue shirt. The round from the M79 hit the tree beside the two men and showered them with deadly bits of wire shrapnel. They both stopped crawling and lay still in the leaves as the side of the tree smoked from the explosion.

Jeff sank back down into the cover of the bush. He pushed the locking lever of the M79 to the right, broke open the breech, and extracted the spent shell. His left arm stung as he reached for the last gold tipped round in his vest. He held his breath listening to the sounds of the battle as he closed the breech. The fighting beyond the upper edge of the gully was moving away with the gunfire becoming more sporadic. Jeff inserted a finger into the bullet hole in his sleeve then tore away the material until the hole was large enough for him to view the wound. The bullet had failed to penetrate the arm but had left a bloody crease several inches long. Blood seeped out of the wound, mixed with Jeff's sweat, and flowed down his bicep toward his forearm.

Pulling his combat bandage from the carrier on his belt, he tore the metalized foil wrapping open with his teeth. With his right hand, he wrapped the bandage around his upper arm and knotted the trailing ties as tight as he could pull them with one hand and his mouth.

He reloaded the M16 with a fresh magazine before yanking the charging handle back. The bolt gave a metallic clunk as it reached its limit before flying forward when he released the handle. Jeff bumped the forward assist with his right hand to seat the bolt.

A mortar round exploded ten meters to his left and the concussion tossed him onto his back. Hot shrapnel peppered his torn uniform a moment later and found bare skin. He brushed his body as best he could without sitting up as the sharp burning shards shifted down his sleeves. The sound of mortar rounds leaving their firing tubes sounded behind the rifle fire. Jeff scrambled to his feet as he held the M79 aimed outward, the safety off and his finger on the trigger. He shouldered the M16 upside down and dove through the fallen trees up the gully.

The area beyond the trees was vacant. Again, in a crouch, he ran away from the deadly rain of mortar shells exploding behind him. He moved his eyes quickly in a rotating scan with the barrel of the M79 shifting along as though locked to his eye muscles. More mortar rounds left their tubes and the deadly projectiles whistled as they flew above his head.

He slowed his movement forward to a hesitant walk as he listened for voices or equipment rattle. No telltale rattle came with the only voices being shouts in two languages in the distance beyond the edge of the gully. He stopped while focusing his gaze downward scanning the length of the path before him. A leaf three feet in front of him shimmered with wet red blood. Jeff raised his eyes from the ground, stared up the gully, and moved forward again.

He shifted to the right side of the path as he walked slowly while he swung the aiming point of the M79 back and forth from the path to the bushes on opposite edge of the gully. Sweat dripped from his eyebrows down on his nose. He wiped his face with his right hand as he kept his ear cocked sideways listening for sounds up the path, waiting for the danger that would come with the sounds to expose itself. He moved his eyes in sweeps across the gully, taking in both sides and the open space to his front. The blood spots on the vegetation became sparser, but the drag marks continued up the path. Jeff shifted to the center of the path before kneeling to look at one of the splotches on the broad leaves.

The blood did not seem as bright as the earlier splotches. Jeff knelt next to the leaf with blood, rubbing his fingers on it. The blood stuck to his fingers like glue drying on wood. He raised his fingers to his eyes and looked closely at the blood. Clear mucus intermixed with the thick red substance showing that congealing was taking place. This healing indication encouraged Jeff as he wiped his hand on his pants. He shifted to the right side of the gully as he moved forward at a trot.

Bullets zinged above him causing clipped leaves to drift down around him as though the season had suddenly changed and fall was in the air. American tracers hissed with their luminous red tails until the glow disappeared into the foliage to his right and above him. Answering AK47s constantly banged beyond the bushes to the left edge of the gully. Magazines clanked as men stripped empty ones from their weapons and rammed new ones into place. Jeff involuntarily raised the M79 toward the sounds above his right as he moved his eyes searching, ever searching for the next danger.

Singsong commands began anew punctuating the spaces between the rifle shots and magazine insertions. Scurrying feet sounded beyond the bushes above him. Jeff looked quickly for cover, but none was close by. The trunk of a fallen tree lay ten meters further up the gully. He sprinted for it just as four NVA pushed through the bushes on the gully's edge behind him. They focused their attention on the gully below Jeff, not noticing him as he ran. He reached the tree trunk and jumped behind it. Turning quickly yet quietly, he aimed the M79 at the soldiers as they moved toward the fallen trees he had passed through only a minute before. He slowly pulled

Clarence's M16 from over his shoulder until it laid on the ground to his right. He sighted the M79 on the back of the lead soldier and squeezed the trigger. The round flew away in an arc as he rolled to his back, broke open the breech, and removed the spent round. The round exploded behind him and screams bit into the air. Jeff looked up while he reached into his general-purpose bag for another gold tipped quick-arming fragmentation round.

An NVA soldier stood in the center of the gully ten meters away. He stared straight at Jeff with a surprised look as he began to raise his AK47 toward his shoulder. Jeff's breath came hard as he threw the M79 at the soldier and began reaching for the M16. The NVA soldier ducked, disrupting his aim as the bullets from his AK47 flew into the sky. Jeff raised the M16 with his left hand and yanked the trigger twice. The NVA soldier, who had recovered and taken new aim toward Jeff, began firing on automatic and dirt clumps churned upward in a line that raced toward Jeff. The NVA soldier jerked around as Jeff's bullets found their mark. He fell backward while the muzzle of his weapon climbed upward to the right. A last clump of dirt flew into the air between Jeff's thighs, just inches from his crotch. Jeff shuddered as he dropped the M16, scurried for the M79, and reloaded it with a round from his bag as he looked over his shoulder toward the sound of more equipment rattle.

The leaves of the bushes on the left edge of the gully rustled as three more NVA soldiers dropped into the protective cover of the ravine to get away from the murderous fire of the American machine guns. Jeff stayed hidden behind his protective log. He pushed the safety of the M79 forward with his thumb until it clicked with the F exposed. He breathed deep several times, glanced left at the M16, and then quickly rolled to his right as he came up on one knee with the M79 held tight against his shoulder.

Three of the original NVA soldiers lay still on the

ground while the fourth sat cross-legged as he picked at the hot shrapnel that burned in his face. The three new NVA soldiers lay on the slope of the gully directing their attention through the bushes toward the advancing American machine guns. Jeff moved his aim behind the feet of those NVA soldiers and fired. The M79 thudded firmly against his shoulder. Jeff dropped it on the ground as the round raced away. He reached down for the M16 as he watched the grenade round strike its mark. The legs of the center NVA soldier sprayed outward as his head dropped hard to the ground. The explosion threw the two soldiers on each side of him sideways. As the shock of the blast passed, one slowly tried to raise himself while the other convulsed on the ground.

Jeff raised the M16 to his shoulder, centered the sights on rising soldier just as he reached for his AK47, and fired a single shot. The man's body dropped as Jeff shifted the muzzle quickly to the left bringing the sights to bear on the soldier who had been picking shrapnel from his face. He had picked up his AK47 and was taking aim at Jeff just as Jeff centered the sights on him. Jeff squeezed the trigger. A tracer round spit its red luminesce in a line toward its victim. The man flew backward but his trigger finger tightened in the moment of death and a single round left the muzzle. Jeff's head slammed backward as the bullet tore under his helmet. It soared into the air behind him. Jeff fell backward but kept hold of the M16.

The grazing shot distorted the scene around him and Jeff shook his head trying to clear stars from his vision. Three of everything reached from his eyes to his brain. Sounds were suddenly muffled, unrecognizable. His hands did not work as he wanted them to as he tried to pick himself up. All he could do is lay there, hoping that he had cleared the area of danger, knowing if he had not, death would soon be his. For a moment, his thoughts returned to Mama Hazel and her kitchen back in Rocksville. The smell of fresh biscuits penetrated his senses from somewhere as he relaxed, waiting to be in his beloved Great-grandmother's home again. Peacefulness came over his body as he waited.

The thought of Clarence drove the biscuit smell from him. His vision cleared, his hearing sharpened. His hands began to work again. He pushed the magazine release with his finger while he reached into his general-purpose bag to find another magazine. He loaded the full magazine, slapped the bolt release to chamber a round as he rolled, placed the sights back toward the slope, and centered on the man still convulsing on the ground. Jeff held his fire while he surveyed the other two for movement, but their bodies remained unmoving. He shifted his aim back toward the original four NVA. Only stillness filled his sights.

Something warm dripped on his right ear. Wiping his hand across it, loose red blood smeared his fingers. Jeff reached up to his scalp and pain radiated on his head as he touched the open crease left from the soldier's single shot. Pulling his hand back, he gazed again at the blood-covered fingers.

He shifted around scanning the area behind him. His helmet hung from a small branch five meters behind him. He scrambled back to it. Pain radiated as he flung it onto his head when the helmet hit the fresh wound. Jeff bit his lip to muffle a cry while he moved quickly back under cover. He retrieved another round from his general-purpose bag, loaded it into the grenade launcher, and waited. No other NVA moved into the gully as he shifted his eyes across the battle scene with his M79 in his left hand and the M16 in his right. The muzzles of both weapons followed his search.

Jeff rose into a crouch moving again up the gully at a trot. He pushed past another bush but slowed when he spotted a dark red splotch on the corner of a broad leaf. The edge of the slope stayed in his scan as he moved, listening for the slightest hint of equipment rattle. The bushes thinned as the gully widened with the bottom flattening out. Small trees replaced bushes as the prominent feature. The sides of the slopes now ended low enough for Jeff to peek over them as he trotted forward. Several NVA moved from tree to tree to the left on the flat ground, but none looked his way. He bent down as low as he could as he raced ahead.

A crater, still wisping smoke from the 105 MM shell that formed it, came into view ahead of him. He scurried for it. Diving over the loose dirt piled on the side, he rolled toward the bottom as his helmet fell away. His head struck a twisted root from the tree that used to grow there and stars again filled his eyes. Bouncing away from the root, his head hit soft sand. Jeff lay there dazed, unable to focus his eyes. Waves slapped the beach in the distance.

Jeff sat up quickly. Twisting his head first left and right, then up and down, he took in his new surroundings. The sun was low in the sky but had climbed above the soft sand dunes that surrounded him. Seagulls shouted their cries as they circled above him in the ocean breeze. A land crab scurried across the sand five feet from him. It stopped momentarily to survey him as a possible new piece of food. It held its pinchers high while twitching its antennas as it felt the air. The crab fled into a hole when Jeff moved his head again as it sensed the danger of the monster in front of him.

Voices drifted across the gentle wind. Not the singsong voices that Jeff expected, but the sounds of a woman and a man speaking English and laughing. Both voices were as gentle as the soft sand under his legs while the affection attached to them drifted through the banter of southern accents. Excited children's voices came across the dunes to his rear. Jeff rose to his knees until his eyes cleared the top of the dune. He peered through the sea grass while a family, dressed in beach regalia, moved through the dunes from a gravel parking lot. The children, carrying small pails with little shovels and dragging boogie boards, rushed ahead onto the soft sand of the open beach while the parents trudged behind with blankets, coolers, a large umbrella, and a floppy bag that bulged with the implements of a day at the beach. Another man, further down the beach, walked with a colorful dog that jumped into the air around him. The man threw a stick into the surf and the dog splashed after it.

Jeff rose from his private hovel in the sand and brushed the sand from his legs. Traces of mud discolored his knees. His left arm stung as he moved it and he twisted his head toward the pain. Blood seeped from a shallow two-inch gash across his upper shoulder muscle while dried blackened blood surrounded the edges. Jeff gently brushed the sand from around the wound before he picked at individual pieces of grit. He moved his gaze toward his right forearm. Lines of dirt mixed with sweat clung to the adhesive that had held the bandage. Sand was embedded in the remnants of the ointment.

He slowly reached his hand to the right side of his head, grimacing as he touched his scalp. When he brought the hand back down, traces of dark blood stuck to his fingers.

He walked from the dunes toward the surf slowly while taking in each of the sights and sounds that surrounded him. The children laughed at the surf's edge as their parents set up the umbrella and spread a blanket in its shade. The father looked Jeff's way and then glanced at his children before he returned to pushing the umbrella pole further into the sand. The man with the dog threw the stick past Jeff and the dog chased after it. The dog slowed for a moment as it reached Jeff, looked in his direction, wagged its tail, and then splashed into the surf at the stick.

Jeff knelt down when he reached the surf to let the swirling water wash part of the mud from his knees.

Scooping water into his right hand, he poured it slowly onto the gash on his shoulder. The salt stung as it washed the sand and blood from the wound. Jeff grimaced as he repeated the process before softly rubbing the dried blood until the caked pieces broke away and fell into the retreating water. Pink diluted blood moved down his arm, dripping away as he cleaned the last of the sand and crusty blood. He placed his hand over the gash before standing.

The fishing pier jutted into the ocean to the south about half a mile away. Figures stood on the end with their poles angled out dangling lines into the rolling swells. Jeff walked on the packed sand toward the pier as the water from the breaking waves rolled across his feet before retreating into the sea. He kept turning his head as each new sound hit his ears, not sure what each second would bring before the nightmare of the battle returned.

Jeff moved into the long shadows created by the pier and touched a piling. The outer edge of rough wind and water-damaged wood fell away at his touch dropping onto the sand by his feet. He looked up at the planking above him as fishermen trudged toward the end to cast their lines. Their footsteps, muffled by the waves striking the pilings, showed only as shadows in the cracks of the weathered wood.

Jeff reached down to wrap his fingers around a clump of sea grass that had taken root in the water-filled hollow behind a piling. He held it loosely so that the long strands flowed through his hand until the seed plume at the top broke off to remain trapped between his fingers. Lifting the plume to his face, he studied the immature seedpods with wispy hairs of the grass between them. The plume morphed into a clump of broad leaves trapped between dirty sweat covered fingers. Mortar shells exploded behind him.

He dropped the grass and dove behind a piling into the broken surf. He twisted his head toward the sound of the mortar shells, but only saw the man with the dog. The dog seemed to smile as it glanced his way again. Then, with a cock of its head, the dog wagged its tail before returning his focus to the offered stick. A large swell crashed into the pilings behind Jeff and the water washed over his legs before stinging the raw flesh of the wound on his shoulder.

Jeff rose from behind the piling while watching the dog as it moved slowly down the beach a throw of the stick at a time. As the salty water dripped from his shorts, Jeff turned south again and left the shadows of the pier.

Helen's house came into view as Jeff made his way down the beach from the pier. Mutluk and Russ were standing by the water's edge playing with the Frisbee. The bright blue disk wobbled back and forth with their gentle tosses, the bravado of the tosses the day before gone in the early morning relaxation. Helen lay on the beach blanket wearing a red string bikini.

Jeff moved across the sand to the blanket. Reaching it, he knelt down. "Good Morning."

Helen opened her eyes. "Where'd you go? I woke up—" She sat up quickly. "What happened to your shoulder? You're bleeding! And there's blood on your face."

Jeff nonchalantly glanced down at the seeping wound. Thinking fast, he lied. "Oh. I scraped my shoulder on a nail on the pier and then whacked my head on a cross member. It's okay. I washed them off in the surf."

Helen stood and took his hand. "You're as clumsy as you ever were. I don't know what I'm going to do with you. Come on. I'll bandage that up. What happened to the bandage on your other arm?"

Jeff looked down at the adhesive marks that ran in straight lines on his forearm. "Must have lost it in the surf."

"Well come on. You're a mess." Helen reached behind him and pulled a clump of seaweed from the leg of his shorts. "You have seaweed sticking out your shorts and mud on your knees. You can take a shower to clean up before I redress everything."

Giving a little grin, Jeff squeezed her hand. His mind though, stayed on the battle he had just fought. Time was becoming very confused. He wondered how he got into the dunes up the beach.

Jeff showered before letting Helen dress his forearm and shoulder as he sat at the kitchen table in his shorts. She then held his head, twisted it to the right, and examined the scalp wound. Her gentle hands shifted the hair away while she looked at the scrap with practiced professional eyes.

"No way can I put a bandage on this without shaving your head. I doubt you want that. You'll just have to try to keep it clean and wash it whenever you can."

"Think I should wear my Boonie hat or not?"

She pushed his hair around a little more. "I'd hold off on the hat for at least a few days. It would probably just scrape the scab causing it to bleed again."

Helen sat down next to Jeff. She ever so slowly took his hands into hers. "I woke as the sun was beginning to lighten the horizon. You weren't lying next to me. I wasn't sure what was going on. Anyway, I first thought that maybe you hadn't really been here and that you're coming back was all a dream. Then Mutluk and Russ came through the dunes with their Frisbee. So, I thought maybe I scared you with my forwardness so you had left. Please don't let me scare you away."

Jeff smiled. "You didn't scare me. Maybe freaked me out for a little, but I don't scare easily. I just got up before dawn and went for a walk to think. Listen, I can't give you the type of relationship you want. I want to be your friend again and coming back here to relax sounds good, but— "

Helen started to speak but Jeff placed a finger on her lips. She smiled under his finger as he continued. "But— I have to find Clarence first."

Helen grabbed his finger from her lips, kissed it, and then squeezed it tight. "I know you do. I'm sorry if I came on too strong. Anyway, how about I just come with you to help you find him. I have vacation coming. After you find him, we could drive back together."

Jeff grasped her hands between his. "As much as having you around feels good, this is something I need to do alone. I promised you we'll talk before I make up my mind about what I do and where I go next. I meant that. I think I could really use a friend like you again."

"Okay. But you can't blame a girl for trying."

She began to put the first aid kit back together. "Anyway, go finish getting dressed and then go play on the beach with Mutluk and Russ for a little. I'll fix a Southern breakfast for y'all to show you what you'll miss by not staying."

Chapter 9

The muddy rivers and swampy bogs of Georgia morphed into sandy shoulders and salt-water canals along the roads as the truck rolled down Route 17 toward Jacksonville. The air had lost its muggy suffocating feel as the sky shined a bright blue that contrasted with the white puffy clouds dotting the sky. Even the waves breaking along the beaches appeared bluer against the white sand that raced by the windows.

Russ guided them through Jacksonville without incident before he directed Mutluk into the little community of Atlantic Beach. The next venue, a combination concert hall, restaurant, and bar known as the Holiday Beach Club, stood out as the only two-story building facing the beach. Mutluk backed up the truck next the building until the rear end kissed the large loading dock. Ralph, the owner, greeted the threesome as they climbed the stairs from the alley. The stage was just inside the dock's rolling door and at the same level. A curtain that hung ten feet from the back gave room to store the cases. The ceiling of the stage, 15 feet from the floor, had open trusses along the entire width of its large opening.

Russ looked up at the trusses and pointed. "Can I hang my lights from those? There's not enough height for me to lift my own light bars."

"Sure," Ralph said. "That's what most groups do. I have a rolling electric lift that you can use to carry them up."

Ralph walked them to the front edge of the stage. A large area for dancing was surrounded by tables four deep along the walls. A balcony, hanging ten feet above the floor, wrapped around three sides of cavernous space. More tables lined the balcony.

Ralph pointed upward to the ceiling before sweeping his arm toward the rear of the balcony. "There's a hanging tray that runs along the roof trusses back to the control booth at the rear of the balcony. You can use it to lay out your control cables. The electric lift will reach it."

He then led them up a flight of stairs off the left side of the stage to the balcony. "This will get you to the control booth. The waitresses use it to get food and drinks up from the kitchen so it gets a little congested at times during the night, but just stay to the right and you'll be in the flow."

When they reached the top of the stairs, rather than turning right toward the balcony above the dance floor, Ralph turned left leading them to a closed door. He reached into his pocket, pulled out a key, and unlocked the door.

He then turned toward the three and held up the key up. "Who's in charge?"

Russ and Jeff both pointed to Mutluk. Ralph handed him the key before he led the roadies through the door into an apartment above the stage.

"Two bedrooms, a fold out couch, dining area with a kitchenette, full bath. That door over there leads to a deck that has a stairway to the beach."

Russ opened the door to the deck, plopped down in a lounge chair, and closed his eyes. "Man, I could get used to this."

Mutluk leaned against the railing looking out at the surfers and sunbathers. He kicked Russ's foot playfully. "We better get used to it later. As soon as we finish setting up, I'll throw the Frisbee with you."

Russ jumped up from the chair and started down the back stairs. "That sounds like a deal. Come on Jeff. You're between me and a Frisbee."

Jeff laughed and followed the now scrambling Russ.

In the wee hours of the next morning after the band had finished their show, Jeff was sitting on the deck in a lounge chair while Mutluk and Russ threw the Frisbee on the soft sand. A bank of floodlights illuminated the beach next to the club. Occasionally, the Frisbee would fly wobbling off course before disappearing into the darkness of the beach beyond the harsh lights. Russ was usually the wild thrower so Mutluk made him retrieve it from the outer sands.

The parking lot slowly emptied as the evening's revelers finished their last swallows of beer in the fenced outside patio before staggering to their cars. Exhausted from the load-in and set up, Jeff lay back in the chair, his Boonie hat lightly propped over his eyes to block the yellow glow of the porch light. The cool ocean breeze blew gently over his body as he fell into a welcome sleep.

Jeff woke to an empty beach with the patio bar below the deck dark and empty. Mutluk and Russ were nowhere in sight.

The door to the apartment sat shut with the lights off behind it. Jeff rose from the lounge chair, walked down the wooden stairs, and out onto the beach where the heavy surf crashed on the sand beyond the lights. His shadow, sharp and short at first, softened as it lengthened before disappearing altogether when he moved into the darkness toward the crashing waves. His toes touched the hard sand of the recent tide just as the red glow of the crescent moon broke the horizon lighting the surface of the rolling waters of the Atlantic. Sands crabs scurried away from his moving feet as his thoughts turned to Mary, their night on the beach, and her offer of a place to stay in Columbia. Being somewhere that no one knew his past may help him after Clarence filled in the holes that he could. Jeff stopped at the surf line as a spent wave touched his toes.

However, the thought of the promise he had made to Helen weighed into him and dug deep into his heart. She deserved his honesty, even if he may not be ready to stay with her after New Orleans. The answers Clarence may bring could open new questions that might cause him to have to search further for answers. How he ended up on Don and Sally's front porch among them. He didn't want to show up at Helen's door and get her hopes up only to need to leave a week later.

The remnants of a large wave pushed flowing water over his ankles causing Jeff to back away from the surf. As he retreated from the moving water, his ankle caught on a piece of driftwood tumbling him backward toward the soft sand of the undisturbed beach. He rolled when he landed and his shoulder hit his helmet as he reached the bottom of the shell crater.

Jeff clutched his M79 to his chest. His breath came in hard fast spurts as he fought to understand his surroundings. He twisted his head as he searched for danger before he grabbed his helmet and pushed it on. The pain from the gash on his head bit into his brain. Jeff rolled onto his stomach and crawled forward until the top of his head broke above the rim of the crater. He slowly scanned the low edge of the gully. In the forest above the edge of the diminishing rim, running figures dashed from tree to tree as they fired their AK47s from whatever cover the thin trees could provide. Some fell as unseen bullets hit them removing the life from their bodies. Explosions from the grenades of M79s hit the ragged line of advancing NVA soldiers, bringing down more. Jeff turned his gaze to the right to check the area behind the advancing troops. A line of reserve NVA soldiers waited on one knee behind the trees 50 meters back, their rifles and RPGs held at the ready while they waited for the bugle call to advance. Their faces grimaced as they watched their comrades fall, lying still or writhing as they crawled toward the rear. Not one of them shifted their eyes Jeff's way.

Jeff looked up the diminishing path at another blood stained broad leaf. Twenty meters beyond the leaf a clump of flowering bushes blocked his view of the path with the remnant of the gully behind it. He shifted his legs up until they were under him then placed his right hand on the rim of the crater. He glanced again at the reserve troops as he tensed his legs and dug his toes into the soft dirt. An officer with red piping on his collar raised his pistol as the bugler beside him brought the instrument to his lips. The officer moved his mouth in an unheard command and the harsh notes of the bugle raced into the air. The line of troops rose as one running into the fray to their front.

Jeff propelled himself out of the crater toward the clump of bushes. He held the general-purpose bag tight against his right side while he pointed the M79 with his left hand toward the advancing NVA troops. He aimed toward the spot the officer would be when the projectile hit and pulled the trigger just as he reached the edge of the bushes. A hidden root caught his foot just after the round left the muzzle causing Jeff to pitch forward. His nose hit hard sand as the water from the spent wave rushed over his legs into his shorts. He tried to stand, but the retreating water of the undertow caught his legs like the tentacles of an octopus. The force of the water swept him along the sand toward deeper water. Jeff forced his fingers into the sand to drag himself through the turbulent water toward the beach.

Jeff's breath came in short ragged bursts as he struggled back to his knees. He looked at the empty sand around him. The waves crashed behind him creating a thunder like artillery shells exploding. The wind whipped loose sand into the air and the small particles tore at the flesh of his face like shrapnel. Ahead of him, across the sand, the two-story hunk of the darkened concert hall with its single porch light stood in silhouette against the streetlights behind it. Jeff fought the weariness in his legs and the burning in his chest as he struggled to his feet.

His breath still labored, Jeff's instincts of survival took

over. He put one foot in front of the other as he struggled toward the building. His feet sank into the soft sand making his progress even slower toward his goal. Wind driven billowing sand stuck to his wet shorts and bit at his bare legs. A discarded paper bag, lifted into the air by the swirling wind, wrapped itself around Jeff's face like a second skin. He jerked violently, grabbing at it with his hand until it came loose to fly away into the darkness. He pushed his feet into the loose sand as he shielded his eyes to keep them fixed on the wooden stairway. The porch light on the deck above beckoned him onward like the beacon of a lighthouse to a ship tossed in heavy seas. The deck offered a hint of safety as the harbor beyond the lighthouse might to the crew of the ship.

Jeff reached out his hands and touched the rough weather-beaten rail of the stairway as his feet mounted the concrete walk. He trudged up the steps one at a time, his arms pulling him forward until his feet could follow. The final steps with the comfort of the lounge chair loomed ahead of him as his strength gave out. He sank to the planks of the steps under his feet. Wrapping his arms around a rail post, he held fast as the wind whipped his hair around his face.

"Stop!" he screamed to the wind. "Leave me alone."

Jeff dropped his head to his chest as he closed his eyes to the stinging wind. The leaves felt cool across his face as he fell into the clump of bushes. The explosion of the M79 round sounded sharp in his ears with a scream following it closely. Jeff rolled further into the bushes as he held his weapon tight to his chest. He stopped on his back, opened the breech, and reloaded.

The bugler continued to blow notes until the sound stopped short. Pushing himself onto his belly, Jeff lifted his head until his eyes cleared the foliage. The line of NVA troops surged forward as they fired their AK47s toward the American positions. Machine guns answered their charge.

The bullets that made their way past the NVA targets cracked the air around Jeff's head causing clipped leaves to fall by his face. He dropped back to the ground, lay as flat as he could, covering his head as he waited for the NVA charge to fail and the fusillade answering it to end.

Mutluk's voice suddenly replaced the carnage in the air. "Wake up sleepy head."

Jeff sat up from the lounge chair startled. He whipped the Boonie hat from his face and looked quickly around. The morning sun shone brightly against the blue sky as gentle waves broke onto the beach with a soft rolling crash. Seagulls hovered over the deck as they looked down waiting for the humans below to drop a crumb from their breakfast. Mutluk leaned against the rail with a coffee cup in one hand and half of an egg sandwich in the other.

Jeff's shorts were dry with no sand stuck to them or his legs. He fell against the back of the lounge chair as he drew in short quick breaths. The Boonie hat fell to the deck when Jeff raised his hands to his face and buried it in them.

"Didn't mean to scare you, dude," Mutluk said. "Russ is getting some more egg sandwiches downstairs in the kitchen. I thought you might like something to eat."

Jeff dropped his hands while he worked to control his labored breaths. As his breathing slowed, he looked down the stairs at the step where he had collapsed and screamed to the wind. When his breathing returned to normal, he turned toward Mutluk and spoke a lie.

"No problem, man. I was just dreaming I was in a storm."

"Well, you look like you didn't sleep at all. It looks more like you partied all night."

The wooden steps creaked as Russ walked up to the deck carrying a tray with two egg sandwiches and two cups of coffee. He smiled at Jeff as he held the tray out to him. Jeff took a sandwich and a coffee.

Russ put the tray down and picked up his own egg sandwich. "Bar owner said there's a coin laundry about two blocks down the street. Trouble is that they don't let coloreds use the machines. He said the closest place I could do my clothes is about a mile away."

Jeff stopped chewing and shook his head. "That's the stupidest thing I've ever heard. Are they afraid your sweat is going to taint their clothes?"

"Don't know man. He said Mutluk couldn't do his either."

Mutluk shrugged his shoulders. "We'll just take the truck to go to the other place later."

"No need to do that," Jeff said. "I've got a few things I'd like to wash. I'll just take everything down there and do it all. Y'all can relax and throw the Frisbee around."

Russ looked at Jeff with grateful eyes. "You sure, man?"

Jeff chuckled. "Yea. I'll even tell them whose clothes they are when I'm done."

An hour later, Jeff walked out of the coin laundry after starting three washing machines. He had dumped the contents of Mutluk's and Russ's laundry bags on the floor after deciding that he could mix the contents and sort by color as his mother had taught him years ago. The difference in sizes between Mutluk and Russ's clothes were enough to tell them apart. He knew his own small piece of the load. As Jeff walked in, heading straight toward the machines, the frown on the manager behind the counter made Jeff glad that the bar owner had given him enough change to feed the washers and dryers so he didn't need to deal with her. Smiling, he looked forward to telling her the secret of the clothes when he finished.

While the clothes tumbled in the washers, Jeff leaned against the building watching the people as they moved along the sidewalks on both sides of the highway. They ran the gambit from beachgoers in bikinis and swim trucks to grandmotherly looking women carrying shopping bags from the stores. Jeff's gaze followed the sashay of a tall young woman in a bikini as she passed. His thoughts went back to Helen. Her offer of coming back to stay for a while entered his mind again, but then something else said that wasn't where he belonged. A young woman, with hair like Mary's, walked by and Jeff's thoughts turned to her offer to visit. However, that same inner voice told him that wasn't the place to go either.

An old black man, his skin as black as Clarence's, moved down the other side of the road. Walking along the edge of the sidewalk with his eyes downcast, he stepped into the gutter each time he met a white woman going the other way. Several grizzled old white men, sitting on a bench across the street, stopped their conversation to stare at Jeff. Jeff focused his own stare at the men until they turned their eyes. Their attention then turned to the old black man as he moved up and down the edge of the sidewalk until he gave up and just stayed in the gutter.

Another group of young women in bikinis moved past Jeff, their voices laughing at some joke one had told. One, with red hair only slightly browner than Helen's, turned her head as she passed and kept her eyes fixed on Jeff. Jeff smiled back at her before she buried her face back into the group laughing along with them. The women moved down the sidewalk until disappearing when they turned toward the beach.

Jeff looked back across the street just when the old black man stepped out of the gutter as he reached a side street. A tractor-trailer rumbled by heading south momentarily blocking Jeff's view of the other sidewalk. After it passed, Jeff refocused his eyes where the old man had been, but he had disappeared. In his place, a young white man, dressed in army fatigues, stood at the corner looking up the street. Blood and sweat trickled down the right side of his face. His army fatigues, torn and blackened from explosions, hung from his slender frame and his helmet sat skewed on his head. His right hand stayed wrapped around the pistol grip of an M16. Jeff recognized the man as McAvoy, a member of his platoon. The man's left arm was missing.

The crowd continued to walk on the sidewalk passing by the soldier without giving him a second's notice. Jeff started moving down the sidewalk while he watched the busy traffic for a break. As he moved into the street between two cars, he shifted his gaze back toward the soldier just in time to see a passerby walk through the man. The soldier's visible eye opened wide in terror as the passerby walked on without a backward glance. Jeff yelled at the soldier and he turned his head toward Jeff. Jeff stopped short and recoiled slightly as the left side of soldier's head came into view. The left half of his face was gone with only blood and ragged shards of bone defining the left edge of his head. The soldier collapsed to the concrete as Jeff pressed through the traffic. As he reached the final lane, the air horn of another tractor-trailer blared causing Jeff to step back to the yellow striped line as a truck bore down on him.

The driver shook his fist at Jeff as the truck rumbled by. "You drunk hippie. Get out of the road."

Jeff darted around the back of the truck after it passed and rushed forward. The spot where the soldier had been standing was vacant. A pool of blood lay on the concrete beneath his feet where the soldier had stood. It slowly faded as though it was draining into the hard surface. As Jeff watched, the last of the stain disappeared as the concrete turned back to a dry dirty gray. He dropped to his knees and ran his hands around where the pool of blood had been.

The rough surface of the concrete stung his hands as he moved them around on the surface. He lifted his hands to his face staring at the gray dust and small pebbles that stuck to his skin. Voices whispered behind him.

Jeff looked up at the faces of the stopped pedestrians that stared down at him. Several young girls standing down the sidewalk shirked away from him, afraid to pass. An old woman walked around him with a look of distaste on her face. Jeff flinched as a pair of hands touched his shoulders. As he jerked his face toward the owner of the hands, he saw it was a young man with hair as long as his. The man gently helped him stand.

The man quietly spoke. "It's okay, man. It's okay."

The man guided Jeff down the street away from the stopped crowd. Soon they had traveled a block. The sidewalk traffic moved along without a second glance toward the two men.

The man released Jeff's shoulders. "You okay?"

Jeff straightened himself up as he glanced around at the people on the sidewalk. "Yea. I thought I saw someone I knew."

The man looked into Jeff's eyes. "How long you been back?"

Jeff stared back at the man with no real answer to his question. "How did you know?"

"I can see it in your eyes. Vets have a certain stare that doesn't go away for a while. You having bad dreams?"

"Yea. I guess that's what you'd call them. Only they don't seem like dreams, they seem real."

"Don't worry, they'll go away. It'll get better. By the way, my name's Robert."

"Thanks. I'm Jeff."

"You got a place to crash? A couple of guys and I rent a house down the way. We're all vets just trying to adjust to being here. You're welcome to stay on the couch."

"Thanks, but I'm just traveling through with some guys. Look, I better get back to the laundry before the manager throws my wet clothes out."

Robert pointed toward the south. "Okay. But, if you

want to talk or just visit, we're down on Redgate at number 45. It's a green house with yellow shutters."

Robert took Jeff's hand into his and held it tight. "You take care, brother. It'll get better."

Robert moved quickly down the street. Jeff watched him as he faded into the crowd, then waited for the light to change before he crossed the street. He headed straight back to the laundry. Scantily dressed women walked by, but Jeff didn't notice them. His mind no longer went to memories of Mary or Helen, only the thought of finding Clarence stayed in his mind.

Jeff yawned as Mutluk locked the rolling door of the trailer. Slowly walking up the passenger side of the truck, he climbed through the open door as Mutluk settled into the driver's seat. Russ's low snore came from the bed behind the cab. Both Jeff and Mutluk pulled their doors closed with a muted click. The silence ended as Mutluk turned the key and the low air alarm filled the dark cab. Mutluk quickly moved his hand to a switch next to the alarm and flipped it.

"Whoops."

Jeff laughed softly as Russ's snore turned to a snort before it settled back to its rhythmic cadence. "There doesn't seem to be much that wakes him once he's back there."

As the cylinder heater light went out, Mutluk twisted the key and the diesel rumbled to life. "Not much. I've found food works. If we stop to get something at a diner later, his head will be between the seats looking for his before we close the doors."

When the needle on the air pressure gauge moved into the green, Mutluk flipped the switch to rearm the alarm. "Russ installed that switch after the first night load-out of the tour back in New York. He does like his beauty sleep."

Mutluk pulled the truck away from the loading dock

then turned south on the highway. Traffic was light and the sidewalks contained only the last of the bar hoppers as they staggered slowly toward their destinations.

Mutluk reached down into the door pocket, pulled the map out, and threw it over to Jeff. "Since Russ is asleep, you'll need to be navigator until he wakes up. We stay on highway 90 the whole way. The only tricky part might be as we head thru Tallahassee, but it should be light by then. Once we get out of Jacksonville, you can catch some shuteye. I'll wake you if I need you to check the map."

"You want me to spell you on the driving any?"

Mutluk smiled as he turned his head toward Jeff. "Thanks, but I do all the driving on this tour. Maybe next tour."

"Are you asking me to stay with y'all after New Orleans?"

"I think you'll stay."

"Thanks for the offer, but until I talk to Clarence, I can't say what I'm going to do."

Jeff turned his gaze toward the highway. He focused his attention on the cross street signs before he turned back toward Mutluk. "Do you have any idea what your next tour is?"

"No. We won't find out until we finish this one."

"Where do you go after New Orleans?"

"We head home after that. Then we'll find out what's next."

Jeff pointed toward a directional sign out the window. "Highway 90 coming up."

Mutluk turned the truck west toward the lights of Jacksonville. The streetlights of the little beach town faded in the rearview mirror as the glow of the lights of the city ahead grew in the windshield. The truck was finally heading west toward New Orleans and Clarence. Jeff smiled at the thought of seeing his friend again.

Soon, the truck climbed the metal bridge over the St.

John's River and the city of Jacksonville opened up before them as they reached the apex. The road deck beneath them rumbled a lower note when Mutluk downshifted as they descended the bridge toward the city. Jeff searched the signs on the side of the bridge for any indication of turns they needed to make. A sign appeared on the side of the road.

"Looks like a left coming up to stay on 90."

"Got it."

Mutluk slowed the truck as they left the bridge and turned at the yellow flashing light. As they left the intersection behind, a sign on the side of the road showed that Tallahassee was 200 miles ahead. Mutluk held the speed down below the limit until he accelerated the truck through the gears when the speed limit increased to fifty-five. The lights of the city fell behind them.

"You go ahead and catch some sleep. I'll wake you if I need help."

Jeff pulled his faded army fatigue coat out of his pack. Rolling it up like a pillow, he stuck it against the doorframe, leaned his head against it, and then placed his Boonie hat over his eyes. Headlights of the cars heading into the city flashed under the brim as Jeff closed his eyes. Visions of Mary and Helen momentarily entered his mind before his thoughts settled on Clarence's face with his bright white smile.

Clarence's smile morphed into bloody lips and his eyes turned puffy and swollen. Jeff seemed to float up above Clarence's body until his view expanded with the entire scene opened before him. An NVA medic worked to wrap a combat bandage around Clarence's calf as a soldier stood nearby with an AK47 in one hand and Clarence's flak vest in the other. Nearby, another NVA soldier sat on a tree stump with a radio handset pressed to his ear as an officer with red piping on his collar studied a map. Clarence opened his eyes and stared toward Jeff. His mouth moved slightly.

"Help me," he moaned softly.

Jeff willed his body forward toward his friend. He cried out as he bumped the still tender head wound on the hard metal dash of the cab. He grabbed his head at the point of pain.

"Oww!"

"You okay?" Mutluk said.

Jeff settled back into the seat, shifted his Boonie hat to his lap, and felt his head before checking his hand for blood. The dim light of the predawn sky filled his vision through the pain on his forehead. "Yea. Just woke up too fast I guess. I was dreaming about my friend."

Mutluk turned his head toward Jeff while casting glances at the highway racing toward them in the fading glow of the headlights. "Well, don't worry. We'll be in New Orleans on Friday so you'll find him then. Go ahead and get some more shuteye if you want. We're still an hour out of Tallahassee."

The almost specter-like vision of his friend returned to his mind. "I'm awake now. I don't think I could go back to sleep."

Mutluk turned his head back toward the highway. "Suit yourself."

Jeff faced out the window toward the dimly lit side of the road racing by. His thoughts went to Clarence and the vision he had seen. Russ's low snore came from the bed behind him.

Chapter 10

Mutluk guided the truck through the lunchtime traffic along highway 90 as they crossed the bridge over the coves at the end of Escambia Bay and entered the city of Pensacola. The flat landscape across the Florida panhandle had been one large forest, punctuated only by the occasional farm field or small town. Though he had looked out the side window most of the morning, Jeff had seen little of the trees. His thoughts remained focused on the vision of Clarence calling to him for help.

He turned away from the breeze of the open window and toward Mutluk. "When we get to the club in New Orleans, how much help are you going to need before I can head out to find Clarence?"

Russ pointed from behind the seats toward a sign on the side of the road. "You need to turn left up ahead to stay on highway 90."

Mutluk turned on the blinker before he eased the truck from the right lane to the left. "Well, the road manager said the load-in is easy but we have to block a lane of traffic while we're doing it. The good thing is that we don't take everything into the club there. You can head out after you help us get what we need unloaded and stacked on stage. Also, you'll have to catch up with me later to get the rest of your pay. I need to get some more cash from the road manager."

"Thanks. After I find Clarence, I'll get him to come back with me to catch the show."

Russ pointed out toward the blinking yellow light strung above the intersection ahead. "Here's the turn."

"I see it," Mutluk said. He shifted his glance toward Jeff as he slowed the truck to a halt while he waited for the oncoming traffic to clear. "Are you going to stay with Clarence at his place or with us at the hotel?"

"I don't know. I guess I need to see what's going on with Clarence first."

"I'll have them bring in a roller bed in case you need a place to crash. You're also welcome to catch a ride with us when we head out."

"I'll let you know. I guess my life is pretty much on hold until I find Clarence."

A hole opened up between the cars going the other way and Mutluk eased across the opposing lanes. He shifted into second and accelerated away from the intersection.

Russ looked down at the clipboard in his hands. "Okay, now we go just under 4 miles on this road and the club will be on the left. It's a blue building with a red marquee. We back into the alley on this side. The stage door is toward the end."

Jeff reached for the clipboard. "Let me see that."

He studied the sheet of paper for a moment. A questioned looked came across his face then he held the clipboard up toward Mutluk. "So we're heading to the Exchange Club?"

"Yea. You know the place?"

Jeff held the clipboard toward Russ. A grin, his first since the vision the night before, came over his face. "Yea. When I was in high school at the military academy in Virginia, I dated a girl that went to the girl's school across town. She was from Pensacola. I visited her for a couple of weeks the summer after our graduation. Her brother worked as one of the bouncers at the Exchange Club and he let us in the backdoor a few times."

Russ took the clipboard back. "Does she still live here?"

"I doubt it. She headed to Vassar College in New York after that summer while I headed to VPI in Virginia. I wrote her while I was in college and got letters back, but after I dropped out, I never heard from her again."

Mutluk smiled and glanced over toward Jeff. "You ought to try looking her up. Invite her to see the show."

Jeff looked down at the floor. "I don't know. It was years ago. She's probably still up at Vassar with a new boyfriend. Heck, she may even be married by now."

Russ punched Jeff playfully on the shoulder. "Do it man. If you don't, you'll be talking about how you wished you had while we're rolling out of town and I really don't want to listen to that all the way to New Orleans."

The memory of Pat pushed his thoughts of Clarence to the side. "Okay. If it will make you happy."

The phone on the other end of the receiver rang for the fifth time. Jeff started to hang it up when the ringing stopped. A woman's voice came through the earpiece.

"Hello."

"Hello. Is this the Thomas residence?"

"Yes, it is."

"My name is Jeff Briggs. Is this Mrs. Thomas?"

The woman's voice turned questioning. "Yes, this is Mrs. Thomas. How can I help you?"

"Do you have a daughter named Pat?"

"What's this about?"

"Pat and I dated back in high school. You might remember me from when I visited the summer after graduation before we both left for college. I'm passing through and thought I'd call to see how she's doing."

Mrs. Thomas's voice became soft. "Oh! I remember you now. Pat's fine. She's actually here in town."

Jeff's heart skipped a beat and he hesitated. "She— She's in town?"

"Yes. She dropped out of Vassar after the first year. We keep hoping she'll go back, but she's happy working at a camera store."

Jeff's voice rose slightly. "When does she get home?"

"Oh. She doesn't live here. She has her own apartment near the beach in Navarre. Let me give you her number. I'm sure she'd love to hear from you. She gets off work at eight tonight."

Jeff copied down the number as she read it twice. "Thanks, Mrs. Thomas. I'll call her tonight."

"How long are you in town for? We'd love to have Pat bring you over for dinner one night."

"I'm here for just a few days traveling with some people. I leave Thursday morning."

"Well, talk to Pat. Maybe you can work something out with her to get over here."

"Okay, Mrs. Thomas. Thanks. Goodbye."

Jeff replaced the receiver on the hook and leaned against the pay phone. He held the piece of paper with Pat's number up to his eyes and then looked over at the clock above the bar. Five o'clock. Three hours until she got off work. Three hours until he could talk to her again. Three hours.

The clock over the bar read nine-thirty as the band left the stage after they finished their first set. The sailor in front of Jeff stormed down the hallway after hanging the phone receiver hard into the cradle. Jeff picked up the receiver, dropped a dime into the slot, and dialed Pat's number for the sixth time.

The crowd of mostly young sailors lined the hallway while they waited for their turn in the toilet. Bantering coursed through the air as alcohol-induced bravado pitted unit against unit. The ring in the receiver was faint so Jeff brought his right hand to his ear to try to deaden the hallway noise. The ringing stopped and he placed the palm of his hand tight against his head.

The voice on the other end of the receiver took him instantly back to high school. "Hello."

Jeff hesitated in his response, swept up in emotion as the sight of Pat waving at him as the train pulled away after their parting kiss flew into his mind.

Her voice spoke again through the receiver. "Hello."

"Pat, it's Jeff."

Her response was questioning. "Jeff?"

Jeff's heart sank slowly into his chest. "Jeff Briggs. You may not remember me, but—"

"Jeff, My god, of course I remember you. I could never forget you. Where are you? I thought you had..."

Jeff listened as the voice trailed off before he spoke. "I'm actually in Pensacola at the club near the air base your brother worked and he would let us—"

"I'll be there in 20 minutes. Don't leave."

"Come to the stage —" Dial tone hit his ear.

Jeff headed back to the control booth where Mutluk and Russ were sitting with beers in their hands.

Russ offered a beer to Jeff from the cooler on the shelf under the soundboard. "Here you go, Jeff. The bartender sent these over and said we could drink for free tonight."

Jeff swallowed a long pull. "Listen, I just talked to my old girlfriend. She's on her way here. You mind if I visit with her?"

Mutluk smiled. "Sure. Go ahead. Just let me know if you leave. Russ and I can handle things here. Everything worked fine the first set."

"Thanks."

Jeff drained his beer as he made his way to the stage door. He showed his backstage pass to the bouncer stationed there telling him he would be bringing back a friend in a little. The bouncer gave a slight nod as he pushed open the door into the empty alley. The light over the door flickered and died as the door slammed behind Jeff. He hesitated in his steps as his eyes slowly adjusted to the new darkness.

The street at the end of the alley teemed with off-duty

sailors, some in uniform and others not, but all identified by their identical haircuts. When his night vision improved so he could see the ground before him, Jeff moved toward the bustling flow. When he reached the end of the alley, he stepped onto the sidewalk pushing through the throng to make his way to the street beyond.

Jeff leaned against a light pole at the edge of the street while he scanned the sidewalks on both sides. Cars parked haphazardly in the vacant lot across the street and people moved from the lot toward the bar through the slow moving traffic. Pat had parked in that same lot when she had driven them here during that wonderful summer after graduation. Jeff hoped that she was still a creature of habit. The same way she had always used her left hand to caress his neck after their lovemaking. The vision of her face looking at him as she rested her chin on his chest filled his mind.

The vision left his mind as he heard Pat's voice call his name. She waved excitedly from the other sidewalk as she pushed through a crowd of people then waited for a break in the traffic. Her long dark hair sashayed freely on her back as she left the curb and stepped onto the street. A car honked making her hesitate in her movement. Jeff left the light pole and started across the street just as Pat raced from her waiting spot. Their bodies met on the yellow line in the middle. She wrapped her arms around his neck and held him close then she moved her lips quickly to his. They held this pose as drivers honked and hooted at them.

Jeff broke the kiss before he guided them both out of the street and back to the alley. He held her tight to him so that her body never left his side. Once out of the flow on the sidewalk, Pat pulled Jeff tight to her before placing her hands on each side of his head.

She hungrily kissed his face and neck. "My god...I can't believe... this. I thought you... were gone from... my life... forever."

She stopped kissing him and held herself tight against his chest. Tears flowed freely from her eyes dampening the front of his t-shirt. Jeff kissed the top of her head while letting his fingers flow through her hair to her waist as he had done so many times long ago. Strangers on the sidewalk looked into the alley at the two but, with the exception of the occasional remark about them getting a room, no one interrupted them. Time was lost as their souls reconnected in the dim light. Jeff finally broke the silence as he placed his hand on her chin to raise her face toward his. "Let's go in. I hear the band starting back up."

"No," she said as she wiped tears from her eyes. "Let's go back to my place."

Jeff smiled down at her. "Okay. But I need to tell Mutluk I'm leaving."

Pat looked questionably at him. "What's a Mutluk?"

Jeff turned to the next page of Pat's high school scrapbook as she poured the last of the wine from the bottle into his glass. He pointed to a photo of the two of them standing in front of the reviewing stand on the parade ground. She was wearing a light blue sundress with matching hat. He stood at attention in his full dress uniform including saber and wrap.

Her bright green eyes sparkled as he looked into them. "I think of this day often. You looked so beautiful in that dress. I was so happy to have you walk with me as my sponsor in the parade."

She leaned against his shoulder as she looked down at the photo. "That was fun. The only bummer was that I had to leave for home with my parents right after that and missed the graduation parade."

She twirled a strand of his hair in her fingers. Smiling, she looked up at his hair. "You know, I really like your hair like this. It's a lot better than that buzz cut you had back then."

He lightly kissed her lips before putting the scrapbook on the coffee table and picking up his glass of wine. "Those were fun days we had together back then."

She placed her wine glass on the table. Her arms went around his neck. "We could have fun like that again. The biggest mistake I ever made was letting my parents talk me into going to Vassar. They said I would get a better education and set myself up for a better life. I finally realized that all they wanted me to do up there was meet some rich guy to marry."

Jeff smiled at her. "Did you?"

"Did I what? Get married? No!"

"Did you meet any rich guys?"

She pulled herself close to his face. "A few. I even tried dating one a few times. But all I did on every date was compare him to you in my mind."

"How'd he measure up?"

She smiled as she brought her lips close to his. "Not even close."

Her lips pushed into his. She kissed him deeply. She ended the kiss, pulled away, and got up from the couch. "Wait here. I have a surprise for you." She disappeared into her bedroom, shutting the door behind her.

Jeff drained the last of the wine from his glass as he leaned back on the couch. He then looked around the room. The apartment was so much like Pat. An eclectic collection of photos hung neatly on the walls. Mountain scenes were interspersed with those of speedboats, horses, cats, dogs, and buildings. Sunsets hung next to sunrises taken from the same location. A photo of the two of them at some dance at her school hung next to the bedroom door.

The walls were two different colors that contrasted each other, yet somehow worked together. Even the wine glasses she had set out for them were different styles. His was long and slender while the one she had used was short and curvy. They were a perfect match for the two of them.

The door to her bedroom clicked opened. Pat stepped out, a grin on her face.

Jeff broke out laughing as she strolled over to him dressed only in one of his old cadet dress shirts. The top three buttons were undone while the bottom one was missing. Only the two in the center held the shirt semi-closed. She had rolled the sleeves up to the middle of her forearms. The frayed collar hung loose.

"I can't believe you still have that shirt."

Pat moved in front of him and climbed onto his lap. Jeff ran his finger down the front opening until his hand touched the space between her breasts. She gripped his hand, holding it tight to her heart.

"I would never have gotten rid of this. It was all that I had left of you after my letters to you were returned."

"I'm sorry about that. When I joined the army after dropping out, I guess I didn't think about putting in a change of address. I just thought that my mail would find me. When I didn't hear from you, I figured that you stopped writing because you had found someone else to date."

A tear ran from her left eye. It fell onto her cheek. "You're back with me now. I really want to pick up where we left off. I have never loved anyone but you."

Jeff pulled his hand from her heart. He gently placed both hands on the sides of her head. "But you don't know me anymore. I'm not a cadet on the parade ground playing soldier anymore. I've killed men in battle without remorse. Something I never thought I would be able to do."

Pat grabbed his hands, held them in hers, and smiled up at him. She spoke softly. "I read something in a book of poems while I was at Vassar. It took me straight back to us. I memorized it so I could say it to you the day I found you again.

She leaned back slightly as a scholarly look came over her face. "You are attracted to a person's body, you become friends with a person's mind, and you fall in love with a person's soul."

She leaned toward him again. Placing her hands around his neck, she looked straight into his eyes. "I fell in love with your soul years ago, Jeff Briggs. And your soul never changes. I love you and I'm never going to let you go. I won't lose you again."

Jeff kissed her deeply before hugging her to his chest. She looked up as tears fell from her eyes. "Please don't ever let us be pulled apart again. Stay with me. You can stay here and we could have a wonderful life together. If you don't want to stay here, I'll follow you wherever you want to go."

He ran his fingers through her hair. The straight strands cascaded down her back before they flowed around her thighs. Turning his head upward, he stared at the ceiling. The promises he had made to Mary and Helen flew through his mind. He looked down at the top of Pat's head tight against his chest. Hopefully, they would understand how things had changed. Everything was different now that Pat was back in his arms.

Well, almost everything. His loss of memory, his need to find Clarence, and his quest for answers still remained. "I've told you that I have to find Clarence to get answers to a lot of questions. I won't know where I belong until I get those answers. I will promise that I won't lose contact with you again. I want you in my life. I've always wanted us to be together. I'm just not sure what my life means anymore or where I should be."

"Let me drive you to New Orleans. Together we'll find your friend. Whatever you decide to do after that, we'll do it together. I'm not going to let you go again."

He looked into her quivering eyes and his heart tore apart. The pieces sank to the bottom of his gut. "I'm sorry. But this is something I need to do alone. I can't explain it, but that's how it has to be. I can only promise that I will come straight back to you before I do anything else."

A look of total devastation came across her face. She then rose from his lap, walked into the kitchen and opened a drawer. Her hands rummaged through it until she found what she was looking for. She grabbed a piece of paper stopping to write on it before she walked back over to the couch. She held up the piece of paper in one hand, a key in the other.

She spoke with determination as she pushed the paper toward him. "Here is the address to this apartment. This is the key. When you get back, just let yourself in any time day or night. My home is forever your home. My life is forever yours. I've also written down my work address and telephone number. Call me if you need a ride after finding your friend. I'll come get you anytime, anywhere. We'll go wherever you want to go. I won't lose you again without a fight." She folded the key into the piece of paper and shoved it into Jeff's pants pocket.

Pat straddled Jeff as she climbed back on the couch. Her eyes softened and she kissed him lightly on the lips. She leaned back, grabbed the bottom of his t-shirt, and pulled it over his head. After she threw it across the room, she reached down to unfasten the remaining two buttons on her shirt. Letting it fall from her shoulders, she took Jeff's head in her hands and guided his lips toward hers.

"Now, we have some catching up to do."

The morning sunlight filtered into the bedroom through the sheer curtains as a tender ocean breeze rippled them into the room. The rhythm of Pat's soft breathing matched the breaking of the waves as they folded into themselves on the beach beyond the windows. She lay tightly against Jeff in the crook formed by his bent legs, their naked bodies nestled together like two pieces of a puzzle. Her hair, draped across her shoulder, cascaded over his side before it disappeared behind him. Jeff's left arm lay under her head while his right hand lightly rested on her thigh.

For all the times they had clandestinely been together in high school and even when Jeff visited her after graduation, this was the first time they had ever been together until morning. Jeff breathed in Pat's morning smell through the salt air. A light hint of lilac shampoo melded with the dried sweat left from their exuberant lovemaking the night before. A dream formed long ago, longed for during a thousand nights at the academy, became real in the beauty of the moment. His heart stirred when she gently turned toward him smiling as she looked at him with half-opened eyes.

"Good Morning," she whispered.

He brought his arms around her back squeezing her tight to him as though she might disappear if he let go. "This is a dream come true. I always wanted to wake up with you. I hated it when one of us had to leave to sneak back to their own bed."

"Never again."

She suddenly opened her eyes fully as she turned away from him. "Shit! What time is it?"

She grabbed the clock from the bedside table holding it in front of her face before dropping it to the floor. "Shit!" She turned back to Jeff, kissed him before she jumped out of bed, and ran to the bathroom. "I've got to get to work. I'm supposed to open the store this morning. You go ahead and stay in bed if you want."

Jeff pulled the pillows against the headboard and laid against them as the sound of the shower came through the open door. The shower shut off a minute later and the bathroom door closed. It opened a few minutes later as Pat came out with her hair pulled back into a tight bun with a towel wrapped around her. She dropped the towel by the dresser as she pulled out a bra and panties. She turned toward Jeff as she hurriedly put them.

"Why don't you just hang out here until I get home? I get off at three today. There's food in the fridge and the beach is only a block away."

She grabbed a blouse from the closet. Her fingers raced to button it.

Jeff lifted his arms and placed them behind his head. "I'll need to get back to the club this afternoon to see if Mutluk needs me to do anything before the show tonight."

She pulled a skirt from the closet and stepped into it. "We can head over after I get home and grab some dinner there if you'd like. I hope he will let you come home with me again tonight."

"I'm sure he will."

Pat reached down to pick a pair of shoes off the floor before she moved over to the bed. She kissed Jeff tightly on the lips. "Please be here when I get home. Don't leave me again."

"I'll be here."

She ran from the room. She scurried around in the living room before she raced out the front door slamming it shut. Seconds later, her car started and the tires squealed as she pulled away. The gentle breaking of the waves on the beach replaced the flurry of activity of Pat's departure. Jeff slid slowly down the bed, turned on his stomach so that his nose pressed into the pillow she had slept on. He covered his head with the other pillow. The lingering scent of her lilac shampoo filled his nostrils as rough leaves scratched his face.

Jeff opened his eyes. A smashed flower sat beneath his nose. The fusillade of gunfire above his head had slowed to sporadic as the NVA charge faltered. A singsong command voice called out the retreat. Jeff rose up on his elbows looking through broken branches and torn leaves at the NVA troops as they filtered back toward their prepared bunkers. Their focus stayed toward the American lines as some dragged wounded comrades while others provided covering fire.

Jeff shifted around inside the bush so that he could

check the path that headed further up the disappearing gully. He looked once more at the retreating NVA while he gathered his legs under him preparing to dash forward. An American machine gun opened fire forcing the NVA to drop to the ground. Jeff sprang from the bush staying low as he ran up the remnant of the path. A light blood mark shimmered on a broad leaf as he passed it. He ran on staying alert for more troops.

The American machine gun stopped its firing just as Jeff raced out of the last of the gully. He headed toward another clump of bushes that grew next to the path, rounded them, and dropped to his knees with the M79 pressed to his shoulder. The NVA had not noticed his rapid movements as their focus remained on the American lines. Jeff kept the M79 pressed to his shoulder and pointed toward the NVA while they continued their retreat. He glanced at the path.

The drag marks on the ground had ended and no traces of blood clung to any leaves. Whoever had Clarence must have picked him up and was carrying him now. The empty path was Jeff's only clue to which way they had taken him. Jeff moved slowly from tree to tree while he checked the surrounding land for danger.

Equipment rattle came from the direction of the NVA bunkers. Jeff turned toward the sound as he walked backward, his M79 raised toward the noise. He glanced behind him every few steps to stay next to the path. A stray round from an M16 clipped a leaf near his head forcing him to squat down into a backward duck walk. The M79 remained aimed at the NVA bunkers as he slowly moved away.

Jeff glanced over his shoulder again. His heart fell from his chest as the path spilt in two. One path went straight and the other went right. Jeff rose from his duck walk turning toward the paths as he ignored the danger of the equipment rattle behind him. His knees followed his heart as they hit the ground while he looked down each path in turn. No evidence presented itself to provide a clue as to the right direction. No blood or broken twigs pointed which way to go. He closed his eyes as he prayed for help to find his friend. The key turned in the lock of the apartment door.

He opened his eyes just as Pat backed through the front door as she finished a conversation with someone in the hallway. Jeff blinked rapidly and realized he was sitting on the couch as naked as he had been when Pat had left him in bed that morning. A half-drunk cup of coffee sat on a coaster on the coffee table. His pack lay next to the coffee table with the contents strewn beside it. His Boonie hat hung over the back of a kitchen chair.

As Pat shut the door, she turned toward him and stopped short. A smile came over her face as she dropped her purse on the floor and kicked her shoes off. She reached behind her head to pull several pins from her bun. Her hair cascaded down falling to her waist. She unbuttoned her blouse as she slowly moved forward.

"I dreamt all day that when I got home you would be sitting on my couch waiting for me. But I never even dreamed you would greet me naked."

The blouse fell to the floor, her bra followed quickly. "I am so glad right now that I didn't invite Mrs. Simpson in to meet you."

Unzipping her skirt, she stepped out of it before she came around the coffee table until she was in front of him. She climbed onto the couch, straddled him, and smiled. "Didn't we just do this?" She held his head in her hands as she moved her lips toward his.

Jeff kissed her back, but his mind stayed focused on the spilt in the path. Pat stood from the couch, took Jeff's hands into hers, and pulled him toward the bedroom.

Jeff and Mutluk rolled the last of the large cases up the

ramp. The smaller cases sat alongside the truck laid out neatly in their rows by Russ. Pat was standing next to the wall. She held her head down, occasionally wiping her nose with a tissue. Mutluk looked at the stack of small cases and then over at Pat.

He turned toward Jeff. "Why don't you take her to get a cup of coffee to say goodbye? Russ and I can finish up here. She doesn't look too happy."

Jeff looked over at Pat. "Yea. She really wishes I would stay."

Mutluk looked at his watch. "Take your time. We've got about an hour before we need to pull out. Mobile's not very far."

Jeff laid his hand on Mutluk's shoulder. "Thanks."

He then strolled over to Pat. "You want to go get a cup of coffee?"

Pat wiped her nose once more before she put the wet tissue in her purse. "Sure. That sounds good."

The two sat in a booth at the diner not speaking for several minutes after their coffees arrived. Pat continued to stir her spoon long after the sugar and cream had turned the coffee to a light brown. Jeff, holding his cup just below his mouth to let the smell envelop his nose, worked on what to say.

He finally spoke. "Listen, I—"

"Don't say it Jeff. It's just that I made the mistake of letting you get away before and I don't like letting you out of my sight again. I'm afraid you may not come back."

Jeff sat silent for a moment staring into her eyes. His resolution faltered as the life he had dreamed about with Pat took over his thinking. Walks along the beach, making love under a full moon, marriage, and children flashed through his mind. "Well, I guess I could..."

The vision of Clarence flying end-over-end into the gully raced in front of his eyes. He knew what he had to do. "I have to go. I promise I'll call you after I find Clarence and have a chance to talk to him. I won't lose contact with you again."

"But what then? You don't know what's going to happen after you find Clarence. Let me come along. Let me help you with whatever you find. Please don't leave me here alone."

She burst into tears as she buried her head in her hands.

The waitress and several customers looked toward Jeff from the counter. Jeff pulled a napkin from the dispenser and lightly touched Pat's hand with it.

She looked up, took it from him, and wiped her eyes. "Thanks."

Jeff placed his hand on her arm. "Finding Clarence is something I need to do.

"But why can't I come along?"

"It's something I need to do by myself. Clarence has got answers to questions that I don't want you to hear until I understand everything. After I find him and I'm ready to leave, I'll call you so we can talk about what's next. We'll figure it out together. Whatever comes next, we'll do it together."

Pat's mouth shifted into a slight smile beneath her puffy eyes. "Promise?"

"I promise."

The two stayed in the booth holding hands and drinking coffee as they talked about their lives in high school. They both laughed hardily as Jeff reminisced about the time the housemistress had knocked on Pat's door in the dorm for a bed check while they lay wrapped in each other's arms under her covers. Her roommate had been away on a field trip and Jeff dove into the empty bed. He had to escape the dorm wearing the roommate's robe and a wig Pat had for a stage production. The conversation lagged as the clock above the counter counted down the minutes. Pat looked up as the door chime rang when Russ walked in.

The waitress looked up from her newspaper. "What do you want? We don't serve coloreds in here."

Russ looked at the waitress before he cast his eyes toward the floor. "Sorry, ma'am. I just needs to tell my boss that we's ready to go."

The waitress went back to her paper. "Well, hurry up and get out."

Russ walked quickly to Jeff's booth. "We's ready boss. Mutluk got da engine warmin' up jest like you said for him to do."

Jeff almost broke out laughing but held it in. Pat smiled as Russ winked at her. Jeff slid out of the booth and extended his hand to Pat. "Will you come say goodbye to me?"

"Wouldn't miss it."

Russ held the door for the two as they walked out and then moved ahead of them toward the idling truck. Pat touched Russ's arm with her hand. "You spoke pretty good Jim Crow back there. If I didn't know you were from New York, I would have sworn you were a local boy."

Russ looked over his shoulder and smiled. "Didn't Jeff tell you? I hope to be an actor on Broadway when I get tired of being a Roadie."

She smiled up at Jeff as she placed her arm in the crook of his. "Well, Jeff and I will just have to come to New York sometime to see you perform."

Russ climbed up the step of the truck cab and slid between the seats into the back as Jeff turned toward Pat. He took her hands into his. "I'll call you as soon as I can. I promise."

Pat placed her hands on both sides of Jeff's head. "I'm going to hold you to that, mister." She pulled his lips down to hers, kissed him deeply, and then released him as she stepped backward. "Now get out of here before I fall apart again."

Climbing into the truck, Jeff shut the door as Mutluk shifted into first and pulled away. He stared back through the side view mirror at Pat as she waved goodbye. The wave was the same one he had seen from the train at the end of his visit after graduation. A tear fell from his eye as the truck turned onto the highway and he looked forward to the street.

Mutluk looked over at him. "Nice girl. Seems like she means a lot to you."

Jeff kept his misty eyes focused toward the street to their front. "Yea, she does. But, until I find Clarence and get some answers, I don't know what I going to do or even where I belong. But, I'll tell you something I didn't tell her. I just have this stinking feeling in the back of my mind that I'll never see her again."

Mutluk faced forward and shifted into third gear. "I'm sure you'll figure it out."

A low snore came from the bed in the back.

Chapter 11

The truck rumbled northwest on Highway 90 with the morning sun behind them. Soon the shops and houses of Pensacola gave way to the farmlands of the Florida panhandle. Small patches of pine forests interspersed the fields. The sun slowly warmed away the mist of the morning making the view of the road ahead grow clearer. Mutluk stared straight ahead at the approaching road as he worked the gears up and down as the speed limit demanded. An occasional bug splattered on the windshield in front of Jeff like a liquid bullet meant for him. He held his hand unconsciously out of the window letting the rushing air blow it up and down as he played with the breeze. Although he faced the oncoming road, his mind saw nothing outside the windshield. It oscillated between Pat and the split in the path.

Jeff forced his thoughts to leave Pat and return to the split in the path. He concentrated on the vision that remained in his mind of each path looking for any signs that existed that might have led to his friend. His heart raced as a panic set in that Clarence might not be in New Orleans, but might be rotting in a jungle somewhere, still captured, helpless, dying. If only Mobile were not in their path, he could be at Clarence's house this afternoon. Pulling his hand in from the breeze, he rolled the window up until the noise of the wind subsided. Russ's low snore once again filtered from the back as the cab grew quiet.

"So why the one night stop in Mobile? How come we don't just head straight to New Orleans?"

Mutluk shrugged his shoulders. "I don't know why the

tour manager does stuff like this. It's not that big a hall so the money can't be that good. However, it's not as if we have a choice. We go where we're told."

"Do we leave tonight right after the show?"

Mutluk looked over at Jeff, smiled, and swept his hand upward then toward the back of the truck. "Why? Are you getting tired of all this? You know, the life of a roadie?"

"No, it's not that. I just want to see my friend."

"We'll be there soon enough. Anyway, from what the road manager told me on the phone, the load-in will take your mind off your friend."

"What do you mean?"

"He said the alley behind the hall is too narrow for me to back in and there's no parking on the street in front. We're going to have to park on the side street, roll everything up the alley, carry it up a flight of stairs to stage level, and clear the truck off the street within an hour. Also, there are no lights in the alley so we can't load-out until the morning. In addition, we have to clear the truck off the side street by nine o'clock. So, we're going to pack everything up right after the show, spend the night on the floor in our sleeping bags, then get started on the load-out as soon as the sun comes up."

"That sounds bad."

"It makes the load-in and load-out in that second story place in Richmond where we picked you up look like a dream. You'll earn your money on this one."

Mutluk turned his head toward Jeff as he smiled again. "Do me one favor though."

"Sure. What?"

"Don't tell Russ. I want to see his face when he finds out."

Jeff laughed as he rolled his window back down to stick his hand out into the rushing wind. Just as his hand hit the air, a large bug slammed into his hand causing him to jerk it back in.

"Oww." He looked at the red splotch left by the unlucky creature.

Mutluk glanced over. "Watch yourself. It's dangerous out there."

An hour later, the low skyline of Mobile came into view as the truck approached the bridge over the end of Mobile Bay.

"Wake Russ up so he can navigate," Mutluk said.

Jeff reached back and shook Russ's shoulder. "Wakeup sleepy head. We're coming into Mobile."

A minute later, Russ sleepily stuck his head through the gap in the seats and stared through the windshield. "That's it? That's all there is to Mobile? Why is the band playing here?"

Mutluk lifted his clipboard from the seat and held it back toward Russ. "Don't know. Don't care. Just guide me to the hall so we can get this done."

"Okay. Don't get your Canadian shorts in a freeze."

Russ looked at the clipboard then out through the windshield. "We stay on highway 90 until we get to Conception Street. It's four blocks after we cross the bridge into the city itself. We take a right there."

Russ pointed out the windshield after the truck crossed over the bridge and rolled down into the city center. "There it is. Turn right, go three blocks to St. Francis, and the alley to the loading dock will be half a block up."

He turned toward Mutluk. "Why'd you wake me up? Jeff could have followed these directions."

"Just do your job."

"Okay. Okay. There's St. Francis. Look for the alley."

Mutluk slowed to a stop as he pulled up next to the narrow alley.

Russ looked down the alley and then turned toward Mutluk. "How are you going to back down that?"

"I'm not. We have to carry everything in."

"What? Stupid tour manager. You wait until I get my

hands on him. I'll never work for that guy again."

Russ slid back between the seats while he kept ranting. Mutluk pulled the truck forward until the end of the trailer was just past the alley entrance. He pulled the airbrake handle as he turned toward Jeff and motioned with his eyes toward Russ. "See? Wasn't that fun?"

Russ continued to complain from the back.

The next morning, just before eight o'clock, Jeff walked up to the rear of the trailer as Mutluk pulled the sliding door down. Russ leaned against the side of the trailer. Sweat stained his underarms.

Jeff smiled as he held up a bag. "Got us a bunch of bacon and egg sandwiches for breakfast and cokes to drink."

He opened the bag on the ground before handing a paper wrapped sandwich each to Mutluk and Russ. The cokes went on the ground in front of them. Jeff sat down on the curb, unwrapped a sandwich, and hungrily took a bite. Warm egg tinted with bacon grease covered his tongue. Mutluk knelt while he popped the tops off the three cokes with his knife.

As Jeff savored his breakfast, Russ smiled through his egg-covered teeth. "Took you long enough. I thought you had left us here hungry while you were sipping coffee with the good old boys."

Jeff swallowed. "Mutluk's idea about me being able to get served in one of the local diners didn't work. The first two said they didn't serve my kind. Guess they meant my hair. I finally found a diner about eight blocks away run by a colored couple that served me."

Mutluk swallowed his bite of his sandwich as he took a sip of coke. "Let's hurry up and get out of here. I don't like this Province."

Jeff looked over at him. "Province?"

"I meant State."

Mutluk pointed up the block. "A police car keeps passing through that intersection up there. It slows down and the driver keeps looking over at us. I want to leave before it comes back again."

Jeff stood and picked up the bag. "Let's go. I'd rather be in New Orleans anyway."

All three men moved quickly into the cab of the truck. Mutluk started the diesel. He let it idle for a few minutes as the air pressure built up in the brake reservoir before he put the truck into gear and drove off.

"Guide me out of here Russ."

Russ read from the clipboard while he continued to talk through his breakfast. "Take the next right, go down two blocks, and then take another right. That should be Royal St. We take it to Government St. which is highway 90 so we take a right on it."

Mutluk held the rest of his sandwich out to Jeff. "Here, hold this until I get out of the city."

Jeff took the sandwich and placed it on the paper on his lap as he watched out the side view mirror. A police car pulled out from a side street behind them. It followed but stayed a block away.

"We got company behind us."

"Just sit back to let me have my mirrors. I'll keep it slow and easy until we're out of the city."

Mutluk made the turns as Russ directed so soon the truck rolled down highway 90. Mutluk scanned the side mirrors as he kept the truck moving just below the speed limit. The police car stayed behind them.

"He's just staying there. Maybe he just wants to make sure we leave town. Hand me my sandwich." Mutluk stuffed the rest of the bread and egg into his mouth. He glanced into the mirrors again before settling back in his seat. As they reached a railroad crossing at the edge of the city, he slowed and the truck bounced slightly as it went over the tracks.

Mutluk stared into the side mirror on his side. "He's turning around behind us. Guess we're out of town." He settled back into his seat and shifted up a gear.

The houses grew sparse and large open fields soon filled the landscape. Young tobacco plants edged up in the fields while lines of black men with hoes moved backward along the rows as they tended the young shoots. The early morning air grew steadily warmer but stayed heavy with moisture. Jeff's t-shirt grew damp even though the wind whipped through the cab. Mutluk kept the truck below the speed limit as they rolled down the road. A sign on the side of the road announced that New Orleans lay only 120 miles away and Jeff's heart lightened as the truck flew past it. Sitting back in his seat, he lowered his Boonie hat over his eyes as the 8-track player boomed out a song over the rushing wind. His mind drifted to images of Clarence with his bright white smile.

A bullet cracked over his head causing Jeff to open his eyes in a start. He was on the forest floor with the two paths in front of him as rifle shots sounded over to his left. He turned his head left and right quickly to look for movement as he listened for equipment rattle. Nothing moved in his sight and only the din of the battle off to his left came to his ears. He stared hard at the leaves on the bushes on the side of each path. No limp broken leaves hung from any bush. Not even a single smear of blood marked the route to his friend. The footprints on both paths ran both ways with neither path having more prints than the other did.

Equipment rattle came from his left and Jeff rolled behind a flowering bush. The scent of the blossoms filled his nose as he scurried to a prone firing position behind it. He carefully broke some small side branches until he could see through the edge of the bush. Two NVA soldiers, hunkered over moving backward, cautiously dragged a comrade by his arms as they pointed their AK47's toward

184

the American lines. Jeff aimed his M79 at the men but held his fire. Their direction of travel took them away from Jeff's hidden spot and toward an NVA officer who was motioning to them. Jeff lowered his weapon and crawled back to the junction of the two paths. He stared down each direction again in turn looking for some clue of where to go next.

Both paths looked the same to him but he would have to make a decision soon. He could not remain exposed for long. Equipment rattle continued from the direction of the NVA as they moved along their own lines.

Russ's voice came from behind him. "Jeff, we got company."

Jeff twisted his head around to the left and stared out into the jungle forest. Nothing moved and no one was visible. He gripped his M79 tighter as he looked right and then left again for the source of the voice. A drop of sweat fell into his eye from his brow causing him to blink. The wind noise slowed as Mutluk ran downward through the gears. Jeff sat up in his seat looking around. Another drop of sweat fell from his brow. He pulled his Boonie hat from his head and wiped his face. Russ and Mutluk's faces were tense.

"What's going on?"

Mutluk looked back into the side view mirrors as he slowed the truck to a crawl as he pulled it onto the grassy shoulder. "Don't know exactly. We just went through a little town and as I started up the gears as we got out of it, a police car pulled in behind me and turned on his rotating light."

He brought the truck to a stop and pulled the airbrake control out. The engine idled with a low rumble as he rolled the window down waiting.

Jeff leaned over in his seat and looked out Mutluk's side window. The left edge of the police car was visible in the side view mirror. A pot-bellied policeman in a tan uniform had gotten out of the police car and stared toward the truck. Moisture glistened from his head through the stubble of a crew cut. Mirrored sunglasses hid his eyes while a pistol hung low in a holster on his hip. The man looked at the road behind him before slowly walking up the side of the road toward the front of the truck.

A car door slammed on Jeff's side of the truck and Jeff shifted his eyes to the mirror on his side. Another man in an identical uniform, only with a police hat covering his head, moved along the right side of the truck with a shotgun in his hands. As he got halfway to the cab of the truck, he racked a shell into the chamber of the gun. He circled outward from the truck until he was even with Jeff's window about five feet away.

The policeman on the driver's side stopped even with the door three feet away from it. "Turn your engine off, boy."

Mutluk turned the key. The air grew still as the engine rumbled one last time before it died.

The policeman looked up at Mutluk for a long moment. "You got a license to drive this thing, boy?"

Mutluk reached toward his back pocket for his wallet. "Yes, sir. I've got it—"

The policeman pulled his pistol out of the holster. He held it in both hands pointed at Mutluk's head. "Nobody told you to move, boy. Show me your hands."

Mutluk raised his hands into view.

"You got that side covered, Billy Ray?"

Billy Ray called out as he pointed the shotgun at Jeff's head. "Got him covered Sheriff."

The sheriff dropped his left hand from the pistol but kept the barrel pointed toward Mutluk. He grabbed the low handle on the door and pulled it open. "Keep your hands in sight and step down from the truck."

He backed into the road away from the truck. "Get the other one out of the truck and to the back, Billy Ray."

Billy Ray kept the shotgun aimed at Jeff's head as his

finger touched the trigger. "Okay, open the door real slow and step down, boy."

Jeff kept his hands away from his body as he slowly climbed down from the cab. Russ slid from between the seats with his hands raised as he moved toward the door.

"I got two over here, Sheriff. White guy and a nigger."

"Bring'em both."

Billy Ray swung the barrel of the shotgun back and forth between Jeff and Russ. As Russ stepped down to the ground, Billy Ray swung the barrel up into the cab. "Anybody else in there? You'd better come out now."

Russ turned his eyes toward the ground. "Ain't nobody else in der, boss."

"I wasn't talking to you, boy. Shut up 'for I slap you."

"Yes'em."

The deputy transferred the shotgun to his left hand and placed his index finger on the trigger. He kept it pointed at the two as he pulled his pistol from its holster. "Both of you move away from the door toward the back of the truck."

Jeff and Russ both stepped slowly sideways.

"That's far enough."

Billy Ray stepped to the door of the cab and looked around. Holstering the pistol, he took a two-handed grip on the shotgun while he kept it aimed at Russ and Jeff.

"Go on. Get to the back of the truck."

Billy Ray followed the two to the back of the truck stepping away from them as they turned the corner. Mutluk was standing against the tailgate, his hands still over his head. The Sheriff holstered his pistol as Billy Ray brought the shotgun to bear on all three.

A grin crossed his face and he looked over at Billy Ray. "Now what do we have here? An Injun, a nigger, and a hippie driving through my county. Just doesn't seem natural, does it?"

Billy Ray smiled.

The Sheriff turned back toward the three roadies. "Turn around, lean forward, and put your hands on the tailgate." He frisked Mutluk first. Pulling the wallet from Mutluk's back pocket, he opened it and held out the cash stored inside. "Where'd you get all this money, boy?" Mutluk spoke without turning around. "The road manager of the band we work for gave it to me for fuel, Sir. We're heading to New Orleans."

He held the bills from Mutluk's wallet up for Billy Ray to see. "Must be two hundred dollars here, Billy Ray. Just doesn't seem natural for an Injun to have that much money."

"No sir, Sheriff. It don't."

The Sheriff dropped the money to the ground and pulled out Mutluk's license. "What's this name you got, boy? What kind of name is Mutluk? And where's this place you're from? I ain't never heard of Weagamow Lake."

"It's in the Canadian Province of Ontario, sir."

The Sheriff dropped the wallet and license to the ground as he grinned again. "So you're a Canadian Injun. Now ain't that special."

He moved next to Russ, patting him down before he pulled Russ's wallet from his back pocket. He opened it, removed the driver's license and money, and gave a low whistle. "This one's not just any nigger, Billy Ray. This one's a New York nigger with lots of cash. Whatcha you doing down here, boy? Trying to stir up trouble?"

"I jest works hauling crates. Ain't lookin' for no trouble, sir."

The sheriff slapped Russ upside his head. "Well, you got trouble now."

He dropped Russ's wallet and money to the ground as he stepped behind Jeff. The sheriff roughly moved his hands up and down Jeff's sides before he reached into Jeff's back pocket and pulled out his thin wallet.

He removed the driver's license from the wallet, looking

in it then held the open wallet upside down. "Tell me this, boy? How come the Injun and the nigger have all money and you don't have any? It just ain't natural."

Jeff motioned toward Mutluk. "I work for him. Like he said, we're the road crew for a band. We're heading to—"

The sheriff slapped Jeff alongside the head. Jeff tightened his torso as the hairs on the back of his neck stood. The sheriff grabbed Jeff's head as he yelled into his ear.

"Shut up, you nigger loving asshole. I didn't ask for your damn life story."

He pushed Jeff's head into the rear-rolling door, and then released him.

He stepped backward as he lifted Jeff's license to his eyes. "Lord, Billy Ray. This hippie's a Virginia boy. Didn't know there were any hippies in Virginia. I bet his daddy's real proud of his little girl."

The sheriff dropped Jeff's wallet and license to the ground but stayed standing behind him. "You know what I think we got here, Billy Ray?"

"What's that Sheriff?"

"I think we got us some drug smugglers. I bet if we take them and this truck back to town, we'll find a bunch of loco weed hidden in the back."

Jeff bent his head over until he could see the sheriff's boots on the ground. The sheriff stood with one foot slightly behind the other with the toe of the rear boot behind the heel of the front boot. A kick to the closest knee would send the man over on his back. The shotgun in the deputy's hands was the problem. Jeff turned his head slowly until he could see the deputy out of the corner of his eye. The deputy had the shotgun draped lazily over his shoulder with his finger outside the trigger guard.

Jeff tensed his left thigh as he rose to the ball of his left foot. He shifted his weight to his right hand, bent his right elbow slightly as he prepared to spin left so his right foot would connect with the sheriff's knee. He hoped that Russ and Mutluk would react when he yelled for them to drop. If he could jump on the sheriff and get his pistol, he may be able to shoot the deputy before he could react to bring the shotgun to bear. Jeff began a slow count to three inside his head.

Before Jeff reached three, the sheriff backed up toward the deputy. "Give me the shotgun, Billy Ray. Get on the radio to Susie. Have her get Sam to bring Junior out here. He can drive this truck back."

He took the shotgun, leveling it at the three roadies. "You boys turn around and stand against the back of the truck. Keep your hands above your heads."

The three turned and backed against the cold metal of the truck. Their hands went above their heads. The sheriff was standing out of reach of any kick Jeff could hope to muster as he held the shotgun leveled at Russ.

The sheriff took a step closer to Russ as a sneer came onto his face. "Course, I'm not really interested in having a New York nigger in my jail. Maybe you better run, boy."

Jeff looked over toward Russ. "Don't do it Russ. He'll just shoot you in the back."

The sheriff swung the butt of the shotgun around and punched Jeff in the gut. Jeff grabbed his stomach as he fell to his knees.

The muzzle of the shotgun touched Jeff's face. The barrel felt as large as Jeff's old M79. "Shut up, boy. I don't want to kill a Virginia boy, but if you push me, I will."

He shifted the shotgun back toward Russ. "I said run, boy."

Jeff looked to his left. A large rock lay in the grass two feet away. Jeff moved his hand toward the rock as he looked back toward the sheriff.

The sheriff continued to rant at Russ. "I said run, boy."

Jeff had just touched the rock when the deputy stepped out of the car. "Sheriff, we got to go. There was a prison break in Gulfport. They killed two guards and a gas station attendant. Several prisoners stole a car and were last seen coming this way. They want us to set up a road block at the 607 intersection to block them from getting into the swamps."

The sheriff looked back at the three roadies slowly swinging the shotgun back and forth, his finger twitched inside of the trigger guard. He stepped forward toward Jeff while lowered the barrel to Jeff's face again. "You're real lucky, boy. Any of you show up in my county again, you're dead."

He raised the barrel and turned toward the car. "You drive, Billy Ray."

Jeff slowly stood as the sheriff got into the passenger seat and Billy Ray started the engine. The lights and siren came on and the tires spun in the grass as Billy Ray turned the car hard left. The shotgun leveled out the passenger window as the car swung left toward the road.

"Duck," Jeff yelled.

The shotgun spit flame as the three dropped to the ground covering their heads. A ricocheting hot pellet landed on Jeff's neck but he dared not move. The tires on the car squealed, smoking as they hit pavement and the car began to race away back up the road toward Gulfport. Jeff looked up as the car disappeared around the curve with only the wailing siren leaving any clue of the danger that had just passed.

Russ quick crawled across the grass to grab his wallet. "Let's get out of here before he comes back."

Mutluk was scrambling across the ground grabbing the money that had blown around in the wind caused by the departing police car. "Good idea."

Jeff grabbed his wallet then turned toward the back of the truck. Eight fresh dots of bare metal, dented in slightly, showed in the sliding door where Russ's chest had been only a moment before. Russ moved up next to Jeff and looked at the dots of bare metal. He placed his hand on Jeff's shoulder.

"Thanks."

Mutluk had finished gathering his wallet and the money from the ground. "Get in the truck. We're out of here."

He raced around the driver's side of the truck as Russ and Jeff ran toward their door. Mutluk started the engine and then jerkily pulled the truck back onto the highway. The truck accelerated quickly as Mutluk made the gear handle fly from position to position. Whereas normally he kept the truck below the speed limit posted on the side of the road, now he pushed the truck faster and faster. The engine roared as they flew past a sign saying the border with Louisiana lay five miles ahead. The road behind them stayed empty. No one passed them going the other way. Only the swampland on each side of the highway witnessed their race toward safety. The forest on each side of the road ended as the metal trusses of a bridge loomed in front of them. The whirling of the tires changed to a rumble as they hit the metal deck that signaled relative safety.

Chapter 12

Mutluk lifted his foot from the accelerator as soon as the rear wheels touched the bridge over the narrow river signifying that the truck had crossed the state line into Louisiana. It was below the speed limit by the time they reached the other end of the bridge. The shores of Lake Pontchartrian welcomed them as Mutluk guided the truck past Fort Pike with its houses that lined the highway. The water of the high tide lapped at the rocks below the highway as the truck followed the curve onto the first of the levees.

All three remained silent, staring straight ahead out the windshield. Russ was the first to break the silence as he sat with his head sticking out between the seats. "You think we can find a different way home? I'm not going through that state again. In fact, I don't think I'm ever going to leave New York City again."

Jeff placed his hand on Russ's head. "It's okay, man. That's behind us now. It's a clear ride to New Orleans. I'll even buy you a beer when we get there."

Russ disappeared through the seats and curled up on the bunk with his face turned toward the back.

The truck moved into the outskirts of the city as the long string of levees that held back the lake ended. Mutluk lifted the clipboard off the seat holding it out toward Jeff. "You mind guiding me in? I don't think Russ is up for the job right now."

Jeff took the clipboard. "Sure."

He studied the directions for a moment before looking out the side window toward the street signs. "I don't know where we are exactly, but we stay on Highway 90 'til we get to Canal Street and then you take a left. We cross Saint Bernard, Esplanade, and Orleans Avenue before we get to Canal."

The truck rumbled down the highway as the city closed around it. A graveyard of above ground tombs stretched for three blocks on one side while classic shotgun style houses lined the other. These gave way first to the fairgrounds and then to low commercial storefronts with a French flair to the motifs of the window displays. Traffic increased as the truck closed in on the taller downtown buildings. Russ pushed his head between the seats every few minutes only to disappear again when a police car came into view. After they passed the lead-in streets, the stoplight-controlled intersection with Canal Street approached.

"You take a left onto Canal," Jeff said. "Then after we go about three-quarters of a mile, you take another left onto Bourbon Street."

Mutluk made the turn onto Canal, staying in the left lane. Streetcar tracks ran down the center divider. Passengers sat staring out the open windows as the trolleys pushed up to the intersection stops. Benches lined the sidewalks with large trees, planted a century or more ago, spreading their branches across the sidewalk and out over the road.

No Jim Crow separation presented itself on Canal Street.

Pedestrians of all colors strolled along on the sidewalks or sat together on the benches, their conversations punctuated by laughter with smiles between them. Some of those on the benches had paper bags across their laps while they ate sandwiches under the shade. Mason jars of brown tea waited on the ground by their feet.

Russ pushed his head forward again through the spilt in the seats. He gripped the seat backs tightly with his hands as he stared out the side windows at the crowds. His grips loosened as he took in the scene around him.

A smile came over his face. "What street are we looking for?"

Jeff turned and looked at Russ's smiling face. He smiled also as he turned forward again. "Bourbon Street. Should be about half a mile further."

Russ reached forward. "Give me that clipboard. Navigating is my job."

Sitting back in his seat, Jeff handed the clipboard over. He let his thoughts go from the intersecting streets to the spilt in the path back in the jungle. He concentrated on the undisturbed leaves and the scuffs in the dirt left from passing sandals. What clue did he miss that would have exposed the correct path? Which trace had led the right way?

When Mutluk turned left onto Bourbon Street, the texture of the surroundings changed from the downtown look of Canal Street to one of a colorful party. Gone were the gray granite buildings with sidewalks twenty feet wide and window displays full of stylish summer dresses.

The shops now sported clapboard facades of faded greens or blues with pink trims. Narrow metal-railed balconies shaded brick sidewalks that were barely four feet wide. It was as if the truck had been magically transported from a modern city to a small town in France.

The sides of the truck barely cleared the distance between the parked cars on the right and the sidewalk on the left. Mutluk stopped as he approached a stylish lamppost, reached out his window, and folded in the side mirror. The mirror still missed the lamppost by only an inch as he slowly advanced the truck in first gear.

Tourists in shorts, most carrying cups of beer or drinks sprinkled with pieces of fruit, strolled under the balconies while they wandered from neon sign to neon sign. They moved along the sidewalk looking into the windows of each bar as though the party from the night before still continued with new friends yet to be found.

Russ looked down at the clipboard before he pointed up the street. "We go five blocks and the club is on the left. Number 633."

Mutluk slowed the truck as it neared a bar with dark green shutters folded back into the building. A group of people had stumbled out of the multiple openings that stretched half a block and were weaving down the center of the street. The carousers ignored the truck behind them as they pointed toward other open bars and balcony signs that advertised party rooms for rent. Mutluk broke their ignorance of him with a short toot of the air horn. They all looked around, smiled, and waved him forward as they moved to the side. One girl stepped onto the passenger running board of the creeping truck and stuck her head into the open window. Jeff leaned away to avoid her rum-laced breath.

She stared into the cab for a moment before she spoke with a slurred accent. "Where's y'all headin'?"

Russ laughed at the intrusion into their mobile office as Mutluk gently stopped the truck and turned toward the girl. "We're going down to the La Roux club. Come see me later and I'll get you in free."

"Cool. See y'all later."

She slid off the running board and stumbled back toward her friends. Letting the clutch out slowly, Mutluk moved the truck forward. He chuckled as the crowds thinned so he was able to shift into second gear. "I wonder if she'll realize that nobody down here charges a cover."

Jeff looked into the side view mirror back at the girl as one of her friends held her hair back while she puked into the gutter. "I wonder if she'll remember her name later."

Russ pointed to a green painted bar as the truck approached the intersection with Saint Louis Street. The bar stretched half a block before them. Faded blue shutters lay folded outward and were pinned to the wall by elegant cast iron stays. The dimly lit inside beckoned to drinkers looking for a cool place to escape the sun.

A line of trash cans sat in the street in front of the club. Mutluk stopped the truck while gesturing toward them. "Jeff, go move those cans out of the way. They put them there to hold the space for us to park for the load-in."

After Jeff cleared the cans, Mutluk pulled the truck into the space. Within minutes, he had the roll-up door open and the ramp out. "We need to get everything out fast. Parking is at a premium here so the other shop owners will complain if we take up half a block for long. We're using the house sound and lighting systems so we only need the stage equipment loaded in."

Jeff looked through the openings into the club. A small stage sat barely twenty feet from the open doors. "This place is way smaller than the other places we've been. Why are they playing here?"

Mutluk moved to the top of the ramp and began handing out the upper cases. "The drummer got his start here and told the owner that if he ever made it big, he'd come back to play for free. I think it's sort of a payback. Come on. Enough talk. Carry."

The load-in went quick and clean as the practiced motions of the three looked like a dance routine. The few lunchtime drinkers at tables near the stage moved away to avoid the activity. Cabinets were carried to the stage and placed without a word spoken. Microphone stands and auxiliary cabinets were put to the side and lids popped opened. Within a half-hour, Jeff and Russ sat at a table waiting for Mutluk to come back from parking the truck in a lot three blocks away. They each held a glass half full of beer. Jeff's pack leaned against his leg.

Russ took a sip from his glass. "I hope you find your friend quick so you can get back here soon. I'm kinda used to you being around now. Sure you don't want to head back north, I mean Virginia way, after we finish here to work another tour? It would be a shame to let all that training I did with you go to waste. To tell you the truth, you're a lot more help than Sam ever was."

"Thanks. It's been fun, but this just doesn't feel like it's what I'm supposed to do. I'll find Clarence and see what happens. I hope that I'll find him quick and we'll be back for tonight's show. I think you and Mutluk will like him. He always had a huge smile on his face that showed his big white teeth and he used to make me giggle all the time. It'll be damn good to see him again."

Mutluk strolled in from the street and walked over to the table. He laid a pile of twenty-dollar bills down in front of Jeff. "That's what I owe you plus a little extra. You earned every penny of it."

Jeff scooped up the bills without counting and struck them into his back pocket. "Thanks. After I find Clarence and we have a chance to talk, I'll bring him back here."

Mutluk nodded his head. "You do that. I'm looking forward to meeting him. Must be quite a friend for you to want to come this far." He motioned to Russ. "Finish your beer. We need to get set up so the band can do their sound check." He stuck his hand out to Jeff. "See you later."

Jeff stood and grabbed Mutluk's hand. "Thanks for the ride."

Jeff released the big man's hand, lifted his pack, and walked over to the bar. Mutluk and Russ moved to the stage and started placing the microphone stands into place. Pulling out his wallet, Jeff removed the piece of paper with Clarence's address. He waved the bartender over and held the paper out.

"Can you tell me how to get to this place?"

The bartender looked at the piece of paper. He then eyed Jeff with a questioning look on his face. "Algiers? Are you sure you want to go there? That's across the river."

"Yea. Why?"

"Well, it's just that's not the part of town many white

people go walking around by themselves." He gestured toward Mutluk and Russ. "Are your friends going with you?"

"No. I'm heading there to look up an old Army buddy."

"Okay. Well, I can tell you how to get across the river, but I don't know the streets over there. You'll have to ask directions once you get across. But you may want to consider waiting to take one of you friends with you."

"I'll be fine."

"Alright, but don't say I didn't warn you." He pointed with his left hand. "Head back down Bourbon until you get back to Canal. Turn left and take Canal down about seven blocks to the river. There's a ferry terminal there. Take the ferry across the river. That's Algiers."

"Okay. Thanks."

"Good Luck."

Jeff lifted his pack to his shoulders as he headed out the open doors. The temperature had risen forcing the tourist crowds off the sidewalks into the bars seeking refuge. Deliverymen rolled hand trucks loaded with kegs of beer and cases of liquor into the dimly lit saloons. Jeff walked down the sidewalk against what little foot traffic the afternoon had to offer. Even the cars and trucks that moved along the narrow street seemed to travel in slow motion. Sweat formed on his brow so he pulled his Boonie hat from his pocket placing it loosely on his head.

The crowds, present when they had driven by in the truck earlier, had also thinned on Canal Street. The benches under the trees were empty now and only a few shoppers moved from store to store. Sweat began to drip down Jeff's back as he moved purposely toward his goal. As the blocks went by, the faces of the few people around him grew more solemn, but Jeff did not notice. Only the joyous thought of finding his friend filled his mind.

When he reached the river, wooden signs directed passengers onto the ferry. The deck of the large flat decked craft vibrated to the rumble of the powerful diesel hidden somewhere below. Climbing to the upper deck, he moved to the rail and looked across the river toward Algiers. He wondered what answers lay there for him. Would Clarence solve the mystery of the last two years or would his journey need to continue elsewhere? His thoughts turned to Pat and the life he might have with her if he just turned around and called her to come get him. The sound of the rumbling diesel changed as the black deckhands released the ropes from their moorings. The ferry rocked gently as it cut through the flowing river toward the other side.

The ship docked minutes later and the moorings were made fast. Jeff stood back from the crowd of people that waited for the deckhand to remove the chain across the gangway. When the way was clear, the crowd moved onto the ramp away from the terminal. Another crowd waited behind a gate for the ferry to empty and their time to board for the trip to the city side. Their eyes followed Jeff as he strolled past them up the ramp on his way to dry land. Many hesitated for a second as the gate opened, their gazes fixed upon the back of the single white face in the terminal. Then, the crowd behind pushed them forward onto the boat.

Sweat coated the back of Jeff's t-shirt and the pack weighed heavy on his shoulders as he moved down the street. Storefronts with plywood protection over missing glass lined the right side of the road. The predominate advertisement on each storefront was the For Rent signs plastered over soaped-out windows. The left side of the road held only the remnants of burned out buildings with the flowing river beyond. Several young black men, probably in their early twenties, walked along the other side of the road heading toward the ferry terminal. After they passed him, Jeff noticed that the sound of their feet moving changed. They left the dirt shoulder and crossed the street. Their voices remained quiet while they reversed direction. The distance between them and Jeff grew ever smaller. The hair on the back of Jeff's neck stood on end and it broke through the covering sweat.

He crossed a side street as he approached a store with baskets of garden vegetables stacked on old wooden chairs along the front. Several young black men were sitting on old empty crates. Their faces turned toward Jeff as he approached and their mouths went from smiles to tightly closed grimaces. One large man stood and blocked the sidewalk in front of Jeff. Mirrored sunglasses, beneath a black beret with a red patch of a raised black fist, hid his eyes. The footsteps behind Jeff closed the distance, ceasing as they blocked Jeff's rear. He could sense the men were standing only a few feet behind him.

The man to his front angled his head down toward Jeff causing the reflection in his sunglasses to show the two men standing within an arm's reach behind Jeff. No one moved for several seconds. Jeff stared back at the man as a slight grin, actually more of a smirk, crossed the man's face.

He parted his lips. Bright white teeth shined against his coal black skin. "What you doin' over here white boy?"

"I'm trying to find an old friend. Do you know where Laboeuf Street is?"

"Never heard of it. You might just be in the wrong part of town."

The feet behind Jeff shuffled. He stared into the man's sunglasses again. The men behind him had moved closer. He tensed his stomach muscles while he rose slightly onto the balls of his feet.

"Do you mind if I go inside and ask if anyone in there knows where Laboeuf is?"

The man grinned harder. "Sorry, they're closed for lunch."

A voice came from behind Jeff. "What's in the pack white boy?"

Jeff shifted forward to bring his leg within a knee's reach of the crotch of the big man blocking his path. The man changed his hands slowly into fists as the feet behind Jeff shuffled again. Someone grabbed Jeff's pack pulling him backward. The man in front of him advanced with his fists raised.

A woman's voice called out from the store. "Leroy! What's going on out there?"

The large man to Jeff's front stopped his advance while dropping his fists back into open hands as he backed up slightly. His gaze stayed fixed on Jeff's face. The hands holding Jeff's pack released it and Jeff stumbled as he regained his footing.

The large man turned toward the door. "Nothin', momma."

A short heavyset woman, a green bandanna tied around her head and a colorful apron around her waist, walked out the door with a broom in her hands. She looked at the large black man, then at Jeff, then at the men behind Jeff. She raised her broom off the ground and pointed the bristles toward the men behind Jeff.

"You boys go'on now. You got no reason to block the sidewalk scaring my customers. Git."

The men behind Jeff backed up. "Yes, ma'am." They turned heading toward the ferry as they laughed between themselves.

The woman pushed past the large black man and stepped up to Jeff. She looked inquisitively at him. "What you doin' over here, child? I never get white customers."

"Sorry ma'am. I'm just trying to find an old friend that lives around here."

The woman's face softened. "Who you looking for?"

"His name is Clarence, Clarence Washington. The address I've got is on Laboeuf Street."

Her face broke into a smile. Perfect bright white teeth beamed out. "That's my nephew. How you know him?"

202

"We were in the army together."

"What's your name, child?"

"Jeff. Jeff Briggs, ma'am."

Leroy's tight lips opened into a smile exposing a full set of bright white teeth behind his dark lips. The woman broke into laughter as she lowered the end of the broom to the ground and leaned on it. Jeff cocked his head at the two, not knowing what to take from the reaction to his name. The woman finally regained her composure as she wiped her eyes.

"I'm sorry about laughing Jeff. It's just that Clarence used to send letters from Vietnam that I'd read to the family at Sunday dinner every week. He mentioned your name often, but he never said you were a white boy. Just doesn't seem like something he'd forget to mention."

"Well, ma'am, he never really mentioned it to me either."

Leroy burst out laughing and slapped his thigh. "That's just like Clarence. Always leavin' out the good parts."

The woman held out her hand. "My name's Cynthia Thomas. This here's Leroy, my son."

Leroy nodded toward Jeff but did not offer his hand. His smile lowered back into the tight grin that seemed to be his natural pose.

Jeff shook the woman's hand. The smoothness of her skin reminded him of Bessie's. "Pleased to meet you, ma'am. Could you tell me how far I am from Clarence's house?"

"It's about 8 blocks from this here spot. It's easy to find." She turned toward Leroy. "Leroy, you take Jeff on to where Clarence's house is."

Leroy's mouth changed from the remnants of a grin to a scowl. "Yes, ma'am."

Cynthia creased her brow and raised the broom into her hands. "And Leroy, you makes sure that he stays safe."

His eyes narrowed as he looked at Jeff. "This way."

Leroy turned and, not waiting for Jeff to move, walked down the street.

Cynthia grabbed Jeff's hand before he could turn. "You take care, child. And you stop by here 'fore you cross back over the river. I'll give you a soda and a peach to quench your thirst. You go'on and follow Leroy now. He'll git you there."

"Thanks, ma'am. Thanks for all your help." Jeff raced after Leroy.

Cynthia called out as Jeff moved to catch up with Leroy. "Leroy, don't you dally after you show Jeff where it is. You git on back here quick as you can. I've got groceries for you to deliver."

Leroy exhaled deeply. "Yes, ma'am."

Leroy took long strides as he moved purposefully along the sidewalk. Boards were nailed over the windows and doors of most of the buildings they passed. The few that were open sold second-hand clothing or used furniture. Barred windows covered the glass of a Liquor store that rose between the ashes of two burned out buildings on the other side of the street. A crowd of men, both young and old, leaned against the sidewall while they sipped from bottles hidden by brown paper bags.

The road paralleled the river and a rusty ship moved in the channel toward the Gulf. The ship, flowing along with the current, moved quickly past Jeff and Leroy. The large air horn on the peak of the superstructure blasted a long sorrowful note as the ship turned into the bend. An attached Tugboat put out a rhythmic beat as its diesel engine chugged just above idle.

People walking the other way on the sidewalk moved off to the side or onto the street as Leroy passed. Many stopped while Jeff walked by and kept their eyes focused toward him as he followed Leroy. Three young men with black rags tied around their heads turned to follow the unlikely pair for half a block. Leroy seemed to sense their presence as he stopped, turned, and stared hard at them. They meekly turned around and walked away.

Leroy led Jeff past an open area that contained the ruins of an apartment building. Several large concrete pads remained where a playground once stood. Young men dribbled and passed a basketball as they raced around the concrete. They stopped their game to watch Leroy and Jeff walk by on the sidewalk. Children laughed as they kicked a ball in a grassy area next to the pads. The sound of their playing continued as Leroy and Jeff crossed an intersecting street and then walked past shotgun style houses with chain-link fences that secured barking dogs.

Leroy stopped at the next cross street lined with more shotgun houses. The road ended at a clump of trees six blocks in the distance. Light filtered through the thin line of trees with buildings rising beyond the trees.

Leroy pointed down the street. "Clarence's house is on the left by the woods near the end. It's the one with the blue door."

He began walking toward his mother's store. He hesitated in his movement before he turned to face Jeff. "Anyone try to bother you, you tell them Leroy sent you down that way." He nodded to Jeff, turned his back, and moved resolutely away.

Jeff watched the man depart before he turned to head down the street. He moved with a slight spring in his step as his journey's end came toward him. Jeff looked toward the end of the street for the glimpse of a blue door but only thickening woods returned his gaze. Sweat rolled down the back of Jeff's neck and dripped onto his t-shirt. He lifted his Boonie hat from his head and wiped his brow before lightly seating the hat on the back of his head.

No sidewalks existed as Jeff moved down the center of the empty street. Old cars, some apparently in running order while others sat with no tires on concrete blocks, lined both sides of the road. Dogs snapped through the chain-link from many lots. Music played loudly from a house halfway down. It stopped as Jeff approached. The air grew heavy as the silence took hold.

Two men, bare-chested and glistening with sweat, came off the porch of the house and stood by the fence. One had a baseball bat slung over his shoulder.

The man with the bat called out. "You lost white boy?"

Jeff turned his face toward the man, stared into his eyes but kept his pace up. "No, Leroy gave me directions."

The two men said nothing. They simply turned back to the porch. The music blared again as Jeff moved through the next street intersection. He looked toward the end of the street again for his final destination but the blue door was not yet visible. Light no longer filtered through the trees at the end. The buildings beyond had vanished in the thickening dark forest. A path into the greenery exposed itself as Jeff reached the last cross street.

The further Jeff moved down the street, the houses on both sides fell more and more into disrepair along with the fences that surrounded the lots. Plywood became the primary window covering. The front doors of several houses hung open with only the top hinge attached to the frame. An old man, on a porch that looked like it shouldn't be standing, rocked in a rusty rocker while he followed Jeff with his eyes. Jeff's focus remained on the end of the street.

The door on the house second from the end was bright blue. Walking past the weeds that grew through the chain-link, Jeff slowly approached the gate of the fence surrounding the yard. The only hinge on the gate hung by a single bolt. The paint on the house had faded to a pasty green with patches missing along with whole sections that had peeled away from the bare wood. The front door, with a paint job that looked like it had been applied the day before, contrasted the fading walls. Bullet holes pierced the plywood that covered the windows.

The single hinge creaked as Jeff pushed through the

gate and started up the broken concrete walkway. He stopped short as a snake came out of the tall grass onto the concrete in front of him. It slithered across until it disappeared into the weeds on the other side. Jeff resumed his walk toward the door but scanned the grass as he moved.

The closer he came to the blue door, the less the house looked lived in. He hesitated at the porch stairs, staring at the scene before him. The faded green porch swing listed on uneven chains as it hung motionless in the humid air. A rusty chair leaned against the skewed wood frame of the open screen door. The closing spring hung loosely from the wall. The plywood over the windows was a weather-beaten off gray and many of the nails had backed away from their initial seating. Flies buzzed through a two-inch gap between the bottom of the plywood and the windowsills.

Jeff mounted the steps in a slow deliberate fashion as he tested each riser before he placed his full weight upon it. Several moaned under his feet as they took the load as he climbed them one by one to the porch. The paint on the porch curled away from many of the boards. As he moved across the porch, his feet cracked loose pieces of paint that lay scattered from the winds of the last storm. Coolness emanated from the house as he got closer, chilling the sweat that saturated Jeff's t-shirt. He stopped facing the front door. Reaching forward with his left hand, he hesitated for three seconds before he knocked lightly.

Chapter 13

A hollow sound answered his knock as if the building was dead. Jeff stood back and examined the door closely. The paint, which now resembled the color of a morning sky after a spring rain, seemed new with drops splashed upon the worn handle. Spillage had also splattered on the threshold.

The heavy brush strokes crossed from the door onto the frame with the dried paint forming a seal between the two that would probably require a knife to break.

Moving over to the window, he knelt down until he could look through the gap at the bottom. Cold air filtered across his face as his eyes adjusted to the darkness within. The light of the afternoon sun penetrated only an inch onto the inside sill. The holes from the stray neighborhood bullets placed pinpoints of light against the far wall through the gloom. As Jeff stared into the black slot in front of him, the slight breeze of cool air from the inside wavered as if a body had moved across the window. One pinpoint of light suddenly came closer and then receded back on its original spot.

Jeff grabbed the sill with both hands and placed his mouth on the edge of the hole. "Hello. Hello. Is anyone there?"

The cool airflow across his face became a torrent of frigid coldness, blasting his face away from the sill before it stopped. His damp t-shirt chilled as the hairs on his neck stood at attention. The room inside lightened slightly and shapes of old furniture materialized in his view. A soft scraping sound came from the direction of the doorway.

The door handle squeaked as it turned. Jeff ran to the door as it opened a crack. He searched the beam of light that ran across the floor from the crack for some sign of life, but the only movement came from dust dancing in the beam. Cold air flowed through the crack further chilling the front of his t-shirt. He leaned forward and brought his left eye to the crack.

A cataract-covered eye stared back at him. Jeff recoiled back almost losing his footing as the door opened fully. A blast of cold air from within hit him while he staggered before he caught himself and straightened his body. Goosebumps covered his arms and the hair on the back of his neck stretched to its limit.

A short, emaciated black woman stood centered in the open doorway. Her cheeks were sunken and hollow as though no teeth existed beyond the skin. The cataract-covered right eye glared a dull white while the other eye was a deep brown. The iris of the good eye opened and closed rapidly as if it had not seen light in the recent past. Her skin had a gray hue to it.

A housedress hung loosely from her tiny torso. The dress wasn't black or gray, it was without color. Frizzed hair sprang from the top of her head at all angles. Skin hung loosely from her upper arms as if she had lost weight and the skin had never caught up.

The goose bumps on Jeff's arms subsided as he leaned slightly forward toward the woman. "Excuse me, ma'am. I'm—"

The woman stopped his speech with a raised hand. A voice as hollow as his knock kept him from starting again. "I knows who you is. Why you here? Clarence need help. Why you here? Go back! My boy need help."

The cold air from the inside became a gust that caused the goose bumps to return on Jeff's arms as he leaned forward to keep his balance.

He shouted into the wind. "Where's Clarence? I'll help

him. Tell me where he is."

The woman moved silently from inside the house onto the porch. Jeff stepped backward down the steps as she approached. Her mouth opened and bright white teeth shown through the parted lips. She reached the edge of the porch and stopped. She focused her good eye toward Jeff.

"Why you here? Clarence need help. Go back! Go back!"

Jeff backed down the walkway while never taking his eyes off the woman.

"Where is he? Show me where Clarence is."

"Go Back! Go Back!"

Jeff reached the gate and backed onto the sidewalk. He turned to head back up the street but a frantic shout from the woman stopped him cold.

"No! Go da way."

Jeff looked back at the woman as she stood on the edge of the porch. She raised her arm and pointed her finger, which was more bone than skin, toward the woods.

"That way. Go Back. My boy need help."

Jeff looked at the thick woods then back toward the woman. He nodded his head slightly as he came to understand the truth of his surroundings. She smiled as she nodded back at him. He ran toward the woods and crashed through the brush. Her voice touched his ears before it faded from reality.

"Go right, Jeff. Go right."

The sunlight grew dimmer as he moved through the outer brush into the thick woods. The ground squashed beneath his feet as branches snapped backward while he pushed through them. No other sounds emanated from the forest. Jeff looked rearward toward where he had entered the woods. No trace of the houses existed; only trees and bushes filled the way behind him. He turned forward as the sting of cordite touched his nostrils. He stopped, lifted his helmet from his head, and wiped the sweat from his forehead with the sleeve of his uniform.

Mismatched shapes covered in leaves disturbed the serenity of the path to his front. As he shifted behind a tree trunk, he knelt. Raising his M79 to his shoulder, he pushed the safety off. His breath stopped as the shapes morphed into NVA soldiers with camouflaging leafy twigs protruding from their packs. Jeff aimed the M79 at a large branch above the path and about forty meters in front of his hiding place.

A singsong voice came from the left just as the first of the soldiers crossed beneath the branch. The soldiers stopped and dropped to their knees with their weapons raised to their shoulders. They pointed the muzzles forward, left, and right. Jeff moved his finger into the trigger guard, pulling back on the trigger until the slack was gone. He would fire as soon as the men rose and moved toward him again.

The NVA officer Jeff had seen earlier off to his left rose from his hiding place to wave toward the troops kneeling in front of Jeff. The lead soldier on the path waved back then signaled with his hand to his men. The column turned right as it headed toward the officer with their weapons still at the ready. The NVA officer dropped back into his fighting hole. Jeff relaxed his finger but shifted his aim to keep it centered on the troops as they moved away from him. Jeff lowered himself to the ground, shifted around the back of the tree, then crawled beside the path toward the spilt.

Reaching the split in the paths, he looked down each again. The old woman's voice echoed in his ears so clear that he had to look around to see if she was standing next to him.

"Go right."

With a backward glance toward the camouflaged NVA troops, he rose and headed at a trot down the path to the right. Gunfire erupted behind him. Bullets clipped the leaves beside his head as he pushed his legs into a full run.

He turned his upper body until he could sight the M79 toward the firing troops and pulled the trigger.

As he watched the round fly thru the air, an American machine gun fired on the standing NVA troops. Several fell as the others dropped to the ground then scampered for the cover of the prepared positions. His round exploded in the midst of the troops, but Jeff had faced forward by then.

Bullets stopped passing around him as he moved down the path out of sight of the NVA. He loaded a fresh round into the breech and snapped it shut. The hint of a singsong voice reached his ears. Slowing to a walk, he raised the M79 to his shoulder aiming down the path.

The voice became clear so Jeff slowed further until his movement forward was a halting series of steps that resembled a bridesmaid's journey up a church aisle toward the altar. He shifted off the path and moved quietly through the trees toward the voice. Movement ahead caught his eye. He dropped to the ground with the muzzle of the M79 pointed toward the shadowy shapes. He focused his eyes on the movement as he moved slowly forward. It morphed into an NVA officer with red piping on his collar and a piece of paper in his hands. The officer walked up to another NVA soldier who was sitting on a tree stump talking into a radio handset. Jeff crawled forward as he scanned the area for the other two people he knew were there.

A third NVA soldier, the AK47 held loosely in his hands pointed downward, leaned against a tree with his eyes cast downward. From his position, Jeff could not see what the man was looking at, but in his mind, he knew it was Clarence. Jeff shifted his crawling approach until he was at a point he could fire at the soldier. He scooted his body behind a tree before placing the M79 on the ground. Ever so slowly, he removed Clarence's M16 from his shoulder, brought the weapon up, and centered the sights on the man's chest. He pulled the slack from the trigger as he let out half his breath.

He released the tension on the trigger as another NVA soldier with a shoulder bag walked up beside his target. The man with the shoulder bag knelt two feet in front of the soldier holding the AK47.

Pulling the slack of the trigger up again, he held his breath before quickly firing three shots. The NVA soldier fell hard as Jeff dropped the M16, grabbed his M79 with his left hand, and rose from the ground. He fired the M79 toward the NVA officer. The round flew true and exploded in between the two men. The blast sent both of them backward and their bodies lay weirdly positioned on the ground. Dropping the M79, he picked up the M16 and raced forward toward the fallen guard. He shifted the muzzle between the fallen guard and the other soldier, who was now back crawling away. The guard had landed on his side was not moving. Two holes in his chest dripped blood and the Corporal's insignia on his right shoulder hung torn halfway off by the third shot. Jeff shifted the muzzle of the M16 until the sights centered on the last NVA soldier. The man stopped his backward crawl as he raised his hands.

Clarence's voice cut through the air. "Don't kill him. He saved my life."

Jeff continued to hold the M16 pointed at the soldier as he shifted his eyes quickly toward the sound of his friend's voice. Clarence lay on the ground next to the crumpled body of the NVA guard. A light green bandage was wrapped tightly around the lower part of his left leg. A stick protruded from each side of the bandage as blood seeped from under it. Clarence's flak vest lay underneath the splinted leg and held it up above the dirt.

Jeff shifted his eyes quickly back to the soldier sitting with his arms raised then over toward the direction of the two NVA he had fired the M79 at. Neither body showed signs of movement. He moved his gaze back to the live soldier and re-centered the sights on the man's chest. He shifted left to Clarence, bent down, and laid his left hand on his friend's chest while keeping the rifle aimed at the NVA.

"How you doing man?"

"Could be better. Leg's numb. He gave me a shot of what I guess was morphine."

"Can you aim this?"

"Sure."

"Keep him covered for a minute."

Jeff handed the M16 to Clarence and drew his pistol from its holster. He scurried over to the other NVA bodies and kicked both with his boot. Neither man moved. After holstering his pistol, he picked up the map that the officer had been holding. Jeff then drew his knife from his boot scabbard before slicing off one of the insignias of the NVA officer. He moved back over to Clarence's side shoving the epaulette and map into Clarence's shirt pocket.

"Souvenir for you. Think you can walk?"

"No way, man. It's broke with the bone sticking out."

"Okay. Let me get my stuff."

Clarence grabbed Jeff's shoulder with his left hand while he held the M16 aimed at the NVA medic with his right. "How'd you find me?"

"Your mother told me which path to take."

"Huh?"

Jeff pushed Clarence's hand down. "Just keep him covered for now. I'll tell you everything when we get back to base camp."

Jeff retrieved his M79, loaded a fresh round into the chamber, and then emptied his general-purpose bag onto the ground. He clipped the Purple smoke grenade onto his webbing and placed three fragmentation M79 rounds into pockets on his vest. He threw the remaining M79 rounds into the forest around him. Picking up the two last full magazines for the M16, he slid them into his right side pants pocket before moving back to Clarence's side.

Jeff talked fast. "We've got to go. Someone's gonna be here quick to find out why the radioman isn't talking anymore. I'm going to have to carry you piggyback. You hold the M16 in your right hand so you can fire forward if we need it. Keep your right leg curled up tight against me in case I have to release it and fire the 79. I'll keep my left arm under your left thigh and hook my thumb onto my belt. I'll try to warn you if we're gonna have to hit the dirt."

Clarence motioned with the M16 toward the live NVA soldier. "What about him?"

Jeff aimed the M79 toward the man as he motioned in the direction away from the NVA main lines. He yelled in Vietnamese for the man to run. The man scampered to his feet and took off running in the direction Jeff had indicated. Jeff kept the M79 aimed at the man until he disappeared into the forest brush.

Jeff gently lifted Clarence's leg and pulled the flak vest from under it. Shifting Clarence into a sitting position, he threaded Clarence's arms through the arm slots of the vest. Jeff then knelt and turned until his back was to Clarence.

"Grab me around the neck."

Clarence reached his arms around Jeff's neck as Jeff stood. Using his arms while maintaining a grip on the M79, he shifted Clarence upward until the weight rested on his back.

"Ready?"

"Yea."

As fast as Jeff could move, he headed back down the path toward the gully and the American lines.

Chapter 14

Gunfire erupted to their front as they approached the intersection of the paths where the NVA had spotted Jeff and shot at him. Jeff shifted his route to the left off the path as he headed thru the trees. He flicked his head to indicate the path to Clarence as they moved away from it.

His breath came labored as he quietly spoke. "The NVA... have prepared positions up that way...Keep an eye out...to the right. We better...head this way until we reach the gully... We can find a spot to cross...and then stay behind tree cover until...we get our lines."

"Think they're still there?"

"There's only been... a few times I've heard Hueys close by...Not enough to signal a pullout. Probably... Medevacs... From the machine gun and rifle...fire I've heard, I'm guessing our guys...are consolidating their...positions now...I'm hoping that the line is...still near where it was."

Hunching over further, Jeff shifted Clarence upward slightly as he pushed his forearms deeper under Clarence's thighs. Clarence winced, tensing his arms in reaction to the shift. An exhalation of pain came from his lips into Jeff's ear.

"You okay?"

"Yea. Just keep going."

Jeff quickened his pace as he angled away from the NVA positions toward where he thought the gully should be. Small branches slapped his thighs so he twisted sideways as he ran into them trying to protect Clarence's wounded leg from further abuse. Constant rifle fire combined with periodic bursts from machine guns punctuated the forest air. Three-round missions from a mortar crew blasted in the distance beyond Jeff's view. Ahead and to his right, the thunk from the muzzle of an M79, followed by an explosion where he thought the NVA lines should be, provided Jeff with confidence that his choice of direction was right.

Jeff kept up his pace for another minute before he moved behind a tree and fell to one knee. Sweat dripped from his nose as he hung his head gulping air. "I've got to... catch my breath... God... my head hurts... Try to see if there's... any sign of the gully off to the right."

Clarence pushed upward with his good leg to take some of the weight off Jeff's back. He tilted his head to the right around the tree. The gunfire diminished from both sides as though commands had been issued. Only the occasional sniper round cut through the air. Wispy smoke from exploded grenades and mortar rounds drifted across the area in front of them like a morning fog near the seashore. Clarence focused his vision as a hint of movement appeared just beyond the drifting remnants of the cordite. The unmistakable shape of two NVA sun helmets moved just above the ground before they disappeared as if they had been apparitions.

Clarence pulled his head back until his mouth rested next to Jeff's ear. "I think the gully is just ahead to the right. It looks like there're NVA moving in it. Stay left."

Jeff grunted as he tightened his grip beneath Clarence's thighs, stood, and lumbered forward again. He moved from tree to tree, never stopping fully at any tree large or small, but hesitated as he identified the next one that could provide them cover. At each point of hesitation, he held his breath while he listened for the telltale sound of equipment rattle. The slap of a rifle stock against webbing filtered from the right. A clunk as a nervous soldier slid back the bolt of his AK47 to check for a round in the chamber came next. Finally, the sound that Jeff had been waiting for came across the quieting battlefield. To the right below his line of sight, rubber soled boots thudded against the trunk of a tree. Jeff turned toward the noise, stopping behind the trunk of a large tree. To his front, bushes, like those he had pushed through several times on his journey to Clarence, defined the edge of the gully.

Jeff dropped to one knee behind the tree. "Think you can stand on your good leg and cover me for a minute?"

"Sure. You goin' left or right?"

"Left."

Clarence placed his weight on his right leg as he leaned into the tree. He slid his mangled left leg from around Jeff's back while he shifted his shoulders so he could aim and fire. Jeff stood behind Clarence, reached into his side pants pocket, and retrieved the two full magazines. He slid them into Clarence's right side pocket as he moved up next to him.

Jeff pointed toward where the slight sound the boots climbing the tree trunk came from. "I'm going to crawl over there to take a look. If I remember it right, that may be a good place to cross the gully and head to our lines."

Clarence touched Jeff's shoulder before Jeff started to move forward. "Be careful."

"Always."

He moved in a crouch to about ten meters from the line of bushes and then dropped to the ground into a crawl. Removing his helmet as he reached the bushes, He slowly pushed the muzzle of the M79 through the lower branches. He let his head follow the weapon until only a few leaves were between his eyes and the gully. Down in the gully to his left, fifteen NVA soldiers crowded toward a hole created by two others holding back branches of the fallen tree. They mounted the trunk one-by-one, disappearing to the other side. Jeff pushed his body quietly back, grabbed his helmet, and crawled over toward Clarence.

After he was away from the gully, Jeff rose back into a

crouch moving toward the rifle muzzle aimed in his direction. He slipped behind Clarence and took up aim on the bushes from the left side of the tree. Clarence shifted the muzzle of his rifle left and right along the line of bushes.

"What'd ya see?"

"Looks like they're moving down the gully and getting ready to hit the right flank in force. There's a fallen tree that will block their view so we can cross, but we're going to have to slide you down into the gully and climb the other side."

"If they start their attack while we're moving, everybody's goin' to be shooting everywhere."

"I know. But there ain't no other way back to our lines. Let's move."

Jeff shifted his M79 to his right hand and grabbed Clarence around the waist with his left arm. Clarence placed his right arm over Jeff's shoulder. Together they hobbled toward the gully. Jeff helped lower Clarence to the ground at the edge of the bushes and then pushed his head under. The NVA soldiers had finished crossing the tree trunk and light sounds of equipment rattle emanated from beyond the blocking trunk. He pushed back and turned his head toward Clarence.

"I'll go through, then pull you in. I'll slide you right down to the bottom. Try to raise your leg after you clear the bush."

"Okay."

Jeff crawled through the bush, quickly turning around and grabbing Clarence's' outstretched hands. He backed up sliding his friend to the bottom of the gully. Clarence winced as his leg struck a branch.

Jeff whispered. "You okay?"

Clarence gave a slight nod as he motioned with his hand for Jeff to keep moving. Jeff dropped his M79, lifted Clarence by gripping him under the armpits, and pushed him up the other side. Clarence grabbed branches with his left hand as he held his rifle with his right. Jeff shifted down and pressed against Clarence's right boot. Clarence slithered beneath the bushes.

"Clear," he whispered back.

Jeff pushed under the bush and crawled on his belly beside Clarence. A clearing opened up thirty meters through the trees in front of them. Five dead NVA soldiers lay strewn in it. An American helmet was sitting upside down next to the tree line on the other side. An M16 barked twice from the trees ahead and a bullet zinged above Jeff's head. Jeff and Clarence pushed their bodies lower into the leaves and twigs. A leaf, loosened by one of the bullets, floated from behind Jeff's head and landed in front of them.

Sergeant Slattery's voice whispered roughly through the open space before them. "Damn it, Jackson. I said hold your fire until you have a target."

"Sorry Sarge. I thought I saw movement."

Muted equipment rattle came from down the gully behind them. Clarence turned his head toward Jeff placing his mouth next to Jeff's ear. "What we gonna do? Pretty soon everyone's gonna be shootin'.

"Hold on a minute. I've got an idea. Let's get behind cover."

They both inched backward to take cover behind a tree. Jeff rolled onto his back, unclipped the purple smoke grenade from his vest, and handed it to Clarence.

Jeff pulled himself up to Clarence's ear before he whispered. "Put a fresh magazine in. I'm going back into the gully. I'll create a diversion that will get everyone looking and firing toward the gully below us. As soon as you hear me fire a round, pop the smoke, throw it as far as you can toward our lines, then roll on your back. The wind's coming from behind us, so the smoke will drift toward our lines but still give us cover from the gully. I'll get back up here, grab you, and carry you toward the line.

You be ready to fire toward the gully. I want everyone on our lines to hear M16 fire as we come through the smoke."

Clarence grabbed the smoke grenade as he whispered back. "Be careful."

"Always."

Jeff carefully turned around and slithered through the bushes until his eyes could see into the gully. No NVA soldiers were visible and his M79 still lay where he had dropped it. He rolled down the side of the gully, picked up the M79, and moved to the fallen tree. A small patch of leaves had been torn from the branches of the trunk and provided Jeff a patchwork view to the other side. He removed a round from his vest before dropping the vest from his shoulders onto the ground while he peered through the hole. Working silently, he carefully broke a few more twigs away until he had a decent sized firing hole and NVA soldiers down the gully were clearly visible.

With their weapons held at the ready, the NVA stood in two ranks down the center of the gully fifty meters away. An officer knelt near the edge of the slope peering under the bushes toward the Americans. He looked down at his watch as he raised his other arm above his head. The soldiers nervously repositioned their feet as they prepared to rush up the side of the gully to storm the American lines.

Jeff aimed at the slope behind the officer and fired. Without waiting for the round to hit, he broke open the weapon, extracted the spent round, and loaded the fresh round. As the first round exploded throwing the officer forward, Jeff aimed the muzzle toward the soldiers in front of him as they jerked their heads his way. He fired again, dropped the M79, and scrambled up the side of the gully.

Rifle fire came from the lines in front of him as he wiggled under the branches, but no bullets whipped above his head. He pushed to his feet when he had cleared the bushes and bent down as he came to Clarence's upstretched arms. Grunting as he picked up the man, he kept his momentum forward as he ran toward the purple smoke billowing in front of him. Clarence fired in the direction of the gully as they entered the swirling acidy smoke. Jeff sprinted as he dodged to the right around a tree.

Sergeant Slattery's voice rose above the fusillade of fire in front of Jeff. "Briggs is coming in. Covering fire everywhere except into the purple smoke. Reserves to the right flank. Concentrate fire toward the gully."

The trees ended as Jeff raced through the thinning purple smoke toward the firing M16s. Bullets cracked past his head from the left as the NVA soldiers overcame his disruption and pressed their assault. The comforting thunk of an M79 firing from the American lines hit his ears as he outraced the smoke and the helmets of his comrades came into view ten meters away. He pushed his legs harder, prepared to drop Clarence as soon as he passed the line.

He aimed toward a space between two firing riflemen and let Clarence's body start slipping toward the ground when two long steps remained. Sergeant Slattery stood and reached his arms out to catch Clarence as Jeff crossed past the bullet-spitting muzzles of his friends. He let Clarence drop as Sergeant Slattery took hold of the man's torso.

Two bullets entered Jeff's left side as Clarence dropped into the Sergeant's arms. The first tore through his spleen and exited on the right leaving a four-inch hole that spurted blood and green bile. The second entered higher, tearing through his heart before exiting and lodging in a tree.

As Jeff fell, images of an eighteen-year-old Don, an eighty-year-old Mama Hazel, a nine-year-old Helen, and an eighteen-year-old Pat flashed in front of his eyes. His vision returned momentarily as his head hit the ground. Clarence's anguished face centered in Jeff's eyes as darkness engulfed him.

Chapter 15

"Nooooooooooooo!"

Pat threw the covers off her body and sat up straight in her bed as she grabbed the sides of her head.

"No! No! No!"

Across the small room, Betty, her roommate, flipped on her light, jumped out of bed, and raced to Pat's side.

"What's wrong?"

Pat buried her head in her hands. Her screams had turned to guttural convulsions as tears fell past her fingers onto her lap.

Betty wrapped her arms around Pat's shoulders holding her close. "It's okay. It's okay. What's wrong?"

The dorm room door burst inward and the Resident Assistant raced in carrying a baseball bat. Other young women crowded the doorway looking in at the unfolding scene.

The RA scanned the room quickly. "What's wrong? What's with the screaming?"

Pat wiped her eyes with the left sleeve of the old gray men's shirt that she used as a nightgown before she ran the right sleeve against her nose. She feebly smiled up at the RA.

"I'm sorry. I was just having a nightmare, but it seemed so real. I'm okay now."

The RA glanced around the room again, looked down at Pat, and then at Betty. "Well, okay, then go back to sleep."

She turned around to face the crowd of young women that were now standing in the room or still crowded around the doorway. Some worn nightgowns and others were clad only in old oversized t-shirts. Later arrivals wore robes that they clutched to their necks. Night curlers adorned the heads of several, but most sported long straight hair parted in the middle of their scalps and hanging down their backs.

The RA herded the women from the room with her hands. "Everyone get back to bed. Just a bad dream. Come on. Get back to bed. We all have school tomorrow."

The RA looked back into the room as she started to close the door behind her. "You can keep the light on for a little if you need to talk to calm her down some more."

Betty raised her head from Pat's shoulder. "Thanks, Stephanie."

The door clicked shut and Betty rose from Pat's bed. She grabbed a box of tissues from her nightstand dropping them on the bed next to Pat. She then sat down on the end of the bed as Pat took two of the tissues from the box and blew her nose. Pat wiped her nose as she finished, dropping the crumpled tissues to the floor. She grabbed two more to wipe her moist eyes.

Betty reached down the bed and touched Pat's leg. "You want to talk about it?"

Pat wiped her eyes again, looked up at the ceiling, breathed hard, and then turned her head downward.

"The dream started out so nice. I was living in Pensacola and my old high school boyfriend, Jeff, had come to visit." She smiled as she looked up with puffy eyes. "It was wonderful. He was there with a band on a tour of the south. We made love in my bed and woke up holding each other. We had dinner in a restaurant before we went for a walk along the beach."

She hesitated as the smile left her face. She took a ragged breath inward. A tear dripped from her right eye and she wiped it away with the wet tissue. "Then I came home from work and Jeff was sitting naked on my couch. I pulled him up off the couch and was leading him to my bedroom. All of a sudden, he was dressed in an army uniform with a helmet on."

Pat broke into sobs again and brought her hands back to her face. The words struggled to get out. "His chest... exploded...I...was covered in his blood."

She wailed for a moment before her distress turned to sobs. She did not speak again for several minutes. She then wiped her eyes, looked at the ceiling again, and then back toward Betty.

"Why did I let my parents make me come here? I should have gone to VPI with Jeff. Then maybe he wouldn't have dropped out and gone into the army. I haven't heard from him in over a year since he left school."

Betty patted Pat's leg. "Come on Pat, it was just a nightmare. I'm sure he's okay. This damn war's got everybody on edge."

"I've got to find out what's going on with him. I just don't know where to start. I tried talking the army recruiter in town, but he said he couldn't help."

Betty smiled. "I tell you what. As soon as our classes are over on Thursday, why don't we drive down together to that town where the two of you went to school? Maybe the alumni office at his old academy has a current address."

"You'd do that?"

"Sure. What are roommates for if they don't help each other? I'll even pay for half the gas and a night in a motel."

"Thanks. Let's do it."

Chapter 16

Helen turned off the main highway and drove through the stately gates of the Old Rocksville Cemetery. She guided the car past the weathered unreadable stones that belonged to the veterans of the War Between the States, then past the family tombs of the town's old money, parking on the road in the newer section that had opened in 1890. The air was still and no birds sang as she opened the door, got out, stretched, and looked around the placid scene.

An old man, probably from the Baptist church that had accepted responsibility for maintaining the graves of the long forgotten soldiers of the South, slowly pushed a ratcheting rotary mower along an orderly line of graves. Behind him, a black child raked the loose grass into piles before carrying them to a green canvas tarp. An old woman pulled a red wagon along the slightly overgrown path stopping every so often to gather the faded silk flowers with their false crystal vases. She filled her wagon then moved behind the cutting of the blades of the mower before placing the flowers randomly on the now fully exposed graves.

Helen reached into the backseat of the car and lifted the bouquet of Gardenias, a single red rose, and a jug full of water. Taking care not to step directly on top of any grave, she walked through the line of family plots. The old woman looked up and waved feebly to Helen. Helen lifted the bouquet for the woman to see. Helen wanted the bouquet to stay where she placed it and not become part of the general honoring of the dead.

The freshly mowed grass at the family plot was damp. The crystal vase with its brown crusts of the previous bouquet still adorned the space just below the center of the double headstone. Helen gently lifted the fragile stalks from the vase and placed them to the side. She slid the new bouquet into the vase before adding water to the dry bottom. Helen moved up to the headstone and placed the red rose on top over the newer of the two carved names. The final date carved under that name was July 17, 1965.

She then walked back to the footstone and sat on the ground. Her finger traced the initials carved into the footstone before she spoke.

"Hi, Mama. Sorry it took so long for me to get back up here. I could lie and say it was school or work that kept me away, but it was really Jeff that did it. I just couldn't bring myself up here to tell you about him. Then I realized that you already knew and are probably sitting with him in heaven drinking sweet tea."

She wiped a tear from the corner of her eye. "Anyway, I'm driving from here up to Arlington Cemetery near Washington to visit his grave. I went by your old house and the Andersons let me pick a bouquet of Yellow Jasmine from beside your old steps for his grave. They are keeping your old place up really nice, but I guess you already know that."

"Anyway, I did want to tell you that I had a nice dream about Jeff before we found out he had died. He had come down to Savannah to visit. It was really nice. He even made peace with my father." She chuckled softly. "That's when I realized I was dreaming. Anyway, it was a nice final memory of him, though I wish I could have seen him for real. I really miss him so much."

"Anyway, I better get going. I stopped at the colored cemetery on the way here to place a bouquet on Bessie's grave. Her family keeps her grave really clean and fresh, kinda like I wish I could do for you, but Savannah is so far away."

"Anyway, I'll stop back by on my way home to tell you what Jeff's grave is like. Please say hello to Jeff for me and tell him that I miss him."

Helen slowly rose to her feet and lifted the bundle of dried stalks from the ground. She dropped it into the pile of grass clippings on the tarp. Walking to the car, she slid into the driver's seat, drove out the gates, and turned toward Virginia.

Chapter 17

The black limousine turned into the gates of the White House then drove up the curving drive until it pulled under the North Portico. As it came to a stop, the Marine guard stepped to the rear passenger door, opened it, and returned to the position of attention as he held the door. Major John Smith stepped to the open door and extended his arm into the car. From inside the car, a hand accepted the arm. Mrs. Hazel Briggs climbed from the seat stepping out into the crisp air of the Washington morning.

Two men were waiting next to the door to the building. Both stood at attention, though one was supporting himself on crutches with his left leg slightly raised from the ground.

The older of the two was dressed in army dress blues while the younger was in army dress greens.

Major Smith escorted Mrs. Briggs to the two men and stopped. "Mrs. Briggs, I would like to present Sergeant First Class Raymond Slattery. He was the platoon sergeant for your son's platoon."

She accepted Sergeant Slattery's extended hand, lightly shaking it.

"So nice to finally meet you, Sergeant Slattery. Thank you for your kind letter. Reading the circumstances of my son's death was hard, but did help me come to closure."

"He was a brave man," Sergeant Slattery said. "If it wasn't for him, myself and a lot of other soldiers would not be alive today."

Major Smith turned to the other soldier. "Mrs. Briggs, this is Private First Class Clarence Washington. He was the soldier that your son rescued from the enemy and, according to his company commander, was your son's best friend."

She lightly touched Clarence's arm. "Jeffery wrote often about you in his letters home. Thank you for being my son's friend. And I do hope your leg is going to heal completely."

Clarence's smile showed his bright white teeth. "They tell me it will be good as new in a few more months."

Mrs. Briggs turned back toward Sargeant Slattery. "Will you and Clarence be at the luncheon? I would so like to talk to both of you about Jeffery."

"Yes, ma'am. We were both invited."

"Did the two of you drive in together?"

"No, ma'am. This is the first I've seen Private Washington since he was medevacked from the battlefield back in January."

Major Smith touched Mrs. Briggs' elbow. "If you'll allow me to escort you inside, the President is waiting. The ceremony will be in the East Room"

Mrs. Briggs took Major Smith's offered elbow and he guided her toward double glass doors flanked by two Marine guards. As they approached, the guards first saluted and then held the doors open while they returned to the position of attention. Sergeant Slattery and Clarence followed them through the door into the Entrance Hall. A Secret Service Agent waited as they came through the door. He guided them down the center hallway into the East Room.

Members of the media, military officers in full dress uniforms, members of Congress, and members of the White House staff filled the chairs in the room. TV and movie cameras perched on tripods on a platform in the rear of the room. As they entered, Major Smith turned Mrs. Briggs toward the front while the escorting Secret Service Agent directed Sergeant Slattery and Clarence toward the rear of the room.

Two seats remained unfilled on the left side of the aisle of the last row. Neatly printed name cards reserved the seats for them. Sergeant Slattery looked first at the seats, then at Clarence's left leg before he walked across the aisle to speak quietly to the two staffers sitting there. The two women stood, gave a nod to Clarence, and moved to the two seats on the left side of the aisle. Sergeant Slattery motioned to Clarence as he dropped into the inner seat.

Sergeant Slattery held the crutches as Clarence lowered himself into the aisle seat. He leaned over and whispered into Clarence's ear. "This way you can stick your leg into the aisle."

"Thanks."

Everyone in the room stood as a voice came over the speakers. "Ladies and Gentlemen — the President of the United States."

Clarence struggled to stand with the rest of the room but stopped as Sergeant Slattery laid his hand upon his shoulder. The Sergeant stood remaining at attention as the President moved to Mrs. Briggs, shook her hand, and said a few unheard words.

The President then moved to the podium. "Please be seated."

"One of the greatest honors that I have as Commander-In-Chief is the awarding of the Medal of Honor to our brave soldiers. Conversely, one of the saddest duties that I have is making such awards to the members of a deceased soldier's family. Such is the case today."

He turned the page on the notes that lay before him. "Corporal Jeffery Briggs was operating as a grenadier in Company A, 1st Battalion, 417th Parachute Regiment when they were ambushed by a superior enemy force near Plei Me in the Central Highlands of South Vietnam. During the early stages of the battle, Corporal Briggs witnessed a fellow soldier thrown by a rocket explosion to a position where he was captured by enemy forces. Corporal

Briggs, without regard for his own safety, undertook a one-man rescue mission. During the course of this rescue mission, Corporal Briggs broke up a counter attack by the enemy that saved the American positions from being overrun. He then resumed his mission going deep behind enemy lines, killing an estimated 30 of the enemy as he worked his way to the location of the captured and wounded comrade. Those killed included the NVA Colonel that commanded the enemy forces in the area."

The President continued speaking as Sergeant Slattery leaned over toward Clarence and whispered into his ear. "I never did understand how he ever found you back there."

Clarence whispered back. "I asked him that when he found me. He said that my mother told him where I was."

"That's weird."

"Tell me about it. My mother passed away five years ago."

Chapter 18

The waves broke gently on the sand bar. Russ's laughter touched Jeff's ears as he opened his eyes into the brim of his Boonie hat. He pushed the brim back above his eyes enough to take in the scene but still allowing it to block the bright sun that shown against a brilliant blue background of sky. Jeff lay still while the woven vinyl straps of the beach lounge chair pressed against his back as the scene before him came into focus.

Mutluk was standing about 10 feet away throwing a Frisbee out toward the gentle surf while Russ waited to chase the flying disc. After Mutluk threw it, Russ caught it and expertly threw it back. Mutluk caught the Frisbee and launched it back into the air. The beach was deserted except for the three men. No boats or ships sailed across the lazy ocean before them. Seagulls drifted overhead on the ocean breeze. Russ splashed thru the ankle deep water toward the interception point as the Frisbee came arcing down again.

Dried sweat on Jeff's back momentarily stuck him to the straps as he tried to raise his upper body. The pins of the chair squeaked as they strained against the movement.

Mutluk turned his head toward the sound. "Hi there."

He reached his hand into the air without looking and caught the returning disk. He kept his eyes fixed on Jeff as he threw the Frisbee backhanded out toward the waiting Russ.

Jeff turned his head downward to gaze at the crisp clean t-shirt that covered his chest. He brought his hands to his sides running them slowly up and down against the smooth skin underneath. Next, he shifted his gaze toward his forearm and ran his hand over the smooth skin where the shrapnel gouge had been bandaged before. No trace of the wound or the bandage remained. Jeff twisted on the lounge chair and placed his feet on the warm white sand.

"I guess it's over?"

Mutluk smiled down at him with his head slightly cocked. He nodded. "Yea. That tour's done."

"Clarence okay?"

"He's safe and will be fine."

"That's good."

Jeff looked out toward the water as Russ ran up to the pair. Jeff smiled up at him as he stopped next to Mutluk. Both of them had a soft glow around them that filtered the bright sunshine.

Jeff looked past them up the deserted beach. "What happens now?"

Without shifting his eyes from Jeff, Russ flipped the Frisbee high into the air with his left hand before catching it behind his back with his right. "We take you home and then start another tour."

"Can I go with you?"

"Not this time," Mutluk said. "Maybe on a later tour. Folks that have missed you a lot want to see you."

He reached his hand out toward Jeff. As Jeff took it and pulled himself up off the lounge chair, a calming energy filled his body. The troubled tiredness that had plagued him since he had woken up in Don's house was gone. Each new step was a wonderful adventure in peace and awareness of his surroundings.

Mutluk and Jeff made their way along a much-traveled path through the sand dunes as Russ walked along behind them. Russ repeatedly threw the Frisbee high into the air catching it behind his back. As the cab of the truck came into view in the distance, Jeff reached out to grab Mutluk's arm to stop him. Russ stopped and stood silently behind them as he tossed the Frisbee up and caught it with one hand behind his back without looking.

"So, what was this all about?

Mutluk looked down at him with soft eyes that had the same glow about them that his skin did. "The rocket explosion that threw you against the tree messed up your head. That alone should have killed you, but your mind wouldn't let go while your friend was in danger. It kept fighting your spirit to stay until you found him. All Russ and I could do was wait for you to finish and come across for good."

"And all the places we stopped?"

"Sometimes people see their past life flash before their eyes as they move across, sometimes they see what might have been. Sometimes they see both intermixed. As you moved back and forth, you also touched other people's souls in their dreams."

Mutluk turned and started back up the path toward the truck. Jeff followed after a moment of hesitation. Russ remained standing in the sand throwing the Frisbee up in the air.

Jeff moved forward until he touched Mutluk's arm again. The big man stopped. "Can I ask you another question?"

"Sure. You can ask anything."

"How did you get here?"

"I was hunting a bear with a stone ax near my village in Canada back in 1745. The bear found me first."

"And Russ?"

"He was killed during the draft riots in New York City in 1863."

Jeff shook his head slightly as Mutluk started back toward the truck. Jeff then followed with Russ close behind. As Jeff looked down at his hand, his skin began to take on the same glow that Mutluk and Russ had. Jeff turned his gaze back toward the truck as they drew close to it. The paint on the side was fresh and different.

"What's with the new name on the side?"

Russ stepped up to the side of the trailer smiling as he waved his hand toward the new marquee. "Like it? Heaven Can Wait was the name while we waited for you. Now we're Heaven Bound."

Excerpt from

Why The Birds Sing

By Gregory P Robertson

Book 1 of
The Vertical Speed Chronicles

Chapter 1

The lights of Casper reflected off the low clouds to the south. An early fall chill was in the air. Vicki rolled down the sleeves of her flannel and buttoned the cuffs, then pulled the partially open overhead doors fully down and slipped the locks into place. It had been another slow Friday night with only a few gas customers since the dinnertime rush. The other two mechanics had left at five to have dinner with their families.

As the sound of a distinctive engine came to her from the highway, Vicki quickly moved back into the showroom and locked the front door. She scampered to the electrical panel and flipped the cover open. Standing on her tiptoes, she shut off the top breakers. The lights in the work bays and the parking lot went dark. Only the light from the back office showed through the windows of the station. Vicki began to shut the door with thoughts of hiding. However, her truck, parked next to the building, was a dead giveaway to her presence. Watching out the front windows, she hoped the truck would pass by.

The distinctive sound grew louder as the truck sped by on the highway and then slid into a quick U-turn. The tires spun and smoked on the dry pavement as it sped back toward the parking lot. Gravel flew when it left the pavement, and the driver revved the engine in backfiring spurts as the truck rolled past the pumps. Then it stopped directly in front of the door. The driver stumbled out.

Vicki was standing behind the counter, the phone next to her hand.

The man in the passenger seat, Bud, swiveled his head toward Vicki. Silvery sunglasses hid his eyes. He turned his head toward the highway, looking one way, then the other. Raising a whiskey bottle to his lips, he drank a long swallow before returning it to its hiding place. Then he looked at Vicki again. The distorted reflection in the mirrored lenses disturbed her.

The driver made his way to the front door and pulled on the handle. "Locked," he said as he continued to hold it. Vicki could almost smell the whiskey through the door. He stared at the handle before he yanked on it again and then looked up at Vicki. "Open the door, Vicki. I need to use the bathroom."

"I'm closed Eddie. Try the Shell station."

"Come on Vicki. I really gotta pee."

"I never knew you were so particular about when and where you pulled your pecker out."

Eddie smiled through the door. "You got me there. But you have to admit that we had some fun."

"You had some fun. All I got was a pregnancy scare and the sight of your taillights when I told you. Now get out of here before I call the sheriff."

"You want a drink? We could have a little fun again."

Vicki picked up the phone. "Leave!"

"Okay," Eddie said as he moved toward the truck. "See you later."

Gravel flew as the truck skidded back toward the highway. It sped away, tires chirping as the gears engaged.

Vicki turned off the rest of the lights and waited in the dark. The night grew still. Two cars passed by the station headed into town. Her house was less than a mile away, but still, she waited.

After ten minutes, she unlocked the door, then locked it behind her and hurried to the safety of her truck. She scampered in, pushed the door lock down, slipped the key quickly into the ignition, and turned it. When the engine roared to life, the low rumble calmed her nerves. She put the truck into gear to start home.

She rounded the corner onto her street. The lamppost in front of her home cast a warm glow on the empty street. The yellow porch light beside her front door beckoned toward the warmth of an evening fire, but her distrust of Eddie made her err on the side of caution. She pulled into the driveway, stopped, and killed the engine. The key remained in the ignition. Vicki rolled the window down an inch, then listened and watched.

Normal noises filtered through the neighborhood. A muted bark from the Johnson's dog betrayed its desire to come in from the cold. A branch scraped softly with the wind on Mr. Stanley's roof. The neighborhood exulted tranquility. Vicki shook her head as she pulled the keys free and opened the truck door. "This is ridiculous." She walked up the sidewalk and pulled the screen door. It creaked as she reached the house key toward the door lock. A hint of stale oak crept into the air just as someone grabbed her arms below the elbows and yanked her backward. The keys dropped to the ground.

A man whispered behind her ear. "Evening Vicki."

She twisted her head toward the voice and her face reflected in mirrored sunglasses. Something moved in the periphery of the porch light that showed behind her in the lens. She turned her head toward the light.

Eddie placed the whiskey bottle on the ground and grinned. "Told you we'd see you later."

As he took a step toward her, the stink of the whiskey overpowered the night air. He bent down and roughly kissed her on the lips. "Now, let's have some fun."

Vicki, a grimace set into her face, transferred her weight to the balls of her feet and tensed her calf muscles. She stared into Eddie's eyes as she waited for the mistake she knew would come.

About the Author

Soldier in the 60's, Rock&Roll Roadie in the 70's, Skydiving Instructor in the 80's, Pilot in the 90's, and Writer in the new millennium, Gregory P Robertson brings a wide and varied wealth of experience with him to his writing. Along the way, he found time to acquire an Electrical Engineering Degree, obtain Professional Engineering Certification in multiple states, and have a 27-year career with AT&T.

His past writing works include the nonfiction history of the Staunton Military Academy and the first volume of a collection of humorous memoirs entitled "Life As A Cadet – How To Find Humor With A Black Stripe Down Your Leg."

Southern Roadie is his first Novel.

You can view his entire collection of writings at his website **www.gregoryprobertson.com**.

www.ingramcontent.com/pod-product-compliance
Lightning Source LLC
Chambersburg PA
CBHW051426170626
46809CB00006B/2337